Floating in the Middle

Floating in the Middle

"The Future looms. The past haunts."

By Frances Rivetti

Fog Valley Press
Petaluma

Print Paperback ISBN: 978-0-9904921-8-4

E Book ISBN: 978-0-9904921-9-1

Other Books by Frances Rivetti/Fog Valley Press:

Fog Valley Crush—Love at First Bite—At Home in the California Farmstead Frontier 2014

Fog Valley Winter—Pioneer Heritage, Backroad Rambles and Vintage Recipes 2016

Big Green Country—A Novel 2019

The House on Liberty Street— Home of Second Chances—A Novel 2022

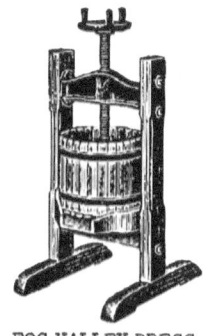

FOG VALLEY PRESS

Dedication

"To old friends and new. And especially to those brave people who are
dedicated to saving our planet, whose tireless efforts inspire hope
and action for a better tomorrow."

"The time seems near, if it has not actually arrived, when the chastened sublimity of a moor, a sea, or a mountain will be all of nature that is absolutely in keeping with the moods of the more thinking among mankind."

—Thomas Hardy

Friday, Mid–Morning

I t's a random encounter I could've easily avoided—if it weren't for my mother issues. But after another tense, guilt-laced call, it feels less like an errand and more an escape to collect my pre-order from a glass-fronted winery overlooking the silver-blue expanse of the Pacific. The wild Sonoma coast calms my nerves, stretching out like something out of a dream—untouchable, beautiful, and just out of reach.

I should've stayed in my car, should've stayed in the conversation, should've tried harder to be the kind of daughter who didn't hang up mid-argument. But instead, with my phone tucked into my jacket pocket and my arms wrapped around a case of wine, I'm headed back toward the parking lot, just a few feet away. The air is crisp and full of salt, when, out of nowhere, a shadowy figure materializes in my path.

I stop.

And there, blocking me, stands a slight, long-haired man—whose presence feels anything but accidental.

"Let me help you with that," he suggests. His gaze is sharp and deliberate. His gravelly voice a level above the rumble of surf breaking onto the beach, below.

I assess him fleetingly, resetting my sight beyond his shoulders, someplace in the distance. My work as a general practice doctor in a coastal region even more remote than this, has me well trained in the art of character assessment, to be my most assertive when caught off-guard.

He's dressed in shades of black, from top to toe—a melodramatic, theatrical get-up which seems to me to be calling for attention over subterfuge. A long, unbuttoned trench coat reveals a faded silk scarf at the neckline, dark jeans and stack heeled buffalo boots. Part rock-and-roll, part Shakespearean cowboy, his man-of-mystery garb is topped off with a black-leather western hat nestled over a pair of salt and pepper braids that rest on the front of his overcoat like weathered ropes of wisdom draped over a treasure chest. Light brown face—thick-lashed, piercing eyes, as dark as obsidian, a prominent nose with a slight hump and a set of ruddy, chiseled cheekbones top his clean-shaven cheeks and chin.

A curious buttonhole of dark feathers adds to the monotone of his stark silhouette. The folds of his black raincoat shifting like polished armor under the morning light.

His moves are fast and purposeful.

I maneuver my body sideways, subtly, instinctively, angling my back as I slither past. Eccentric, clearly. Each to his own. I grant him the courtesy to say his piece before I move on, though I'm not inclined toward small talk, especially this morning.

"All good, thanks," I brush him off, politely, but firmly as I stride on toward my car. I hear the heavy door shut behind him, a resonant *thunk* that lingers in the air, giving way to his footsteps as he follows, eager, yet, to engage.

"Aussie?" he asks. He reaches out and takes a gentle hold of my left elbow as I stand at the trunk of my beat-up Volkswagen Golf. I focus on balancing the case of wine on the trunk. I have no idea what his game is and I shrug him off, drawing the line at his touch.

There are several empty vehicles in the parking lot. He's close enough for me to feel the warmth of his breath on the back of my neck, intimate, unexpected and unsettling. I turn on my heel, ready to confront. There's no place to go, other than to head back into the tasting room, or my legging it through the native grasses and wildflowers along the busy coast highway if it comes to it.

"No, you're totally off-mark." My best, most polished and patronizing British. "I've never even been to Australia," I inform him, primly. "Guess again. Then maybe you'll tell me what it is you're after?"

I'm unable to hold back in correcting a common miscomprehension as to my heritage. If there's one thing that is guaranteed to annoy me, it's a sweeping assumption as to my nationality. Typically, here in California, it's a wild guess at the commonwealth countries, Australia being the number one pick. It's not that I have anything against Australians and their endearing tendency to substitute their Ts for Ds, their elongating of the letter A.

Truth is, after twenty-three years in the States, my accent has mellowed into a confusing blend of British-American. But come on—just because I sound like an East of England tv breakfast show host who binge-watched American sitcoms doesn't mean I'm okay with being tossed, rootless, into the wrong continent!

And my hard-to-place accent is only part of the price I've paid to settle in Northern California since my arrival as a wide-eyed overseas college student back in the day.

"English, actually," I admit, in an effort to avoid a second random stab in the dark.

There is no flinch or flicker in his eyes, it's as if he's weighing my secrets or silently mocking from a higher vantage.

"Same difference," he replies, eventually, standing aloof, rolling his shoulders. Not quite human as his frame shifts slightly forward and up, before sweeping back in a smooth, shrugging motion. "Tourists."

"It's not the same at all," I respond. A bank of white cala lilies sways in the breeze, each petal a soft whisper of elegance against the green waves of their leaves. A waft of sour-creamy, clove-like scent carries on the air.

"And you? Am I to take you as a hospitality ambassador?" I ask, aware that my tone is facetious as I toy with him. I'm all-riled up after my phone call with Mum, so he'd best watch out. I'm generally adept in reading a person, as I've said. But this guy's uninvited interest in my activities is a puzzle.

I take stock. He stands at an average height, his build solid and unassuming. His face bears the deep lines of someone accustomed to the coastal wind and sun. There's an air about him that suggests a deep-rooted connection to this land. If that is the case, then he deserves my respect, not condescension, despite his unorthodox approach.

"Maybe you work for the winery?"

My carefully practiced off-duty avoidance protocol has slipped. I notice the laugh lines crinkle around the corners of his eyes. Well-worn trails on a mountain path, etched by years of journeying.

"Is that it?"

His head tilts slightly. Not with confusion or curiosity, like he's studying me more than just seeing me.

"The Raven is here for renewal. For recovery and healing," he replies, softly, slowly, as he gestures theatrically, first to the sky and then toward the Pacific with a silver-ringed pointer finger. His fingernail is worn smooth like ancient stone. A subtle tilt of the head and a slight hop. It might be part stretch, part preening gesture, or even a way to shake off tension—but it's expressive for sure. Birdman-with-an-attitude, I can't help but think.

It's all so curious. He appears unsettlingly intelligent. What is it about ravens? Smart and expressive, creative. Also, according to native lore, tricksters? Sometimes prone to theft.

"Right then Mr. Raven," I announce, upbeat but ever-more assertively, as I swivel and turn my back to him a second time. My car keys are in my pocket along with my phone.

"Have a spectacular rest of your day. Must be on my way"

I force a smile and cross my arms across my torso in a shield to signal what I consider to be the end of this random interaction.

His head bobs with a kind of knowing rhythm, occasionally tilting to the side as if it's listening to something only he can hear. He's close enough to be touching but not quite.

"Take it easy," he encourages, his turn to patronize, a teasing look on his face. He's chuckling, as if I've been some kind of fool after all to have misinterpreted anything but friendly intentions.

"The Raven is simply reaching out—watching, reminding you to stay mindful of your actions."

I arch a brow and narrow my gaze, sending him a warning. He's clearly set on provoking me—though not quite to the point of real trouble. Yet.

I glance around, reassessing the situation. A couple from the tasting room return to their car. The woman sits down behind the driver's wheel and proceeds to reverse her near-silent electric vehicle in the direction of the highway. I raise an arm and I'm to about to flag her down when the Raven retreats, assumedly having interpreted my body language, if not my words. He's still dancing around, however, hopping from foot to foot, raising his palms in peace.

"I appreciate the warm welcome, but I can take it from here," I say with quiet assurance. "I'm no stranger to these parts. I know my way around." My goal is to bring this interaction to a firm and definite close.

I interlace my fingers in an exaggerated, schoolmarm gesture. But it's clear he's not finished as his hands move to grasp my wrists. I freeze for a few seconds, taken aback by his boldness. This is too much. He's crossed the line. I raise my hands forcefully and release his hold.

"What's your point?" I ask, as a powerful motorcycle sweeps into the lot. I raise my voice now. "I'm asking you politely to move on."

The motorcyclist plants his boots on the ground, then reaches up to remove his helmet. The arrival of this new presence does little to curb the Raven's eagerness to lecture me on his coastal oasis. Instead, he leans in, clearly unable to hold back as he dives into a low-key rant that kicks off with the damage caused by recreational vehicles and beachgoers.

His diatribe shifts, breathlessly, into the topic of second-home owners. He barely misses a beat as he rails on into the collective impact of coastal inns, restaurants, ice cream and gift shops, tasting rooms, galleries and gas stations, concrete foundations and parking lots (like this one), which he insists, as he gestures elaborately with his bony hands, involve enormous amounts of concrete being poured over fragile coastal infrastructure, forever changing the face of the rugged, natural coastline.

Okay, I'm grasping the urgency of his message. He's crusading. And as far as he's concerned, I'm an outsider. Ignorant as to the vital need for the protection of his environment.

"Consider me as a free-agent for the preservation of coastal biodiversity," he validates my assumption, raising his hands to the sky as he further articulates his case. It's not hard to grasp his concern. And yet, what does it have to do with me? I'm neither a tourist nor a second-home owner. I suggest as much.

"Well, you're here, aren't you?" he says, gesturing toward the case of wine. "All I'm trying to do is reach people like you—those who wander into my world, whatever the reason—to educate, inform, and make you aware of the impact your individual footprint leaves behind."

"Thanks for clearing that up," I reply. "I get where you're coming from, and I respect your motive—but if you want your message to land, maybe ease up a bit next time."

He has every right to defend the natural order but the way he's going about it tells me he's maybe more of an evangelical than a peaceful naturalist.

I ask if he was born and raised around here. I'm digging myself in deeper, despite my desire to disengage.

He responds with a smile, this time one of genuine regard, his eyes drifting past me to the green hills in the distance. A small herd of black bovine approaches the fence line, a scatter of ink blots, each one quietly absorbed in its own rhythm, contentedly munching a field of long grass.

"See? Just look around you," he says, gesturing broadly. "It's an honor and a blessing to share this glorious land with countless others—bacteria, fungi, plants, mammals, birds, reptiles, fish, and invertebrates—all of us equal in calling this same place our home." He draws out his syllables with deliberate flair, adding weight to each word. It's almost hypnotic.

"I've no objection to folk passing through in a mindful manner," he concedes. "My purpose is to slow down the unsustainable drain on our coastal paradise. Preserve our precious water and energy."

I nod, gravely, in an effort to demonstrate that I'm actually on his side with all of this. I get it. But I don't have all day. I need to be making my way.

"Experts," he adds for extra punch, "believe we're in the midst of a sixth mass extinction. One that may have been evolving over thousands of years."

"So why target me this morning with this, specifically?" I ask. We're veering into dense territory and what I really need is a second cup of coffee. "All I'm doing is going about my business, visiting friends."

I explain how Serena and River live out here on the coast, full time.

"They're locals. So, you see, I'm not a tourist, in that respect, Mr. Raven, more of an invited guest. Maybe you've seen them around?"

"Well, maybe I have, but that's picking at straws now, lady," he replies, dismissing my claim with a flourish of hand. "And are you hearing what I'm saying? We're each of us complicit in our own neglect."

Fair enough, I reply. "Though it's a little too early for me for the heavy stuff to be honest. And while I'm at it, you'd do better not to pounce on unsuspecting solo travelers," I say. "Especially women. It could be construed as creepy."

The Raven pauses as he mulls over my words. After thoughtful concession, he finally appears to conclude his lecture—though not before making one last declaration. His gaze sharpens.

"I've learned to accept much of it. The power of the relentless waves, the torrential seasonal downpours, an excess of groundwater. But the truth is undeniable. Erosion is happening faster than the local authorities are able to keep up with."

And someone has to challenge the ignorance most everyone else appears content to live with, he concludes.

I see his point. I do. Ignorance is bliss. Temporarily. Denial is too often deadly. I've experienced more than enough of it professionally, especially during the first year of the pandemic. We all carry our own traumas. From my perspective, there was not nearly enough government acceptance and responsibility for its lack of preparedness, the paltry provision of safety measures and less than adequate equipment in our hospitals. Janitors, porters, nurses, technicians, doctors. We were basically treated as cannon fodder—expendable, powerless.

～

I'm to meet Jamie at the harbor, a few miles to the north on the coast highway. I don't have time or appetite this morning for any more of this intense lecturing. Besides, he's clueless to who I am, what I do, how much I know or don't know about the state of our planet and the way we humans treat it.

It's weird, though, as the very reason for my being here this weekend involves the creation of a safety net for the future. A pact born from a mix of youthful adrenaline, idealism and a desperate desire to maintain our bond. A need to be something bigger than ourselves. At the time, it felt like the most important thing in the world—a promise to stick together through thick and thin. Some might question whether it was driven by peer pressure. I wonder why we let it get so serious, why we believed that fleeting moment could define our entire futures. And yet, there's still something hauntingly powerful about those memories—the camaraderie, the intensity of those promises made in the heat of our youth.

"I can assure you, I'm on it," I tell him, as I take my leave, avoiding his hand. "Consider me your poster girl for treading gently on this shore. I promise."

The lanky motorcycle rider has caught the tail end of our conversation. He has a bemused look on his fresh, young face which tells me that he's not overly concerned by the heated interaction he has heard. He appears to be familiar with this peculiar man. He lifts an arm in order to ruffle a head of curly brown hair and shoots me a more enquiring look. I smile to let him know that I'm okay. I've got it.

I haul the heavy case from the top of the trunk and bend my knees in order to place it onto the ground and unlock the trunk. The Raven has read my signal at last and he makes his departure. He's muttering to himself as he retreats toward the tasting room in preparation for his next conquest. I guess he has a goal in mind as to how many unsuspecting tourists he's intent on accosting today. It's not my problem. I've paid my penance. I'm out of here.

"Don't let the Raven bother you none." It's the motorcycle guy speaking, as I'm climbing into my car. He's all blue-eyed and spring-tanned faced, around the same age as I was when I launched into an early adulthood of my first post-graduate years, the early Millennium, a time of ridiculous transition, when life as we knew it first turned on its head. Think about it. The completion of the human genome, the creation of Facebook, of YouTube, Twitter, Netflix, Spotify, the introduction of the iPhone. If that wasn't enough next came the onslaught of AI, driverless taxis, hot on the heels of cloud computing and video teleconferencing technology for heaven sakes. No wonder we're more stressed out than ever, frazzled by so much overload in so short a period of modern history.

"You know him?" I ask. We're fully out of earshot of the Raven, I hope, though I'm careful not to re-engage as I glance back over my shoulder.

"He's harmless enough," the motorcyclist replies. "Legend has it, he's a descendent of a Russian sea captain and his Coastal Miwok wife. He's a smart guy when you get to know him. Deep. Passionate about protecting the coast. But he's not supposed to go around verbally harassing our customers, no matter what. And he knows it."

He's heading in to work his shift in the tasting room, he tells me. He must be over twenty-one to be serving alcohol, but barely. The realization of this makes me feel suddenly quite ridiculously old, even at forty-two. I'm probably twice his age. Technically old enough to be his mother.

"Every now and again the dude is out here, especially on the weekends, lecturing folk on the dangers of drinking and driving. But for the most part he settles for hand-drawing posters. He photocopies them by the hundreds. He and his mom post them on any standing target, all over the place for the visiting public to see."

It's refreshing in a way, the Raven's use of old-fashioned artistry for his analog message. I find myself hoping he keeps up with his planet-saving campaign, despite his impertinent in-person delivery. I'm tempted to donate to his photocopy cause but I'm not willing to risk engaging again. I need to move on.

"Oh well," I appease my baby-faced confidant, "It's certainly unique— his technique, but maybe have a word with him after I leave. Back me up in suggesting he works on adopting less of an aggressive approach. Many women in my shoes would've misread his intentions."

He nods his head several times in agreement. "Sure thing. And don't let it stop you from having a great day when you get where you're going to. Enjoy the wine, Ma'am."

Ma'am. Yes, I know it's intended as polite terminology, especially if you're unaware of a woman's name or age but barely anyone under thirty uses it in common speech in California these days. I'm reminded all the more of my apparent descent into seniority whenever it's applied directly to me.

"The wine. It's not all for me! I'm spending the weekend with my former college roommates," I feel the need to clarify. I want him to see that I'm not a lonely, lush of a certain age. I want him to recognize my vitality.

"Oh yeah. Which school?" he asks.

"We're celebrating our twentieth reunion of graduation. UC Santa Cruz," I explain. "Liked it so much, I never left. In the mountains that is, not on campus! And we've plenty of practice in working our way through a case of wine."

"No kidding," he replies. Undoubtedly, he's heard all the small talk, working a tasting room on the coast. "We're open all weekend if you need to restock."

I keep that in mind as I wave goodbye. The silhouette of the Raven fading slowly into the distance, leaving behind nothing but silence and a faint ripple of unease in the air.

I plug my cellphone into its charger, taking a minute more to compose myself. This, after an especially fraught call with my demanding Mum not half an hour earlier. I check myself in the mirror, release my messy pony tail and brush my hair, spritz a little rose water and orange blossom on my pulse points.

I intend to present as cool, calm and collected by the time I reach Jamie. I really do. Who am I kidding? So much disconnect for so long. I'm determined to meet him and the others where they're at. No judgement. And hopefully they'll feel the same. All of them.

Spring has arrived amidst the cliffside and rolling hills along the stunning Sonoma Coast. I inhale as I press the lever to release the sunroof. It slowly folds into itself until I hear it stick, noisily on the case of wine which means I must jump out immediately and reposition its load in the trunk.

The land is regenerated after a winter of extreme weather and I breathe it in, calming myself once more. Not a mile off shore, the spout of a gray whale making its great migration rises up from the ocean in a plume. Heaven on earth and sea. To the naked eye there is absolutely nothing amiss on such a glorious morning.

Friday, Late Morning

My intention of a carefree, wind-in-my-hair approach isn't quite going to plan. I rub my eyes. My lips are chafed and my unruly hair still a mess. I pull over to the side of the mud flats in an attempt to tidy myself up and regain some semblance of composure.

The first thing I hear is the collective peep-peep of a flock of Western sandpipers pecking intently for small invertebrates in the wet sludge. I gather a bunch of wayward strawberry-red strands into a loose pony tail as the distinctive sound of the pecking pierces through the overlapping orchestra of a low tide.

The peep of the sandpipers and the soft purr of the engine in park are soon obscured by the chug of an approaching fishing boat. I reach over and rummage around in the over-stuffed glove compartment, retrieving the tail end of a hydrating chap stick and a tin of curiously strong mints.

Pungent aromas of dead fish transmit on the breeze. Its collective origin's a long wall of nets and multi-colored floating devices stacked along the roadside.

I'm about to put the car into drive when my phone beeps with a notice of a new voice message. Mum. Again. Damn it. I'd clearly annoyed her even more having cut her off mid-stream. If I don't take the time to listen to whatever it is that she didn't get to say earlier, it will have to wait. And that will irritate her royally. I press my shoulders back into the driver seat, brace myself and hit play.

"Hello darling," her message plays out, "It's only me again. Mum."

Like I wouldn't know her voice. Formality being her middle name.

Picture, if you will, my mother as a woman of a certain age—straight out of central casting for PBS Masterpiece Theater. Doesn't matter which mystery or period piece you choose, as long as it's quintessentially British. Feel free to slot her into your imagination like one of those old-fashioned paper dress-up dolls we were gifted in press-out-books as girls. She'll fit any random role that calls for a well presented, sixty-something, retired English teacher-type. Think persistent lady detective, or, alternatively a respectable villain hiding in plain sight. Simply throw on a floral frock, a hand-knitted cardigan, and place a leather-bound edition of a Thomas Hardy novel in her hands and you've created the perfect caricature.

"I'm mulling over what you said, dear." This is never a good sign. Wait for it, I warn myself . . .

"If you really can't make time to come home this summer, then I'll simply plan on an extended visit to you instead."

I close my eyes in order to better absorb her message. Delivered in her polished Norfolk rhythm and melody—deceivingly pleasant in its sing-songy lilt. I close my eyes and suck purposefully on a second mint, dislodging it from the roof of my mouth with the tip of my tongue. I'm bracing myself for the inevitable hint of neglect. She blames my late father for my becoming a doctor. For everything, really. She was the intensely proud and long-suffering wife of a general practitioner until he left her.

"Lord knows I've been patient with your schedule, Tamsin," she continues. "But if I'm to travel all the way to California, it would be nice to know I'm welcome to stay for a while."

My heart sinks. I should've seen this coming. Mum is in the process of selling her small, rare and used bookstore, once such a lifeline to her community. The charming, decades-old store she took over after her retirement from teaching, catered to summer season tourists, for the most part, visitors to the Norfolk Coast and its holiday cottages and caravan sites. Since the advent of reading tablets and the allure of large font and audiobooks, the demand for used books has dwindled significantly. That little store kept her occupied and busy for years and blessedly out of my hair. Clearly, she's broadcasting her preparedness for another new chapter. And if I'm to feature in its opening paragraph, I'd do best to brace myself for the coming months.

After all, it was she who named me after an especially lac-luster character in Hardy's 1878 novel, *Return of The Native*. I've been fighting the ideal of the wallflower varietal of an English rose since I was old enough to have read the book and judged for myself.

I count to ten, breathing in and out, as I attempt to tune back in to the sounds of the harbor. A second aluminum boat slices through the water, gentle waves lapping onto shore, the white noise of distant sea birds. It would be calming, dreamlike if I weren't so concerned with the realization that there's nothing to keep Mum in the UK other than the cottage she inherited from Gran.

The breathing room the cottage and bookstore afforded me was a life-saver for my own personal development. It took me years to persuade myself that I am, in fact, a grown woman of my own making and not the fantasy-compliant-only-daughter I never had any intention of becoming.

I scrutinize myself in the side mirror, mentally brushing aside my mother's sweeping glance of disapproval—the condescending look she doesn't even try to disguise. In her mind, I've let her down with my lack of attention to polite, daughterly detail and my basic refusal to model my life in the shadow of hers. Her biggest regret what she considered my impetuous choice to stay on in the States, to launch my career, my adult life, here, a world away from hers.

A squirrel darts across the road, narrowly avoiding the wheels of a truck in the opposite lane. Mum wraps up her message with a decidedly curt order, advising me to settle things with Jamie for once and for all. I'd foolishly mentioned I would see him this weekend. It's her dream that I'll give up this American escapade one of these days, my ties to Jamie, my career in California and head on home to her. Maybe she thinks she's coming over to reclaim me.

"Don't you think you've left the poor man hanging long enough?" she'd asked. And then, for added punch: "Who else will want you in your forties, especially if you can't even be bothered to draw up the divorce papers?"

No holds barred once the niceties of her impending visit were out of the way. Now, this is a classic example of my mother taking pleasure in her habitual and uninvited meddling. It doesn't help that she's considered herself the doyenne of marital dissolution since Dad divorced her in my early teens.

The inside of my throat burns with a familiar taste of indignation. I swallow what's left of the mint. The more my mother pushes her agenda, the more I pull away.

Besides, she should know better than to stir the pot with the sensitive subject of Jamie and me. It's taken me the last few years to consider myself as being anywhere near safely out of the woods when it comes to confronting our split. I've had plenty of time to think and reflect on my vulnerabilities, my numerous regrets.

Don't confuse the cliché of my suffering in silence, my British reserve, with a lack of ambition in the love department. That's not it at all. I've subconsciously played the ultimate long game, by instinct, learning to overcome and accept and forgive more slowly. I'm not cowardly, or lazy, or heartless in my holding back on a divorce. I didn't want one. I don't want one. And from his lack of action in that department, for whatever reason, I'm hoping he doesn't either.

I grip the steering wheel with both hands, lean back into my seat and stretch out my spine. This weekend is a real chance to attempt to fix our mistakes, address any lingering confusion. It's why I agreed to meet Jamie at Spud Point Marina this morning. A calculated move on my part. We'll be thrust back into the mix with the others soon enough. It's my intention to have him all to myself for a little while.

I look around me, gathering stray wrappers, empty cans of sparkling water and stuff them into a paper bag to recycle. I can't stand the clutter of a road trip. With the gear in drive, I inhale the salt air and step on the accelerator.

I've been through hell and back in the last few years and it has taught me so much about my emotions, my micro-decision making. If you'd sat at the bedsides of as many dying people as I have, you'd know yourself better, too. There's nothing like a world health crisis to teach us that life is all about love. Nothing else really matters: not how successful we are or how much money we make. It's who is there to love us when it comes down to it and who we love in return.

I'm far more content with who I am now, what I've learned, who I've become. And I need to show Jamie how far I've advanced in my quest for self-acceptance, how ready I am to accept intimacy back into my life. I've changed, inside and out, no longer such a shy, internally uncertain human.

The thermometer hovers in the mid-fifties. I'm bundled up in layers of practical outdoor gear, the damp, chilly air cutting through. I silently will the sun to break through, but as I near the parking lot and peer through the misted windscreen, it's clear that it's not going to happen anytime soon.

Jamie's plan is to dock his boat, *Pearl*, at Bodega Harbor for the weekend. Without a vehicle to get around, he's asked me for a ride up to the beach house—and anywhere else he might need to go. Bingo! He's all mine, at least for these brief moments.

He's standing off to the side, clearly there with intent—his posture alert, gaze scanning, waiting just for me. He looks genuinely delighted the moment our eyes meet, his whole face lighting up with unmistakable warmth. He throws both arms into the air in an eager, unmistakable wave, like he's been holding it in and can't wait another second. I wait my turn in a short line of cars, jostling for a spot among an eclectic range of sleek, brand-new electric models and aging, exhaust-belching rust-buckets that have survived decades of coastal wear and tear.

My heart beats absurdly fast at the sight of his pleasingly open face. Some things never change. Best way I can describe it, is a soul connection, this thing that binds me to Jamie, his optimistic, uncomplicated spirit. The mere thought of him is uplifting, despite our troubles. Seeing him in person is revitalizing. I've missed him. I raise my hand in greeting, open the door and step out onto the gravel.

Jamie is tall and of medium build, resilient against the elements in his sleek-black boating gear, his bags set neatly beside a forlorn, bronze sculpture of a fisherman, dedicated, assumedly, to the countless local lives lost at sea. His head is tipped upwards as I approach, an unruly mop of sandy-hair falling to his shoulders. He's as pleasing on the eye as ever. An unselfish man, morally good at the core, aside from the one major error of judgement, the misdeeds that led to my leaving him. It's complicated. We're flawed, all of us, if we're honest, even the most unadventurous of us. It's figuring out how to live with this, to forgive, that is key.

It really was foolishly optimistic of me to have driven with the roof down. I'm self-conscious enough as it is. I tuck my messy hair behind my ears, willing the sun to make another break through the heavy cloud cover. Sunshine is like a painter's brush, coloring the world in brighter hues, making everything look better.

A crowd of gulls and raptors screeches overhead. Our feathered friends sail and swoop amidst the cloud-troubled ozone. I slow my stride as I make my way over to greet him. What does he care about my hair? I hold a hand on my head to keep it from forming a mask around my face. A secondary ruckus ensues in a bank of trees beyond the row of harbor-front cottages. It's the shrill, rasping squawk of pelican nestlings, competing with the intensifying yelp of the gulls.

Neither of us speaks as we embrace, a flock of aerobatic, white-tailed kite and other coastal birds catching my eye beyond. There's a huddle of them bracing against the chill on the rocks that surround the harbor separating us from the ocean beyond. It's encouraging, these long-term relationships of avian colonies, old friends with common interests and shared-space looking out for one another. It's the kind of mutual benefit society that we're looking for this weekend in a way. Previously segregated humans, pooling our strengths and resources for a few days. What a concept. Nothing wrong with that in theory. The wild card is our shared history. A host of indisputable personality issues.

"Are you ready for this?" I ask.

"Cue the epic soundtrack," he replies. "Let's roll." The grin on his face tells me he's slightly more optimistic than me that things will go well over the long weekend.

It's been close to a year since Jamie and I last set eyes on each other. Last time, we met up for dinner in San Francisco after a conference I attended late last spring. Back then I wasn't ready to risk pushing it any further than a convivial Thai curry and a beer. Seeing him in person is disarming, no matter how composed I am going in. He's a man of few words, sometimes clumsy in delivery, though we've never not kept up with one another by phone or text, given that we're still technically married, though not in the conventional sense. Trust takes time to rebuild and the fact we've remained on respectful terms bodes well at least.

I realize this is confusing. I'll explain more after we settle in. Suffice to say, our arrangement to meet up at noon is working out well, seeing as we're to arrive at the beach house promptly, no later than two after a winding drive north along Highway One.

It's silly, but I'll admit I've built-up quite an atypical romcom, movie-set backdrop in my mind. Jamie and me, center frame, the majestic horizon to our left. The sweeping vista of the Pacific—cattle pastures, wild and rocky hills of green to our right. It's a landscape like no other, the perfect setting for our separate paths to intertwine and fuse.

But first, before I take off my rose-colored glasses, Jamie has the heavier load of his weekend shopping list to fulfill and, as we'd discussed a couple of days earlier by text, we're to combine a quick bite to eat with his shopping assignments on-route.

"Best get our shit together," he suggests as he leans over and positions a large, zippered duffle on top of his solid black guitar case, that he's rested along the full length of the rear passenger seat. He's balancing two crumpled, paper grocery bags under his other arm. One of the bags threatens to spill a yellow mound of Meyer lemons, which he subsequently informs me he has harvested just this morning from a wide-hipped, dewy dwarf tree in his sunny side yard. He drops his aromatic haul on the floor of the passenger seat, by his feet.

It's a joyful scene, an abundant reunion and the simplicity of which is the beauty of it. I'm struggling to maintain my composure when all I really want to do is wrap my arms around him, confess I'm finally over our extended physical estrangement and declare my true intent. I imagine he can hear my heart as it continues beating a drumroll through my sensible, weatherproof layers.

The lemons omit a spicy fragrance of bergamot and thyme. It's as intoxicating as the natural scent of the man who has brought them to me, the man who is still technically my husband. I inhale through my nose and simultaneously run the tip of my tongue over my sea-salted lower lip. I can almost taste the honey-like lemon juice, the fortuitous and tangy result of a cross between a regular lemon and a mandarin. The second bag, he explains, in his characteristic drawl, contains the white-bottomed stalks of a bunch of young, cattail plants, otherwise known to a foreigner such as myself, as bullrushes.

"The supermarket of the wild," he declares with an enthusiastic sweep of his arms. "Darn. A survivalist's top-pick for tonight's spring salad. You secured the wine?" he asks, checking I've made good on my chore.

"In the trunk," I reply, gesturing to the back of me. "Don't worry, as if I'd forget. I'd never hear the end of it, otherwise. One half Chardonnay—Serena's orders, one half Pinot Noir. Sonoma Coast. Cool climate. Only the best. Though there's a story behind it."

"Wine stories never disappoint," he says. "Feel free to spill. First things first though, how was the drive up from our favorite Surf City?"

I left my place in the Santa Cruz mountains just after seven this morning, stopping for a brief bathroom break after a traffic hold-up on the Golden Gate Bridge.

He listens, attentively, as I describe in detail my having cut across through Mill Valley, weaving my way up the longer, scenic route from Stinson Beach and along the shallow banks of Tomales Bay. I share in detail how the mist rose from the rain-swollen, brackish waters as I'd cut inland from the tiny western town of Tomales through to Valley Ford.

"I stopped for a coffee at the cheese factory and bakery before I made my way out to the coast and up to the winery."

"This little weekend away sure has taken some serious collective effort," Jamie replies. "Appreciate the ride by the way. Perfect timin'."

"No problem," I glance his way, fleetingly as I sort myself out in the driver's seat. "And me still driving a car of this age, it's a small miracle that I made it all the way out here in one piece."

Jamie pats the dashboard, affectionately. He knows this old motor almost as well as he knows me. It's as if the three of us are present in the moment, happy. Relieved. There's a sense of nostalgia about this morning. I was driving this old thing back when Jamie and I were together. It was Dad who had taught me to take care of the basics on his prize vintage Jag, how to do a tire and an oil change, that kind of thing, the summer before he died. I pride myself in keeping this old tin can of mine on the road.

"Hey, I'm divin' for sea urchin on Sunday," Jamie says. "Not sure if you're aware of just how awesome the meals we have in store are?"

I glance over at him as I start up the engine. He raises his eyebrows, long eyelashes like two, soft, dark brushes. They sweep across a set of pebble-colored eyes that are virtually dancing in anticipation of his impending mission. "Serena's strict instructions. Uni pasta —Japanese-style, a Sonoma Coast seafood session worthy of a grand finale feast."

I'm reminded of a sea urchin spaghetti dish he used to make me. "That dish, the one with the white wine, lots of lemon and olive oil?" I ask, my taste-memory intact and my tummy rumbling in tandem.

"You remember? That one was an old Italian recipe. What Serena has in mind is a Japanese version, richer. Calls for a heavy cream, white wine, sauteed garlic, shallot, red pepper flakes—it's the sweet and salty flavor from the buttery, rich urchin that takes center stage," he replies, waxing lyrical on the subject as he is wont to do when it comes to fruits of the ocean.

"Okay then," I reply, with a whistle, though I can't help but think of the two of them sharing this decadent dish in some, past, intimate setting. She was licking her fingers in glee, no doubt. I boot this jealous fantasy to the back of my mind. "Sounds delicious. Just promise me those lemons will make an appearance."

Ocean truffles—urchins. Such a delicacy and too pricey to buy in large portions from a fish market. It's just like Serena to send Jamie out on a cold-water fresh urchin dive in order to up her game. I bristle at the thought of her still bossing him around. Seems a tad excessive an ask, given that it's been such unpredictable weather of late. I stop myself from saying as much. It's his thing.

"You still diving this way with your kelp restoration crew?" I ask, gesturing beyond the harbor walls toward the choppy coastal waters. I'm genuinely interested in the program.

"I'm plannin' on getting' back in there on a weekly basis soon as the water warms," he replies. He's facing me as he fastens his belt, his head is dangerously close to mine. Those eyes again, flecked with gold and burned into my soul. It's always been about the eyes for me, especially his. Jamie's intelligence, his natural charm and humor shine through. He has no problem speaking through his eyes. They stop time for me.

My stomach lurches as he gently moves a strand of hair from above my eye. I may as well stick with the roof down now. What the heck.

"*Floating in the middle?*" I ask, staying on topic. "Isn't that the diver's term? That's how I picture you when you're out there on the ocean, Jamie. Floating in the middle. In your element."

I start the car, finally, though I could sit here, truthfully, inhaling his essence all day.

"Ha,' he says. "My happy place. I taught you that, right? A diver must be naturally buoyant to be safe—able to hover motionless in mid-water."

My eyes are fixed firmly on the road as I head out of the harbor parking lot.

"That's me out when it comes to any late career diving," I joke. "Remember the time you talked me into lessons? I sank, miserably. Every single time."

I'm embarrassed to bring it up, but it's no use pretending that everyone is a natural when it comes to flotation. It started for me as a kid. A fear of deep-water drowning.

Growing up with my parents had been a slow suffocation in itself. It had reached a near-strangulation point when Mum discovered that Dad was having an affair with a nurse, at work. A cluster bomb that resulted in a bitter divorce. Traumatic for me as the sole product of their failed union. This is one of the reasons I'm so grateful that Jamie hasn't yet asked me to sign papers. I'm not ready for the finality of drowning in my own isolation.

"Negatively buoyant," he recalls, his hands on his lap. "Yep. Hauled you back up to the surface like a sack a potatoes on more than a few tries. Too bad, as you're such a strong swimmer, otherwise, Tam. These days, I'd be signin' you up to assist, if it was anyway otherwise, urchin removal bein' key to the kelp forest restoration project. Never enough pairs of hands-on-board and in the water."

He rattles on enthusiastically for the next few minutes, despite the wind distorting our conversation. From what he tells me, California coastal diving efforts are starting to reap some significant return in reviving the ocean's health.

Strong swimmer aside, I've yet to adjust to the frigid waters of the Pacific, despite the length of time I've lived here. Doubt I ever will. Yes, I spent much of my childhood on the east coast of England. But the North Sea has nothing on the chill of the Pacific in summer. I also part blame the fact I was raised with sizzling summer holidays camping in the south of France, that is before Dad did what he did and Mum's seismic sense of betrayal, her fury taking over, sending massive ripples into my previously content little world.

Give me warm-water bathing in the Med any day. Don't get me wrong, I love boogie-boarding on a sunny day at the beach at Santa Cruz, but I draw the line at ocean swimming this far north. A wetsuit helps, but even then, it's not appealing to a lily-liver like me.

Jamie on the other hand is certifiably one of the crazy, cold-plungers by nature and birth-right.

Contented deer graze nonchalantly in an emerald green-grassy pasture on one side. The blue-grey Pacific on the other. As advertised. I introduce the topic of the Raven and the general theme of his rant.

It's an issue Jamie agrees on to a certain degree. "There have been several evacuations out here over the past few years," he explains. "Wildfire and storm seasons both. The climate playin' havoc with the meteoric calendar."

It's easy to dismiss the possibility of impending fury as wild flowers cheerily line the edge of the narrow road. Striped coral root, trillium, red-wood violet and thimbleberry. I recognize these colorful plants from the dog-eared California wildflower pocket guide tucked in my daypack. Briny air encapsulates us as we drive by lines of Friday lunch-goers snaking along the sidewalk leading to the Crab Shack.

The sky is the color of a three-day-old bruise. It's not looking ideal for the next few days, weather-wise.

"Good thing you're decked out in that bougie puffer jacket," Jamie remarks, intuitively, as he pinches my upper arm through the layers. "Sensitivity paddin' may be required over the next few days."

I do my best to maintain my focus on the road ahead as I reach out blindly and return the squeeze, nipping his toned bicep in response through a sleek layer of recycled polyester. We pass an RV park and head on up the steep, narrow lane, home to a tree-lined redwood grove with a hand-painted sign for a secret garden.

"Basically, what we're talkin' about is the green-washin' ploy of hospitality marketin' itself as sustainable," he says.

"Huh? Interesting."

Jamie explains how Sonoma County was once at the cutting-edge of California's coastal protection movement. He's being serious now. "This was long before the wine industry and others took hold, stakin' a claim on parcel after parcel of prime agricultural land throughout the region."

"I get it," I add. "I do. My being here. How much work am I prepared to do to minimize my environmental impact during my stay?"

"Kind of takes the buzz out of an innocent little road-trip," Jamie replies, with a shrug. "But it matters. Each time we head out on what we consider a harmless jaunt out to the coast. What we take, what we leave behind."

I'm intoxicated by his proximity. This is ridiculously uncool, I know.

"The ocean takes what it wants in turn," I reply.

"It's good to be here, anyways," he continues, like he's reading my thoughts. "With you."

I turn to look at him, briefly. There's a sense of anticipation in the air, as if the world is always on the edge of shifting—waves crashing or fog lifting, the harbor forever suspended between moments of stillness and motion.

He trains his eyes on the road ahead as if it's he who is driving. "We'll have plenty of time to debate the heavy stuff later. Let's eat first!"

My tummy rumbles as I pull into the parking lot beside the general store overlooking the water. It's packed, given that it's a Friday and lunch time.

I've an urge to make light after diving in deep so soon and I casually hook my arm through his as we make our way toward the store.

He grabs a shopping cart by its rusting handle and I watch as he proceeds to pile in several bundles of firewood from a covered stack in front of the store. Look at us, shopping together, I'm tempted to declare, but I don't. I'd once imagined a life for myself that was completely different from my parents'. A solid guy by my side, a happy, stable, gaggle of kids. I swallow my regret. It had come so close to turning out that way.

"Well, it's gonna be an interestin' weekend for sure. Hashin' it out," he says.

"And why on earth would you think there'll be any drama?" I ask, more than a hint of sarcasm in my voice as we wander overstuffed aisles, side-by-side as in a past life, on a newly-wed, student budget.

"Unfinished business?" I'm making light, but it's true, the two of us are a prime example. The harboring of a wide range of repressed emotions between any number of us could very well blow it all up if we're not careful.

This time it's Jamie who reaches out as he stops and extends a long, steady arm in my direction. We're standing in front of a colorful display of crab nets, kites and jumper cables. He rests his arm across my shoulders for precisely one minute. I'm counting the seconds. I'd forgotten how the touch of an arm, a hand, in the right circumstances, is capable of eliciting such an intense chemical reaction. The tautness of his muscles transforms my shoulders into a set of electrical receptors that shoot a series of sudden sharp signals straight into my heart. I'll take what I can get. I fail to convince myself that this gesture is nothing out of the ordinary, further evidence that I am most definitely not over him.

"We're all human." He eases his arm off my shoulders, letting it fall casually to his side as his eyes scan my face. Then, with subtle precision, he steps back. "Unfortunately, as we both know, some of us—myself included—have a regrettable tendency toward . . . well, having the emotional depth of a puddle."

"Bubble wrap to soften any impending blows?" I quip, my cheeks heating as I motion to a pile of mailing supplies. One of the many things I find attractive about Jamie is that while he never stoops to badmouthing others, he doesn't shy away from owning his own screw-ups.

He orders for me at the deli counter. I find this interesting, endearing and encouraging in equal parts. A Turkey Club on wheat roll for me, mustard, mayo, tomato, lettuce, no onion, avocado extra. For him, an Italian Sub—god-awful, greasy salami, layers of pepperoni, coppa, pepperoncini, lettuce, tomato, onion, oil and vinegar.

"May as well go for it before we get there," he says. "There'll be no such thing as a processed package of meat in Serena's cooler that's for sure."

"What? No watery, out-of-season tomatoes?" I ask.

He throws in a share-size bag of salt and vinegar chips, one of my favorite vices, selected from a rack at the counter. "For you," he says as he detours to pick out three dozen cans of local craft beers from the glass fronted refrigerator. "You're on vacation, Doc. Drink?"

"I'll stick with water for now," I reply. "No drinking and driving and adding to the chagrin of the chap who gave me the lecture, earlier." Besides, there will be plenty of lord-knows-what on offer later.

We eat from thick, pink paper packages spread out on a wooden bench overlooking a pier that's seen better days. The crunch and sharpness of the salt and vinegar chips lingers long after the last bite, leaving me craving more.

An elderly, sinewy man and woman in matching aqua-blue waterproof gear paddle by in a pair of identical orange kayaks. Crows line the deck railing, staring intently, waiting patiently for us to throw them a crumb. The air is thick with a briny, earthy perfume.

"Oh wow, there's one of his flyers. I don't believe it. The Raven." I point to a poster, printed on green paper, pinned to a post on the wooden deck. Its edges are curled and it's taken a beating, but I recognize the *Save Our Coastline* message and the drawings of fungi, fish and reptiles are impressive.

"Good for him," Jamie says. "Maybe it's an omen, him pickin' you out for his sermon."

"What kind of omen?" I ask.

"The kind that keeps us on track with our goal for healthy-intentions this weekend," Jamie says. "We're all on the same page I guess, in theory, goin' forward together as we've planned, but, as you say, there's bound to be differences of opinion."

"Showing up is key. That's the starting point when it comes to the possibility of the seven of us coming to a consensus. Cementing the foundation of deep, consistent mutual care we'd promised each other," I add, serious now.

"Selective kin. Nice idea in theory," Jamie says, offering a thumbs-up and a shrug. He lifts his bottle of vitamin water in a mock toast, taking a long, thirsty swig.

How serious we were back then. The seven of us, senior year—pledging a future bound by blood. We made a pact, solemn and dramatic, pricking our thumbs one by one with a safety pin, its tip briefly kissed by candle flame.

We finish up our lunch, Jamie and me, tossing paper, napkins and the unashamedly emptied chip package into a recycle hole in the trash bin before heading back to the car. Jamie unloads the shopping cart with its considerable haul.

"That's a boatload of firewood," I remark. "Trunk's full, so pile it on the floor behind my seat."

"For the beach," he replies. "There's a pit."

"Ever the romantic." I raise my eyebrows in jest. Half jest. Sitting around a firepit, stargazing with him is as fine a prospect as any.

Jamie wraps a tissue around his pinkie finger and proceeds to wipe a spot of mustard from the corner of my mouth. My heart skips another in its series of enthusiastic, if not ecstatic beats. One of the things I adore about him are these small acts of kindness. Even a tiny gesture like this hits me in the gut. In a good way.

"You missed a spot," he says. "Can't have the good doc arriving disheveled."

I navigate up along the ribbon of silver that is the coast highway as it weaves north and snakes itself inland, breaking away from the hemline of the ocean. We pass a surf shop on the right, a sport fishing shop to the left and a story-book, pink and white store selling colorful wind socks, sand windmills, candy and kites. There is a sign for a farmer's market (Sundays) and another advertising horseback riding on the beach. A turkey vulture sweeps low, its keen eyes scanning the earth like a shadowed detective. Fish and chips, oysters—red pokers and giant purple lupines frame the scene.

Several hairpin turns and I'm mindful of the case of wine I wedged in the trunk as I ruminate on what's in store for the weekend. The wind carries a tangy spray from the ocean. There's a sharpness to it, the scent of unyielding vastness.

Echoes of a ukulele carry on the breeze, tender notes floating through the air. I spot a lone musician, a figure of quiet solitude seated on the hood of his Honda, parked facing the ocean and gazing into the distance from a narrow overlook. His faded flannel sleeves are rolled up to his elbows, his hair a tousled mess. A little ways along, two older men with one large black-and-white poodle resting between them, picnic from a basket at bench overlooking the surf. The table is covered with a red-and-white-checked cloth. The one with a silver pony-tail, is holding a thermos. I notice all the doors are open on their dark green, brand-new Subaru nearby, awaiting its plates.

Further along, a hawk sits sentry on a ragged 19th century fence post, scanning the wide panorama. Wild fennel explodes with frothy green fronds, the vibrant chaos of new life along both sides of the coastal highway. A pack of Lycra-clad cyclists in shiny, black helmets funnels into single file, taking the curves, like a pack of gigantic gnats on a springtime mating campaign.

A sign saying *Your Tax Dollars at Work, Rebuilding California* announces a new stretch of highway.

I wonder . . . am I really strong enough to forgive—not just him, but her too? To release the weight of what happened and still choose to move forward?

Friday, Early Afternoon

A foraging doe and her startled, young fawns scatter like leaves as we navigate down the steep, narrow driveway at Serena's place. A sun-bleached, decorative windsock twirls its silken body energetically, a conically shaped tube, like a giant sock, indicating wind direction and speed.

My stomach is unsettled after having navigated a twenty-minute series of switchbacks along the raw cliff edge.

Picture this—a vintage California beach house, windswept, modest in size, minding its own business, an imprint of multi-generational family as it perches on the edge of the western world. Its redwood exterior never painted, presumably so as to blend into the seascape, as if sprouted, spontaneously from the ground—its rustic walls, windows, doors, roof—on its own accord and at some stage in the first quarter of the last century.

Powerful waves below swoop up sand, scooping it over and over, as since time began, harnessing the power of the ocean—a repetitive motion like a giant sheet of abrasive sandpaper grating against the face of the eroding cliff edge, hour after hour, day after day, month after month, year after relentless year.

"Listen to it," I say. "It's relentless, the pounding." I linger in the driver's seat a moment longer. I'm delaying the moment I'm face-to-face with Serena, held back by the friction we will inevitably generate between us. This place, however, it tugs at me, whispering its loaded welcome on the salty wind. It's as if the house has interwoven itself within me over the years. It's a part of me, of all of us.

"And this old place," I say, motioning to the house. "Inching ever closer to its tipping point." There, I've broken the spell. Spoken the unspeakable.

Jamie nods in agreement. He rolls down the window and rests his elbow on the door frame in order to better assess the stretch of cliff to our right. His career in the building trade has undergone a growth spurt with a bunch of green, sustainable buildings these past couple of years. Jamie's adept at utilizing renewable organic materials such as wood, hemp and bamboo—carbon absorbing plants and trees.

"Any cliff fronted by a sandy beach such as this, well, simple truth is that it's only a matter of time. Erosion happens twice as fast when ocean waves are tearin' into it day and night. And we'd be foolin' ourselves to think otherwise."

"Let's just enjoy the moment," I suggest. "Assuming it's safe enough for one more weekend. Put the future on hold for a few days. Time to turn the clock back a couple decades."

"Good with me," he replies, as he pushes opens the door with the reinforced toe of his boot. "Party time. Let it all go for now. Long as we don't dare forget who's in charge."

Serena. Our host, she's planned the itinerary for our reunion, starting with a commencement hike as soon as we're all assembled and unpacked. The idea being to start the weekend as we mean to go on, communally, foraging seasonal ingredients for our weekend's keep.

Sounds a little idealistic? Elitist even? Rummaging around on the hillside in order to put food on the communal table. I love a farmer's market, don't get me wrong, fresh, local, seasonal. Serena however, she takes the concept to another level entirely, always has. She's hardcore. All about the wild foods. River too, since they've been living out here together. I know it sounds good—intentional and mindful and all that, but the idea of the rhythms and cycles of the land dictating my entire diet is too extreme for me. Nobody here works the hours I do.

Still, neither Jamie or I make mention of our deli lunch with its dubious origins. And I've a secret stash of trail mix and energy bars in the trunk of my car, just in case. Serena greets us, barefoot at the door. She's decked out in a pistachio-green, woolen poncho and a pair of mustard-colored, flared leggings, all dirty-blonde hair and blue eyes, the colors of the landscape. Two black and tan mini dachshund rescues, Minnie and Myrtle yap at her heels. She's every bit the boho-matriarch of her coastal nest and seeing as she's clearly not about to offer a hand to unload, it takes us three or four trips back and forth from the car to offload everything into the house. Jamie carries the wine in first and then the firewood, which he leaves outside, the heaviest items.

"You're the dude," I whisper to him, in passing, as I lug in my duffle and head back out to cover the convertible. It looks like rain and anyway, I know better than to risk any damage from nesting squirrels, racoons and lord knows what else might attempt to take refuge inside of my vehicle.

"Ever the gentleman," Serena remarks, flashing her perfect white teeth in Jamie's direction. "I would've hitched that roof up for the ride, despite what *Tippi* here had in mind."

Sweet scent of lilacs softens her opening attack. Instant nostalgia. The England of my childhood and early teens. It catches me off-guard. I'm surprised that lilacs are able to survive as well as they do out here along this rugged coastline. A strip of long-established, eight-foot bushes benefits, I deduce, from the warmth of the house siding and its protection from frost by the overhead eaves. The first of two annual blooms, this old lilac, I remember from past visits, is blessed with the same romantic fragrance as that of my grandmother's garden.

"It was invigorating," I reply, intentionally sweeping a curtain of dampened hair from my eyes. She's referring to the actress, Tippi Hedren, the one who sported a fur coat and silk headscarf in one of the famous scenes of Hitchcock's iconic 1963 movie, *The Birds*. Unlike me in my rickety, old VW, Tippi cut an elegant and sophisticated figure behind the wheel of her open-top Austin Martin as she motored out in the most glamorous fashion toward the small town of Bodega.

I spot crumbs in the corners of Serena's pink lips, a late lunch of her own, hurriedly eaten in order to fortify herself for the onslaught of the rest of us.

"Wouldn't miss the chance of a full-immersion," I declare, for added measure, forcing a beaming smile. "Bracing in fact."

Jamie turns on his heel and tips his head, tuning out our goading banter as he continues to listen for the ocean. He has an ear for the waves and the cobalt water's changing nature with the wind patterns. I switch from watching him to Serena, she herself intent on gaging my reaction to her jabbing.

If she hadn't called me to re-acknowledge her past wrong-doing and her desire to make amends, I wouldn't be here. There are some pretty strong emotions beneath our diplomatic truce. And she knows, I imagine, she's figured it out. I want him back. And this weekend will be as good a way as any to stress test the viability of our graduation pact.

The air inside the house is redolent of eggs over-easy and toast. Thick with comfort, familiar, a soft embrace. A tea kettle whistles on the stovetop. It's like stepping into a pair of old slippers, coming back.

"It's awesome to see you both," River declares, striding forward and embracing. Their greeting is neither rushed nor stiff, but warm and steady. The comforting weight of a familiar presence. River's touch is solid but not overwhelming, a quiet strength that makes me feel both grounded and safe. An embrace that holds space for a thousand unspoken things since we last met.

"Sure is. We're so happy you're here," Serena adds, sidestepping me and wrapping her arms around Jamie.

Serena and River have been together as partners since the pandemic began. At first it was a trial rematch, they said, though it didn't appear to take much time for them to commit. I couldn't help being jealous of their isolated coastal-front hideout at first, a love nest in a romantic and remote location, away from the coughing, spluttering, infected masses.

But after a while, I grew increasingly grateful for my own small space, my safe haven within a small, caring community in the mountains. The peaceful presence of my neighbors. My work. As terrifying as it was during the early days of lockdown, the silence and the comfort of home was my lifeline in a time of unfathomable loss.

What is it they say? When you live in awareness, you become more in control of yourself? Nothing like a few years of compounded healthcare worker trauma to make a person grateful for the small mercies of life.

While I prized my privacy off-duty, we'd looked out for one another up there in the fire-and-flood-prone mountains, my neighbors and me, grocery shopping for those amongst us who were the most vulnerable, dropping packages of baked goods and pots of soup on porches, splitting packs of toilet paper, flour and butter when they were scarce. In retrospect, Serena and River were far more isolated out here on the rugged Sonoma Coast, loved-up, yes, but detached from the rest of the world for months on end. I guess that's a make or break for any relationship. Somehow, remarkably, it looks like they've figured it out. Thrived even.

River's cropped hair is a statement all on its own—jagged and choppy, like the showy plumage of a bird-of-paradise plant caught mid-flight. A deep claret-red forms the base, vibrant and intense, with bursts of electric blue and bright yellow woven in, playfully. I search their face, discreetly.

The two of them surely had issues to work through after they'd shacked up, but looking at them now, as River tucks a toned, tattooed-arm, its colorful design of doves, skulls and roses showcased comfortably around Serena's slim waist, they're certainly presenting a positive and united front.

Months of navigating personal challenges and dealing with external judgments, I'd imagine, knowing them as I do. River is non-binary, and I'd guess this pair probably drew uninvited attention in such a remote place. Many couples didn't last past the first few months of intense isolation, but Serena and River—well, they seem to have found their rhythm, settling in together with ease.

But then, I notice something— something in River's eyes—that makes me rethink everything I thought I knew.

Friday, Late-Afternoon

———

There was no prior thought to the subject of our sleeping arrangements, at least on my part. Eva, Jamie and I stand side-by-side by the kitchen counter, shuffling our feet, a trio of mismatched socks on a laundry line, awaiting a suitable pairing.

Last dibs are in the form of a nook, a small space which connects to the living room with its single day bed and high window and a double sofa bed in the small sleeping/sun porch.

"I'll take the single," Eva is all too eager and quick off the mark. Billy and Nate have bagged the bedroom at the far end of the main floor.

Serena and River are in a larger, bonus bedroom which Serena's late mother, Veronica, converted years ago in a portion of the basement below the main house. The other half of the downstairs remains in its original condition—dirt floors and rock walls. I wonder if the old cider press is still there. I picture dusty cans of preserves from decades past amongst all the old fishing gear that lurks in the shadows.

Serena outlines our limited options:

"Eva, I'd kinda thought you and Tamsin might be more comfortable sharing the sofa bed in the sun porch," she suggests. She's drawing a small circle on the hardwood floor with her big toe, hoping Eva will not persist. But Eva stands her ground.

We follow one another in single file, like a flock of docile sheep, taking a look at our non-options. The double sofa bed in the sun porch sits under the eaves of a wall of framed and fading Grateful Dead posters. It's covered with a pretty, blue and yellow, handsewn quilt made up of nine same-sized squares pieced in three rows of three with matching pillow covers.

It was one thing for me to fantasize about Jamie and me getting back together, but the prospect of us bunking up with no such thing as a warm-up is a little intimidating. The self-critic in me begins to squirrel away, gnawing at any initial confidence I'd built. I scratch my head. This is moving way too fast. My knees are wobbly. I don't like being put on the spot, feeling vulnerable.

"Oh, get over it, Tam, quit being such a prude," Serena says, eyeing me closely as she pivots in her stance. She had clearly not intended the sleeping arrangements to work out this way, but neither had she taken steps to construe things otherwise. It would require making a scene with Eva to reverse it.

"Top-to-toe, like you set out to do in the first place," she says looking first at me then at Jamie with a studious gaze.

She knows better than anyone how easily even the best-of-platonic intentions may be led astray.

"Fine with me," Jamie replies, casually, shrugging off any awkward decision-making as he bounds off to the entryway like an affable golden retriever, returning to the sunroom with his and my duffle bags in his capable paws. We avoid making unnecessary eye contact with one another, he and I, which is true to form, given our non-confrontational natures.

I offer a polite smile, my neutral expression slowly shifting into a forced veneer of ease, as though I'm completely fine with it all.

And it doesn't help that Serena's on to me like a panther, prowling, stalking her prey. I'll not give her the satisfaction of messing with me today. It's certainly not for her to hit the defrost button, hand us back to one another, serve us up like yesterday's reheated supper.

I watch her closely as she stoops and proceeds to scoop up Minnie and Myrtle, one in each arm. She snuggles them close, planting a series of kisses on one slick head after another.

"Never apart, these two," she says. "And never far from my side. My babies," she adds, in a sugar-sweet tone.

It's getting on in the afternoon. Outside, faint sunlight strains through an overcast sky. It's past time for us to set off for the first activity on Serena's agenda. A row of our freshly deposited hiking boots awaits us in the entryway, alongside the addition of a collection of small, wicker baskets, which makes me think of kindergartners at the tiny Waldorf preschool that's close to my house.

I dose myself with nasal spray in addition to the seasonal allergy pill I took earlier. The moment the nozzle meets the inside of my nostril, there's a sharp, almost electric coldness, a brief, invasive chill that makes my eyes water. I've been suffering spontaneous sneezing fits from the pollen that has settled in my hair and on my face from the drive up. This makes me think ahead to the wine I'll drink this evening and I weigh up whether the addition of alcohol is worth any further suffering. There's an odd taste at the back of my throat, sharp and metallic, as if the mist has traveled too far down and left its mark. I'd forgotten how intense the spring allergens are around here. I probably look like a panda from having rubbed so many circles around my eyes.

I reach up and coil my pony tail into a tight ball, securing it beneath the back of my Santa Cruz beanie.

"Salud!," Eva says as I sneeze, again, less violently this time, into a tissue. She has reappeared from the bathroom having reapplied a rich and indulgent coat of dark red lipstick. She's casting an air of drama and empowerment as she swishes past.

"Allergies, Mija?" she asks. I've missed her occasional colloquial terms of endearment. Eva is good at code switching and doesn't use her parent culture around us all that much. But when it comes to swearing and caring, it rolls off her tongue like a stream of warmth, her syllables dancing in the current between us.

"Yeah," I reply. "T'is the season."

I notice several threads of grey at the temples of her otherwise dark, glossy hair. Her bangs have been newly cut short, drawing attention to a set of impressively sculpted eyebrows. Her wavy, chin-length bob is also new. This is the first time I've seen her wear her hair so short. It's super cute. Sophisticated. I tell her so as she directs her gaze through a pair of oversized, black eyeglasses, first at me, then at Jamie.

"You guys good with that double pull-out?" she asks, a little sheepish. "I'm probably being selfish, but I haven't been sleeping too well and I'd rather not be a pain".

Eva's up-front, sensible-mom-like presence is hard to argue with. She's the most mature of all of us, easily, creating a space between us where we can be ourselves—unjudged and unfiltered. She listens with a genuine, open heart, offering quiet reassurance without pushing me to explain more than I'm ready to share.

"You and me both with the sneezing," she adds, as she hands me a travel pack of tissues and tucks a second into her daypack. She points to a large flower arrangement in the living room. "Those calla lilies, they're not helping any."

Calla lilies are natives of South Africa she explains. I think of the huge patch by my car outside of the tasting room and I picture the Raven. I wonder what he thinks about the degree to which they've naturalized out here along the California coast. A slightly biblical scene in spring. I've been to more memorial services at this time of year than I care to count, and they certainly look good on an altar.

"Nate arrived with an armful he harvested from an abandoned homestead he and Billy found on their way up," she says. "I'm sure the pics will end up on the Gram."

Serena, she says, had obligingly filled a large corrugated metal milk urn with water and arranged the stark, white, trumpet-like flowers on their long, green stems in reverence to Nate's offering. The fact that the living room is infused with only the slightest, most neutral fragrance of the earth stops me from slinging them out of the window, where they belong.

"Serena took the stamens out, so I agreed to have them in the house," Eva continues. "Most of the pollen is gone, but if it gets bad for you, we'll out them to the porch."

Eva's both artist and medical toxicologist, a mix that totally fits her vibe. Creative, curious and analytical—just the right balance for her one-of-a-kind-personality. In my eyes, she's a modern-day goddess—smart, stunning, and brilliant. The first in her vibrant, close-knit Latino family to attend college. She's an inspiration to at least half a dozen nieces and nephews.

Eva's college boyfriend, Joshua—went missing in the devastating 2004 Boxing Day tsunami and earthquake. He had been backpacking solo through Southeast Asia and was on-route from Thailand to Indonesia. His body was never recovered.

We were all completely crushed by the tragedy and his unfathomable loss at the time but nobody more so than Eva. I assumed the grief of no-closure played a major part in her having fallen for the charms of her deadbeat ex. The romantic in her had jumped into early marriage, back in San Antonio, with a handsome but underachiever husband whom none of us liked. But thankfully, logic, ambition, a sharp eye for order and her independent streak took charge the year before the pandemic and, to our relief, she left him and initiated a divorce.

There's something different about her today other than the eyebrows and the edgy-haircut. I can't put my finger on it and I don't want to probe. Anyway, whatever has changed, it suits her. She's glowing. She's more lovely, more Eva than ever.

Rounding up seven friends who haven't spent time together in one place since the summer before the pandemic is like opening a time capsule—once sealed, but now bursting with memories, laughter and the familiar scent of shared history. No one other than me appears to be mindful of the advancing hour, but if we don't get a move on it'll be dark before we return.

"Remember, there are mountain lions, bobcats and coyote out there, guys," I warn, clapping my hands, urging them to get a move on. "Not to mention the occasional mama bear and her cubs." I for one did not sign up for a wildlife encounter in the dusk on day one.

Quirky, adorable Nate is a street photographer and a cyclist who plans green weddings, mostly in his native New York City and surrounding area. I watch him as he pokes through his basket, closely assessing the quality of the clippers, the reusable bags, the scent of a small bottle of organic hand sanitizer. The discreet diamond inset in his slim, gold wedding band twinkles in the late afternoon light. Nate is as lean as ever, super cute, his sculpted, olive-skinned limbs, narrow chest and shoulders encased in an expensive-looking set of top-brand adventure clothing. He's of average height, with a pleasing, curious face. He'd make a good model for an outdoor outfitter catalog.

"How's it going with your business, Nate?" I ask. "Assuming people are still getting hitched these days, you've really carved a niche for yourself, especially after acing it on your own big day." I still smile when I think about their union. Tasteful, intimate, joy-filled. Inclusive.

It was Nate and Billy's outdoor wedding in leafy Brooklyn on a mild, fall day in October 2019 which had drawn us all back together after a far too long hiatus. This having been a few months before lockdown proved especially poignant. I can see them now, suited out as the ultimate pair— dapper, mixed-race grooms buttoned up in complimentary shades of vintage Tom Ford tuxedos. Pale green succulent boutonnières—so tasteful.

"Timing is everything," he replies, his broad smile flashing a set of small, neat, pearly white teeth that light up his face. "Who would've dreamed it all up? Micro-weddings with minimal carbon footprint officially now forever in vogue."

"So, you'll be setting the stage for this evening's supper, I hear?"

Nate runs his hand through his thick, brown hair, sculpted in a recent cut, a soft, modern take on the voluminous, tousled look of James Dean. A longer layer flops adorably on the left side of his forehead. I assume he must've employed the use of a gel product and a round brush, earlier, to blow dry it into place. More work than I've ever put in on my hair, that's for sure.

"I may have some small influence on Serena's table scape," he replies with a wink. His meticulous grooming won't last long this weekend. He appears resigned. He casts a coy glance across the room toward a stack of boxes on the countertop. "Linen, candles, place settings . . ."

"You're not telling me you traveled with that lot?" I ask. I don't suggest the irony of the cross-country haul versus the weekend's preordained green theme.

"No, of course not. She's the queen of repurposing. Most of this belonged to Serena's Grandma, Marie. Some of it was Veronica's. Have you seen the storage shelves in the basement?"

As for Billy, his hair is inky-hued and has been freshly clipped in a no-nonsense fade. He too looks as if he's ready to trek through uneven terrain with a degree of confidence, decked out in his coordinated, sage-green, lightweight, breathable garment selection, curated, I assume, at the same time as his partner's, specifically for packability for their trip out west. The color tone of his outfit compliments his smooth, milk-chocolate skin, perfectly. Always gorgeous and immaculate, if not flamboyant, our Billy.

He crouches to tie the laces of his hiking boots, a versatile, yet stylish design with a combination of smooth suede and waterproof membrane. I hope he's worn them in. They look too new. He tells me how he's taken up indoor rock-climbing since I've seen him last. Billy always stays busy. He walks at a faster pace than most in his regular stride, places to be, people to see.

He tuts, insisting that there's time for the fluffy stuff later, like table décor, after our hike.

"Let's go, babe," he reaches for Nate's hand and steers him, purposefully toward the door. "The great outdoors awaits. The table will still be here, fear not, primed for your touch on our return."

River, as always, is altogether more eclectic in their outdoorsy attire. I expect nothing less. They are rocking a rebel-soul this afternoon in a colorful, tie-dye and bandana ensemble as they round us up into one vehicle, a minivan they use for transporting troubled teens to court-appointed activities. They have been gainfully employed by the county after ditching a lucrative A.I development career in Silicon Valley in the early days of the pandemic. River, passionate about youth mental health, escaped the tech industry as a fierce opponent of A.I. since dabbling in its early stages of development.

"I've seen the devil and it scared the shit out of me," they confessed vehemently during one of our early lockdown virtual cocktail hour reunions. I'll never forget what they said. We hadn't heard too much about it back then. River's life journey has transported them from a troubled childhood of their own into new and unchartered territory and out again, career-wise. They had the potential to earn the big bucks for the rest of their working life. But like many more vocal opponents who were in it at the start of the race for artificial intelligence, they want absolutely nothing to do with it now.

"The bus is leaving," River declares, rotating a contoured set of arms around their toned torso, reminding me of a well-maintained windmill. The antidote to digital overload. "Hop on board or miss the fun."

Billy fusses, bustling Nate into line. He has a big heart and likes to have a laugh, but he's no-nonsense at the same time. "If you pack anything else into that basket, you'll never make it up the first hill," he warns, assessing an assortment of extras Nate is intent on bringing along.

"Is that what I think it is?"

"Bourbon? Hell Yeah. Purely for medicinal purposes." Nate glares briefly at his partner, then attempts to make light. "Mind your own knitting, Billy Boy, husband of mine. You'll thank me later."

Eva overhears. She raises her hands. "You don't change any, Nater Tot. When are you going to quit the predictable party boy meme?" she asks. She's laughing, but I can tell she's serious.

Serena is not as easily amused, or as good at hiding her judgement. "That another East Coast thing?" she asks. "Liquor on a hike?" We all know that Serena's mother died of liver complications leaving her the beach house and very few of resources to take care of it. "Not cool, dude."

"Hubs here never goes anywhere without his Bourbon," Billy says. I watch as he scrunches his right fist, which, in turn, flexes the discernable muscles in his upper arm. Billy's been working out as well as rock climbing. "His liquid comfort blanket," he says.

"One of these days I'm gonna quit," Nate replies. "When I'm a sensible grown up officially, or a doting dad, whichever comes first. Until then, I fully intend to hold on to the last of my vices and savor every second of shameless behavior."

Jamie steps into the on-boarding conversation. "Man, I hate to break it to you buddy, but last I heard, forty-two is pretty much adult even by our lax standards."

River is settled in the driver's seat. Their body reflects the active and grounded strength that comes with age, a balance between youth's softness and the resilience forged over the years. Serena climbs into the passenger seat and buckles in by their side. She could be heading off to lead a yoga session somewhere, her high-rise, stretchy-flared pants and a cropped jacket highlighting her flawless physique.

Billy and Nate pack into the second row. I crawl in beside Eva into the row behind the guys and Jamie squeezes in next to me. His thigh rests easily against mine. It's too chilly for shorts. We're both wearing water resistant hiking pants so there's no skin-to-skin connection. Even so, I experience a definite current racing from my thigh to my core. Blood rushes to my face as I knit my hands neatly together on my knees, pushing thoughts of tonight's intimate sleeping arrangement out of mind. I uncross my legs, cross them again, conscious of every awkward move as I place my hands palm down, one on top of each thigh. What am I, a teenager again?

"Which airport did you fly into, Eva?" I ask, distracting the jitters and the internal chatter with small talk.

"River met me in Santa Rosa this morning," she replies. "Hence the vintage Peanuts attire! Dig it?" She swivels to show me a super cute, though stretched-tight Snoopy t-shirt she's changed into under her open waterproof jacket. It certainly emphasizes her curves.

The airport Eva flew into, seven miles north of Santa Rosa is named after the late, famed comic strip cartoonist Charles M. Schulz who lived in the area for decades.

"Last time I was here I splashed out in the gift store when we stopped in at the Schulz Museum." she replies. "I loved seeing his office and his drawing desk all set up. So cool."

River nods.

"When was that?" I ask. A tendency to feel left out rears its ugly head.

"During COVID, before restrictions were lifted," she replies, choosing her words carefully to prevent any hurt feelings. "No offence, but I figured Serena and River were safe to visit. It's so isolated out here."

"None taken," I say and I mean it. "Though I wouldn't call the Santa Cruz mountains highly populated." I don't need to say that nobody wanted to visit a doctor back then. Still, she and I both made it through the pandemic in various arms of the medical field. It's a miracle we're still here. I think about the work she was tasked with. I broach the subject.

"I thought we weren't talking work this weekend?" Serena asks, turning her head and flashing me a warning with one finger. Her rule not mine.

"Hey hon, it's relevant in this context," River interjects. They turn off the coastal highway and park up on the entrance road to Shell Beach.

Most people have little idea of the on-going work.

"Our understanding of the epidemic continues to evolve on a daily basis, hourly," Eva explains. "The main work now is to respond to and isolate any new outbreaks and other nasty interlopers from taking hold locally, regionally, nationally, globally."

"I guess we'll never truly be done with it," Jamie says. He stretches his arms out and takes hold of each side of the back of the headrest to the passenger seat where Serena is unbuckling her belt. "The denial and the crazy, bat-shit regimens I've heard people came up with to self-treat all the shit that's out there. The mind boggles," he says.

I've seen plenty of this from a country doctor's perspective. From folk drinking bleach and boot-legged liquor adulterated with methane, vaporizing cocaine into body parts . . . you name it, I've seen it and I've been charged with treating it.

"Overdosing in general—it's a problem," Eva says, drawing wide hand gestures in the air via silver-and turquoise-ring-stacked fingers within the compact space before us. "The world has gone mad if you haven't noticed."

"Which is why you are never leaving us, darling," Nate replies. "We are your chosen ones. Don't forget that when the crazies come."

Billy tuts softly, in irritation, as he unfolds himself from the cramped space of the van. "Hysterical, apocalyptic talk is not helpful. Let's keep this weekend civilized please," he mutters.

"What I wanna know is if Jamie here has brought along one of his old man's hunting guns?" Nate asks, peering back into the van. "No one, least of all myself, would trust me with a firearm—that much is certain, but given how isolated we are out here, I wouldn't mind knowing we had a little basic protection on hand."

He waits for Jamie to unfurl his long legs, stretch out and step onto the gravel road. "Well, did you?" he asks, "bring a rifle with you?"

"The two I own are back at my place under strict lock and key," Jamie is quick to reply. He swings his arms as he steps forward and play-punches Nate on the arm. "And no, you're never gonna get your pretty, little man-icured mitts on one of my firearms, that's for sure."

I'm no gun lover. But I've been in the mountains long enough to figure out it's unlikely I'll see an end to the culture anytime soon. Jamie was raised deer and wild boar hunting with his father and grandfather.

"That surprises me," Serena questions Nate. "Are you such a city boy that all this wide-open space is freaking you out?"

We're gathered by the side of the highway, waiting for a break in traffic in order to cross and head on up into the riparian zone, an area above which the Russian River flows on the opposite side to the ocean.

Serena holds up a hand just as Nate opens his mouth. "Time for all the chit-chat later," she says, striding across the highway. The bright yellow laces of her hiking boots stand out like streaks of sunshine, cutting through the grayness of the day. A matching yellow beanie is an added burst of en-ergy and color to her striking silhouette. We follow, like a brood of fluffy ducklings, all fleece jackets and flushed faces as we enter what she describes as an ecotone, a meeting place of both aquatic and terrestrial animals.

Serena intends for us to shave at least two miles off the 6.5-mile-loop through a gateway into Pomo Canyon onto the Red Hill Trail due to the lateness of the hour. The air here smells of

something older, more primordial, as though the very breath of the place is steeped in the ancient history of the damp earth.

"We might time it right to at least see a racoon taking shelter for the evening in a tree trunk hole. They hunt for food down there in the river below," Serena says.

As for me, I'd be happy to catch a glimpse of a woodpecker, a hawk and, maybe even later, if I'm lucky, a great-horned owl.

"River and I stopped in at the bakery in Freestone on our way to the house," Eva announces. "It's amazing. I devoured an entire half-loaf of fougasse for lunch—stuffed with shiitake mushrooms, caramelized onion,

Swiss, jack and smoked gouda. I've never tasted anything like it. I pretty much inhaled the whole thing!"

"You didn't save some for me?" I ask, pouting as I take her arm.

"Oh, don't you worry, sweetcakes," she replies. "We picked out nine entire loaves to last us the weekend, warm from the oven; one of each of the hearth breads baked this morning. Garlic rosemary, olive, pumpkin—all insanely good."

River is close behind. "A morning-pastry-high guaranteed," they say. "We snuck back with quite the decadent haul, didn't we? Scones, sticky buns . . . and enough farm fresh eggs from a nearby stand to feed an army."

"We are an army," Eva adds. "Forecasters. Horizon Scanners. Whatever."

The image of us as a troop is vivid as we plod along on the start our climb in a gradual elevation. Only instead of military or survival packs, we're carrying with us wicker baskets and pricey outdoor-brand day packs.

"Scavengers," I suggest. "That's certainly a better analogy, considering our weekend of seasonal gourmet indulgence."

Serena circles back. "There's plenty of work to do before we start feasting," she remarks as she tilts her pretty head back and gazes into the sky. "It rained heavily earlier in the week. I'm hoping it will hold off until later tonight at least."

It's a gorgeous view from up here, I can't deny that. The ocean is bright blue and the breeze makes for comfortable hiking conditions. We climb steadily until we follow a trail to the left, taking in panoramic views where the Russian River meets the ocean. The scene unfolds like a vivid painting, a winding ribbon of silver, carving through the landscape as it snakes toward the vastness of the Pacific. It's a place where the forces of nature meet in seamless infinity and I feel a sense of calm I haven't experienced in a while.

The path is not too muddy considering the recent rain. There's no one else around at this hour and we traverse along, looping beside a series of babbling brooks and redwood groves above the river. Ferns line the edge of the trail.

"Listen to the wind," Billy instructs. He stretches his arms wide open, pumping his lungs full with fresh, ocean air. "Come on, follow my lead," he urges his partner, as he lifts Nate's arms above his shoulders. The wicker baskets they're holding swing from their hands.

We raise our eyes in unison to the upper limbs of a redwood canopy. There isn't a good deal of sunlight left to filter down, but what little there is bathes us in a soft glow.

"I thought you said it wasn't too intense an incline?" Nate asks River, hands back on hips as he lags, noticeably at the back of the group.

"Don't worry. It's a little steep and sustained in parts, but it's totally worth the effort to reach the summit," River replies.

It's crowded out here on warmer weekends," Serena says. She extends one arm and indicates a spot in which to gather. "Don't sit on the ground until you've double checked for poison oak," she adds. "I should've reminded you to dodge any likely suspects along the trail, though I think we've been spared any obvious offenders, so far. This is ideal habitat, right here. It's donned its leafy cloak with gusto this spring."

She warns us to keep a look out as we progress. New leaves, lobed, reddish, shiny, generally three leaves per stem. "Better late than never," she says. "My bad. Hopefully none of you has brushed up against it already."

I'm reminded of my first spring and summer in Northern California. I had no idea what I was brushing into on a solo evening stroll through the oak forest playground situated above campus. Ignorance is an understatement. I learned the hard way that *Toxicodendron Diversilobum*, the scientific name for the perennial, deciduous shrub, or more accurately, the vine that is Pacific poison oak isn't actually any relation to oak, despite its misleading name.

It's actually chock full of an allergen called urushiol oil, subsequently producing a nasty contact dermatitis in me and other unfortunates. I've been forever on the lookout for it since, especially after discovering on a subsequent occasion that even bare winter branches contain some of its oil.

"Remember that first time, Tam?" Jamie asks. He hasn't forgotten either. "Poor thing. All over your face. We barely recognized you the next day."

"I'd blanked on that," Serena says, though I'm not sure I believe her. She's gathered several pungent bay leaves in her hand and is tucking them into her basket.

How could she have forgotten? My eyes had swollen shut like a prize fighter. Steroids from the campus clinic and seclusion for over a week.

There was little to compare in the UK, aside from stinging nettles. The rashes I'd come home with as a kid after running around the country lanes, bare-legged in a summer dress had subsided effectively in comparison, along with my mother's robust application of simple soap and water and a moistened cloth.

"My welcome to America!" I recall. "Initiation by poison oak."

"This and ticks are just two of the reasons I'm not a fan of foraging," Billy joins the banter. "I like to know exactly what I'm getting myself into out here in the wild, thank you very much."

He broaches the subject of police and rangers in some parts of this country being known to take an anti-foraging approach based on race. I realize this may have been Nate's partial concern when he brought up the subject of protecting ourselves.

"You may not have a care in the world when filling your basket, Serena, dear," Billy says. "Out here roaming the hills like the modern-day Heidi, braids and all. Whereas, take one look at me, the lone black man on the mountain. My helping myself to your native, nutrient-dense wild foods could easily be considered as something else entirely."

We listen as Billy proceeds to outline, matter-of-factly, how ethnicity is as major a consideration out here in the open space as it is in an urban environment.

Am I imagining it, or did I catch a glimpse of someone ahead of us, in the shadows?

"Historically speaking," Billy continues, "foraging has been known to be criminalized as trespassing in regions where systematic oppression still exists."

"What he's basically saying is that he could easily get his ass shot for less," Nate adds.

River shares that the population of Black residents in Sonoma County hovers disgracefully low to this day. "Billy has a point. Think of it this way, only two Blacks in every hundred people."

"On the other hand, Serena here is as white a European American as could be," River adds. "Her family has been merrily supplementing their pantry with food from the region's wild sources since settler days."

I shift uncomfortably, glancing ahead, back to where I'd seen him—or thought I did. The figure, the Raven? No way, surely not. My fingers curl around the edges of my basket, but still, I don't say anything. I can't explain why I haven't spoken up about this feeling. The man, or the spirit of him, lingers in the periphery of my thoughts as Serena continues the conversation.

"That said, wild foods are never necessarily fair game, though, for several reasons," she says. This is her territory now. "Consider the Coast Miwok having managed to subsist for centuries before my lot showed up. It was them, the first people who knew how to truly live in harmony with the land. Early settlers raided vast swaths of their natural pantry, stripping it bare for ranching and cultivation."

We're a captive audience as River takes her cue and launches into the general ethics of foraging today: "It's essential that we know exactly what we can take for free and from where. Everyone's after the same bounty," they say. "Especially wild mushrooms. It's become such a thing that a reduced-bag limit of fungi has been put in place in the state parks."

"Mushroom hunters were making off with thirty or forty pounds of porcini in the past few years," Serena explains. "It had to be contained. Park rangers are carrying digital hanging scales, in an effort to keep a lid on it. We're currently not allowed to take any more than two pounds per person."

We hear how commercial hunters who've made this their business have been forced into more remote locations.

"It's made it difficult for people like Serena and me who only want to take our fair share," River says. "If the forest floors are stripped by professionals and black-market sellers, it becomes totally inequitable and unsustainable."

"Same goes for seaweed harvestin'," Jamie joins in on the topic. "The North Coast is a big draw for those in the know and I'm seein' more and more people out here huntin' and harvestin' seaweed each time I'm out."

A taste for seaweed picked up at a significant pace during shelter in place, he explains as I push any more thoughts of the Raven tracking our hike to the back of my mind. I'm being paranoid is all.

"I suppose the pandemic was the first time in decades that ordinary people gave any thought to foraging," I suggest. I zipper my jacket. I'm chilled when we stop walking.

Serena insists that the ideal practice is to follow the lead of the indigenous first people after all. Observe a wild space such as this for an entire year before harvesting any of its offerings.

"The only way the earth is able to sustain its generosity is if we learn to take no more than what we need and we're consistently mindful of others," she explains. The rule of thumb, according to Serena, is to take only or less than a tenth of whatever is growing at any one time.

"Don't ask us to disclose our secret spots for mushrooms, not least the psilocybe we've squirreled away for this weekend," River adds with a wink.

"Now we're talking," Nate replies. "Good old magic mushrooms with their psychedelic compounds."

River brushes Serena's cheek affectionately with the side of their hand.

"If authorities are to avoid a shut down, then an increase in foraging license requirements is likely, surely?" Eva asks. She's been listening, intently, taking it all in. It's her turn to comment. "Surely people should have permits for specific regions, not just those who are leading tours in state parks? And shouldn't we be required to have some basic training before we plunder and pillage the wild?"

"We do plunge, as a society, so blithely into the wild without so much as knowing what dangers we're getting ourselves into," River replies. "It's important to better educate ourselves before we hit the rivers and lakes, especially the land out here by the ocean."

Eva asks how many of us checked for swimming, fishing and foraging advisories before we set out this weekend.

"More and more people are getting sick from harmful algae and blue/green cyanobacteria as a result of our general ignorance," she explains. "It's shocking." She stumbles, slightly, on a rock in the path. Billy sprints to reach and grab her by the waist, steadying and rebalancing her weight.

Ocean mammals, fish, pets and livestock are usually the first to be affected, Eva continues, barely missing a beat. "They're the most likely to drink from or swim in marine systems and fresh water containing a cyanobacterial bloom. And these hot summers we've been experiencing, well, they only serve to elevate the rate of growth of these microscopic organisms that bloom in our inland water."

"Yikes. The general public is clueless," Nate says, scratching his head. "Myself included. That's why I'll be sticking close to you this weekend, Eva, if you don't mind."

Serena's expression reveals her concern. "It's often a sign of ecological imbalance," she says. "When oxygen levels drop beneath the surface, the water's surface is choked by a thick, swirling layer of green-blue scum. You can see it when it shimmers in shades of turquoise, jade, or even rust-red."

River retakes the lead in our ecology lesson as we walk on. "Sometimes, unfortunately, toxic algae is triggered by agricultural run-off, including sewage discharge, but most times its climate-related temperature shifts that create this paint-like layer on the water's surface."

Seaweed, Eva is quick to add, relies on sunlight and clear, oxygen-rich water to thrive, so algae blooms tend to stunt growth and kill off crops, she says. "Harvesting is often restricted or banned temporarily in areas affected by blooms, preventing contaminated product from entering the food supply."

River explains how in optimal conditions, there is a ten pounds of sea-weed a day limit. "It takes an entire day to process that amount anyway," they reason.

Jamie must have picked up on my sweeping glance into the woodland. He mentions my chance meeting with the Raven, asking River and Serena if they know him. "Evidently an authority on coastal ecology. Dude's a prolific poster, by all accounts. We spotted one of his hand-drawn coast-al-protection flyers by the deli."

"Seems like he'd be someone you must've crossed paths with?" I add, glancing side to side as if he is about to appear. I treat them to a brief summary of my unexpected interaction, earlier.

"Sure thing. He's a legend," River replies. "Never afraid to speak his mind and stand up for our fragile ecosystem."

Serena explains how the Raven lives with his mother, in an ocean-front cabin not far from her place. "A little ways along the coast, though I'm pretty sure we're visible from their porch, with the help of binoculars."

"Bit creepy?" I ask.

"Not really," Serena is quick to reply. "It's not like he's spying on us or anything. He speaks his mind on most matters. He and his mom are local ham radio messengers. Have been for years."

"Who do they make contact with?" I ask.

"You'd be surprised," Serena replies. "Other amateur broadcasters from all over the world, I believe. Except for those countries and regions that we're banned from communicating with."

"Such as?" Jamie asks.

"Oh, I'm not entirely sure. North Korea, Cuba, Iran, Syria, Sudan. They're amongst those that are prohibited for contact for sure. I've seen the two of them set up shop once or twice a week in different spots along the coast. It's all legal, they have licenses, they've told me all about it in passing—they've had training and all."

River says they've seen the Raven and his mother keeping log books of all the contacts they make.

"Some days they reach radio enthusiasts as far away as Japan and Europe, though I assume mostly they tap into others, like them, who are sending out signals from parks around the United States."

"What's the motive?" I ask, all the more intrigued.

"They're hooked up to the Red Cross and other emergency services," River replies. "If there's a wildfire, or a tsunami along the coast for instance, the Raven and his mother would be the first to alert. Who knows, they may have saved a bunch of lives out here over the years."

I'm starting to rethink my take on the Raven. He's even more of a local legend than I had imagined.

This afternoon we're specifically looking for miner's lettuce and lamb's-quarter greens which we're instructed to pick last, to avoid any wilting, along with wild onions, dandelions and herbs. These findings will, we're assured, be of tasty complement to the chanterelles and hedgehogs, otherwise known as sweet tooth mushrooms our hosts have previously assembled in a basket back at the house. Serena has been out foraging earlier this week at a private ranch. She's asked me to make the pastry for a tart for tomorrow's lunch.

My tummy rumbles envisaging the taste of the wild-picked bounty, despite my slight mocking tone, earlier. I'm quelled by the deep, grounding aroma of the forest. I can only describe it as a dark, loamy richness of spirit, of being at one with the damp wood and earth. An other-worldly, soothing allure permeating my five senses as we traverse onwards in the wild, salty air.

My cabin-life in the Santa Cruz mountains connects me to the sacred, seasonal beauty of the giant redwoods as a part of my daily routine. It saved me while I was being re-introduced to myself. Spending time alone is important when you've been through a period of extreme discomfort. It has trained me to become more at ease with myself.

Even though I've survived periods of wildfire, flood and plague to get to this point, it's hard to imagine leaving the mountains. But this is nice around here, I'll admit. There's a profound sense of continuity, as though the redwood forests along the California coast are not isolated groves but rather threads in an unbroken tapestry of time and nature.

I'm lost in thought as we approach a patch of western sword fern, native to North America and older than time. It's growing abundantly alongside the hillside trail in a spot that provides partial to full shade.

"The ancient understory of the forest," River says, eyeing the fern's palm, explaining how recent rains have kept the fronds of the evergreen from developing dry, crispy edges along its delicate, lacy sides.

"Anyone aware that the sword fern utilizes spores to spread and reproduce, as with fungi?" they ask. They run a hand along the edge of a large leaflet, shaped, as advertised, like a sword. "The fern's large root systems serve to prevent soil erosion—see."

"It's these strange-looking, little fiddlehead ferns we're searching for today," Serena adds, nerding-out as she takes her turn in pointing out small, quarter-sized green spheres, the early stages of a new fern frond. "The first people were all over every part of the sword fern. They used them as non-stick berry-drying racks, for lining baking pits and separating food for storage."

Eva's face lights up as she adds to Serena's enthusiastic tutorial: "Fiddleheads came in super handy as medicine and even bedding mats for thousands of years. What's more, these fantastic fronds we're looking at were considered especially delicious this time of year, peeled and roasted over fire pits and served alongside a bounty of salmon eggs."

"Yes, and it only takes a small amount of cooking to make them edible," Serena replies. "They've been known to cure sore throats, ease childbirth and even cure the shits, right, Eva?"

Although they've apparently been making more frequent appearances at farmer's markets in the area these past few spring seasons, our resident toxicologist is quick to remind us that fiddleheads, as with all foraged foods must be properly identified at the correct stage to avoid any nasty mistakes.

"They're tender and edible just as they begin to shoot through the wet, fertile ground and unfurl. But this only lasts a few days," Eva explains. "That's why they are so expensive to buy. The season's really short. "They taste kind of like an asparagus-spinach-broccoli blend if you can imagine that."

Seeing as we've stumbled upon a bright green clump of half a dozen or more of the aforementioned fiddleheads and soon, hundreds more by a stream along the forest floor, Serena declares them ripe for the harvesting. Eva agrees. There's a feathery, brown, paper-like material covering the sides of the coils. She kneels, pinches off and snaps the stem a half-inch to an inch from the coiled head, brushing away the papery material and any twigs and leaves.

"It's vital that we don't pick a clump clean," Serena says. "The last thing we want is for the fern to die."

We're to steam our fiddlehead haul for ten minutes or so back at the house, I learn. After that, we'll sauté them in olive oil and season with salt and pepper and serve them as a side dish with supper.

It's getting late as we loop around and wind our way downhill. A view of the ocean greets us as we exit the forest. The roar of waves is muted by the symphonic cacophony of bird call and all other overlapping sounds. Nature is broadcasting its own auditory information of boundaries, of potential predators, food supply and mates. The air in the elevation smells like heaven, or how I would imagine heaven smells. It is the fragrance of new life on the air.

Fennel is invasive along the coastal route and it's Eva who encourages us to have at it as we descend and approach a bunch of frothy foliage sprouting along the trail edge. "The wispier the shoot, the sweeter and more tender, but don't harvest any too close to the highway," she warns. "Who knows how many pollutants it's been exposed to from all the coastal traffic."

My fingers take on the scent of licorice as I set about cutting stalks, stems, fronds and flowers from a seven-foot plant. "It's okay to pick as much of this as you like," River says, as further encouragement. They explain how every part of wild fennel is edible: "It's actually a highly noxious weed, a European invader introduced into California by the Italians, most likely. And so, we're doing the ecosystem a big favor in trimming it down."

Eva turns full circle to point out a substantial foliage of hemlock growing nearby. "Be sure to always use your nose," she says, pinching hers. "Fennel smells good, like anise, whereas hemlock is stinky and one of the most toxic plants on the continent."

We're instructed to discard all but the young fennel fronds for use in a wild-fennel-cake recipe on Serena's welcome-supper menu as Nate passes around the bourbon.

"Time to get this party started," he says. The rest of us drink from our water canisters, politely passing the bourbon without a single one aside from him, partaking.

"Slow it down, babe," Billy urges, motioning with his palms toward the ground. His forced smile a giveaway in his exercising a familiar patience. "Plenty time to let loose later."

I picture the roots of the redwoods above, stretching and intertwining like a vast, unseen web connecting one grove to another. Similarly, though we have been apart for so long, we're here to reconnect and relax this weekend. It's my hope that we'll figure out a way to share our quiet, secret language of old, not as a collection of individuals, but as an interconnected family of sorts, once again living and breathing together in some kind of harmonious community.

And even though it's clear that no one else noticed, I can't shake the feeling that somehow, that peculiar, bird-like man is watching, waiting, listening too.

Friday Early Evening

The vintage Wedgewood stove is the heart of the kitchen, drawing everyone in. As the seven of us gather around the table, the space becomes more than just a room—it's where connection and comfort come alive, a vibrant hub of warmth and togetherness.

This hulking fossil-fuel burner, which River swears would be the first to go in a remodel if the house weren't so perilously close to the edge, dominates the kitchen. Those of us not seated at the table have to squeeze around a set of high-backed chairs just to reach the countertop, stovetop, and ancient fridge.

"Would you say I'm guilty of over-romanticizing the best parts of our senior year?" I ask Eva. Eminem's "Lose Yourself" is first up on my deep-dive, a nostalgic playlist from 2003, cobbled together in the form of a dusty stack of CDs from our college days. She shrugs her shoulders and smiles, neither agreeing or disagreeing. I simply attempt to do as Eminem instructs and submit myself to sinking into the rhythm of his signature, hypnotic hip-hop.

If you ask me, nothing tops music in scoring the highs and lows, tagging those specific memories and experiences, particular textures, tastes and smells that have imprinted themselves in our brains from the distant past. Music was my learning curve back then, being so far from home. I think back to how I floundered around at first, desperately figuring out who I was, who I wanted to be and who I had already become when this specific song was released. It strikes me even more today that he was some kind of motivational genius for so many young people like me, who were struggling to fit in for one reason or another.

I sweep my eyes around the kitchen, weathered but full of life. An eclectic collection of heavy-duty, cast-iron skillets and patinaed copper cookware hangs from a heavy, primitive wall rack next to an orange clock that is shaped like a cat. Open cabinet frames appear to have been freshly painted a buttery-cream gloss that offsets the original brown-sugar wood paneling of the walls. The crowded Formica countertop from the 1950s sports a groovy cube design in brown, orange and mustard. It's so retro it's back in fashion. The scent of time has settled into the walls.

My foot, in its thick, woolen hiking sock, taps softly in rhythm to the music on a braided, multi-colored rug resting on the beat-up wooden floorboards beneath the table.

"The last days before the world was run by social media," Eva remarks as The Postal Service switches the sound vibe emerging from the old, battery-fed boombox I brought with me for added authenticity. "Such Great Heights"—my favorite track on the one and only album from this distinctive indie-electric pop duo. No doubt about it, "Give Up" was one of the soundtracks to our senior year, the laughter, the tears, the camaraderie, the hookups, the breakups.

"Didn't these two collaborate by sending audio tapes through the mail?" Nate asks. "How quaint."

Serena and River have incorporated a pleasing touch of the outdoors indoors with a well-tended herb garden on the greenhouse windowsill. A hanging arrangement of air plants in urchin shells hovers above. The pragmatic in me is itching to ask questions about the eroding cliffside, but I decide to save my curious enquiry for later. It's hard for me to imagine not wanting to talk about it if this was my place. This enormous rock beneath our feet is more unstable now than ever. Why ignore the inevitable?

"This is the first time I've seen an urchin shell repurposed like this," I remark instead, deflecting my concern, at least for now. Best to bide my time. We're walking on nails with one another, me and her, at the moment. Serena has a way of seeing through me. She pauses before she launches into an explanation of how her grandmother was the ultimate forager, inspiring her from childhood to hang on to any urchin shells that washed-up on the beach.

"She talked often of an old folk tradition in southern England and Denmark," Serena continues. "They imagined sea urchin fossils as thunderbolts, apparently. Not sure how it came about, or if you've any knowledge of it, Tam, but she loved to regale me with stories of urchin fossils in other parts of Europe, where people carried them as amulets to ward off any harm by witchcraft. She said they believed them especially powerful around midsummer."

I shake my head. "Wow. Cool," I reply. I've never heard of such a thing, though it's an enchanting idea.

"Thanks for the folklore lesson, our white witch-sister," Nate pokes Serena with a finger. "Are you casting your spells on Witchtok yet? You could be making a small fortune."

She widens her eyes in mock reproach. "Watch yourself."

I for one am well-versed in Serena's book of spells.

River is quick to point out that nature worship isn't remotely the same as witchcraft. "Pagan, maybe," they say. "Pre-Christian, certainly."

"Well, let's hope you've a spell up your sleeve to stop us sliding down the cliffside this weekend," Nate replies. There, he's said what we've all been thinking.

And it's met with total silence.

Awkward. I avoid catching anyone's eye as I feign interest in re-focusing on my surrounds, in particular, an ordered and substantial spice rack that fills the open wall cabinet closest to the stove. A comforting scent of oil and seasoning clings to this well-stocked, old-school California kitchen, nothing sleek or modern or minimalist here. I don't see a microwave or any large, modern gadgets. Farm-to-table movement pioneer, Alice Waters would happily make herself at home here.

My eyes settle on the adjacent pantry. The concertina door to the narrow pantry is open.

"Take a look, find what you need," Serena offers, following my gaze. Each of us has been allocated a dish to prepare for tonight's wild-food-welcome-supper. My job is to strip the cattails for a salad and fry the fennel cakes. I slide from my seat and walk over to better peruse the pantry.

"It's taken a bit of a beating of late," Serena adds. "I do my best to keep my pantry-staple stocks steadily replenished."

I spy several glass jars filled with bright yellow preserved lemons, bay leaves and peppercorns. A large jar of walnuts is set beside another, filled with what I'm guessing, from the orange hue, are probably dried persimmons. Blackberry jam and mint jelly jars nestle in the forefront.

"The ground meal, right here next to the persimmons is made from manzanita berries," Serena says, proudly, as she selects the largest of the jars and twists the lid. She holds it under my nose. It smells nutty and astringent. "I dry the berries and grind them with raw sugar in a mortar and pestle," she adds. "It started out as a bunch of insanely fragrant pink and white blossoms that smelled like honey."

I ask what she plans to create with her woodsy ground meal.

"It makes for amazing sweet-tart shortbread," she replies. "You wouldn't believe it but you can taste for yourself. I've baked some for later."

I'm intrigued to try her shortbread, to compare it to the traditional, Scottish-style, buttery-version my grandmother served with tea when I was young.

"Manzanita berries were an essential part of the North American native diet for thousands of years," Serena explains. "It's not surprising, as they contain three-times the anti-oxidants found in blueberries."

That's quite the superfood. There's an herbal infusion made from manzanita leaves in my medicine cabinet at home. I'm regretting not having packed it, made more of an effort to avoid the perils of any accidental contact with poison oak. Another Native American use of the plant, a remedy to treat a breakout, the leaves containing mildly disinfectant chemicals.

I'm sure Eva knows a lot more than me about its use in natural medicine.

Although it's one thing to experiment in self-administration, herbal remedies are largely left to the individual to take a chance on in the mainstream medical field. I have little choice but to be cautious in my line of work.

"Eva showed me how to add a little bark into my wildflower meadow tea," Serena says. "Along with some clover, verbena, bay, chamomile and fennel. Manzanita has a mind-blowing range of medicinal purposes."

It was the Spanish who named the plant after little apples, Eva adds.

The others are paying little attention to our conversation as they launch into a spirited sing-along to "Where is the Love?" by the Black-Eyed Peas.

Serena moves closer so that I'm better able to hear what she's intent on imparting. She warns me sternly to steer clear of the stones in the center of the berries.

"They pose a health danger if ingested in any large amount. Kind of like eating too many apple seeds."

At least she's not trying to kill me. She describes in detail how she washes the stick berries first, before she sets about separating the stones from the fleshy part as she prepares her course meal. The more she talks, the less I intend ever to be inclined to embark on such a project. I feign interest.

"Don't be fooled by all this trickery," Billy remarks, with sweeping arm movements as he steps in closer. He's been half-listening after all. He shakes his head and a laugh spills out of his mouth, a warm-hearted, full-throated chortle, infectious, as he stands beside us at the pantry door, an arm now around each of our waists.

"Serena wants us to think she's finally gone full freegan, but I deduce the clever minx has clearly purchased much of these fairly impressive stocks in a general store." He points to lower shelves, stocked with bags and boxes of rice, oats, flour, pasta and other grains, jars of beans, stacked tins of tomatoes, condiments and cartons of mushroom, vegetable and chicken stock, kosher salt, jugs of oils and vinegar, honey, syrup and seeds. The pantry smells of a slight metallic twang, of must and a warm, sugary sweetness.

"What's a freegan, exactly?" Jamie asks. "Remind me." He tunes into our conversation, as he opens the first bottle of wine, the soft scrape of the corkscrew as it bites into the cork, then a small, satisfying pop and a sudden release of pressure as the cork gives way.

"Someone who tries to avoid purchasing anything in protest against the capitalist, consumerist food system," Billy replies.

"You always were a bit of a dumpster-diver, weren't you, Serena?" Jamie asks.

Serena play-swipes the back of his head, her hand lingering a second too long on the side of his neck. "I prefer to think of my student extra-curricular activities as guerilla gardening, thank you," she replies, dropping her hand and scooping up the first, filled glass of deep, translucent, ruby red wine.

There was a period during senior year when she would disappear for hours with her gardening cohorts in an old, unoccupied city park.

"It was pretty dangerous, to be honest," she admits. "But we grew some good shit."

"Weed mostly," River clarifies. "And tomatoes. So many damn tomatoes."

We hear how it was River who spent an entire afternoon earlier this week, cleaning out the pantry and reorganizing the kitchen in readiness for hosting our gathering.

"Serena may put on a good show with her pioneer kitchen, but she's not all that fond of the domestic drudgery on a day-to-day basis, are you sweetie?"

River is pushing it. Serena does not appreciate being called out. She swallows another full mouthful of wine.

"Help is a little scarce out here, if you hadn't noticed," she replies. "So-what if I don't feel like cooking and cleaning every day? I'm not contractually obligated just because I'm technically in charge of the house. But you know, if you'd like to take full responsibility for the *glamorous* role of washing dishes and scrubbing floors, I'd be more than happy to concede."

Expectations, responsibilities and boundaries remain an era and gender-defying subject, despite our best intentions. River leaves the house daily, for work. There's that. And it's become more of a rarity for Serena to leave these days.

River insists they split most of the household tasks based on their schedules.

"Hey, life changes and so do our roles," they say. "Don't be feeling sorry for Serena, despite what she says. We're doing a pretty decent job around being flexible when one or the other has more on their plate."

Considering she had quite the career out of college in fashion merchandising, I figure it must be an adjustment for a gregarious person like Serena to spend so much time at home, far from city life. Since lockdown she's been making ends meet in her buying and reselling of vintage couture online. According to River, a trip to the post office in Bodega Bay is a big outing in Serena's week. I picture her pulling over and chatting to the Raven on occasion that he and his mom are out there with their radio.

"Save us your prickly domestic disputes," Nate pleads, joining the fray. He runs his fingers through his hair. His beard, an addition since lockdown, is neatly clipped beneath a small, round pair of eyeglasses which suit his narrow face. He raises his eyebrows and gestures toward the far end of the kitchen with a sweeping motion, an over-the-top show of enthusiasm. "Your refrigerator shelves are equally as impressive as your pantry, my friends. Plenty of mixers. What are we waiting for?" he asks. "Cocktails?"

He glances between them, a playful smile tugging at the corner of his mouth, but his eyes remain pointedly wide.

Billy turns slowly, crossing his arms with his own raised eyebrow. He gives Nate a pointed look, then gestures toward the empty glass in Nate's hand with a sharp tilt of his head. "You already have a head start on the drinking, hon, so maybe let the rest of us catch up a tad?" He leans back slightly, a casual smirk tugging at his lips, as if daring Nate to challenge him.

Nate snatches the bottle of wine from Jamie's hands with a grin. He pours himself an exaggeratedly generous amount into the cloudy crystal glass he'd placed before him on the table. I fight the urge to interject as he fills it to the brim with theatrical precision, a flourish of his wrist, as if to mock his partner's request. One arm tucked behind his back, he makes the whole thing look like a performance.

"Oh well," Billy shrugs his shoulders. "Do as you please. As usual."

Jamie opens a second bottle with a practiced twist of his wrist, the cork popping with a soft, satisfying *thud*. As he pours, he hums along quietly to the soothing melody of Coldplay's "Yellow," his shoulders relaxing as the music fills the space. His fingers move with a fluid rhythm, almost syncing with the gentle strumming of the guitar, while his gaze drifts lazily toward the ceiling, lost in the music. The corners of his mouth twitch into a small smile as the song swells. He's clearly enjoying the moment of calm amidst the chaos.

"Beer or wine, Tam?" he asks. I gesture to the Chardonnay. "If we're hoping to eat at some stage of the evening, we'd best get this dinner-party-prep started. Assume our duties," he declares.

"Aprons on," Serena instructs, clapping her hands. Aprons were on the list she'd sent us all. Chef's knives also if we happened to possess anything sous-chef worthy and we weren't amongst the three that were flying in. I'd offered to order up a bunch of aprons from an online photo site with our grad group shot and "Class of 2003" emblazoned on the front but Serena had poo-poohed the idea as too corny and/or unnecessarily wasteful.

Billy and Nate don a pair of heavily starched, matching, blue-and-white striped aprons. Brand new, as is most of their gear, given the evidence of post-packaging creases. A bold move, given the declaration by our host to make the weekend all about conservation. Utilizing what we already have. Billy's looking buff these days, whereas I see now that Nate looks a little strained.

Jamie, ever the picture of good health, motions for me to secure the strap of his well-worn, pro-grade chef's apron with its leather neck strap and pockets. Eva gives us a twirl in a cute, cotton "Kiss the Cook" bib that has seen better days.

River is taking a fun-loving approach in a playful apron emblazoned with an image of a cat in space, clutching a cup of coffee and a baguette in its paws. Serena, in contrast to all, appears as if she's about to throw pottery in her linen cross-back baker's apron in a soft-worn lavender-gray with a set of roomy side pockets.

As for me, it's a never-worn Union Jack apron, a Christmas gift from my mother several years ago, its custom embroidery declaring me as a highly unlikely winner of "Britain's Best Chef". Hardly is an understatement. A bad joke on my mother's part as she painstakingly insists that I've never been good for anything in the kitchen other than a TV-supper of beans on toast.

There's already a detectable edge to the collective energy and it's early yet. I sense a pinch of sarcasm, irritation, resentment and competitive edge in the air. Given that our mission is community, if we're to envision any kind of harmonious future in the kitchen, the seven of us preparing regular meals together, maybe taking shifts, then we're going to have to settle our underlying issues. And I'm nervous about the amount of booze that's being downed, before we've even begun. It'll either soften the score or raise any tension to the surface.

It's not for me to judge. And so, I down the contents of my glass in one—its lemon-lime-tartness puckering my lips as I set my glass aside in order to scope out the cooking utensils that I'll need to concoct my share of this evening's meal. I notice Eva is making eye contact with Billy as she lays a hand over her glass, discreetly, passing on the first pour.

Friday Evening

Evening casts its purple shadow over our meal preparation. We're laboring in the low light of the kitchen's underperforming overhead fixture. And yet there's a magic quality to the glow of the vintage glass pendant and a steady focus in our slicing and chopping. A dusky-pink luminosity highlights the golden strands of Jamie's sandy-brown hair. I spy a light row of frown-lines formed in concentration on his forehead, though the rest of his face is softened pleasingly by the peachy low light. I try not to scrutinize him too obviously and he doesn't seem to notice as he deftly slices a bunch of lemons for Billy and Nate's oyster appetizer.

I've assembled a large, wooden chopping board, knife, fennel, cattails, egg, olive oil, garlic breadcrumbs and parmesan. This is going to be good. Even I'm able to manage this. A rare swell of contentment settles into in my core. It's been a while since I've felt this way. I've clearly grown way too comfortable with my basic cooking and company. Not a bad thing, but the pleasant buzz I'm experiencing from the wine, the camaraderie and the general group energy is surprisingly potent.

Eva works beside me diligently. She's sliced a garlic rosemary loaf into a basket and is starting in on arranging a warm, wilted dandelion salad in an earth-hued, ceramic bowl. The rich, toasty aroma of the brick-oven bread is firing up my taste buds. I reach out for the heel from the crust-end of the loaf.

"Go on, dip it in a little balsamic and olive oil," Eva suggests, digging her elbow into my side. This girl is always so confident and solid, spreading joy and love like an elixir. She adds a heaping teaspoon of dried red chili pepper flakes into the concoction in a small, hand-thrown dipping bowl.

I taste an explosion of flavors, the garlic sharp and fragrant. The rich, fruity oil adds a velvety, peppery base against the tangy sweetness of the balsamic. The chili flakes providing a layer of heat that lingers on my tongue.

Serena is making no secret of the merits of the fiddlehead fern and wild mushroom ragu she's making. I switch my attention as she bustles about, bossing River around, instructing them to boil salted water, prepare an ice bath to transfer the greens.

"Pass me the parm when you're done grating, Tam." She barks her orders across the kitchen as she rustles around in an overstocked utensil draw and pulls out a vegetable peeler. "Better yet," she corrects herself in motion as she passes the peeler. "Cut me a bowl of parmesan curls, please."

Serena resumes her talk about her grandma, Marie. "When she was a girl, just after the Second World War, almost all of the protein that appeared on the family table in their seaside community of Bolinas, was hunted or fished from the wild. Rabbit, wild turkey, deer and duck."

We listen, transfixed as she describes how Marie would talk of having caught steelhead trout with her hands as a young child.

"My great-grandfather, he was a minister, his wife a school teacher before she married. Marie was born in 1936, their only child. This would've been a good thirty years before Bolinas became hip."

"How on earth did she become a Deadhead?" I ask. Ever since I first heard about Marie having been a beatnik hippie in her thirties and forties, I've been dying to learn more. All I know is that she hung out with the Grateful Dead. It was Marin County where the groovy naked-party enclaves were located, before and after the Summer of Love.

I learned all about the Grateful Dead from Serena—me not having much reference of the legendary rock band formed in the mid-1960s, from my vantage point as an 80s born Brit. Famous for an eclectic blend of rock, folk, blues, and jazz influences and known for their loyal and ever-growing fanbase, affectionately called Deadheads, the band remains a symbol of the American counterculture movement. Their long, improvisational jams and laid-back, free-spirited approach to music may have captured the hearts of a generation, but it was Northern California's Stinson Beach, Novato and Mill Valley that were among the iconic places where the Dead's fan base gathered for concerts, parties and their infamous "family" vibe.

"All that peace, love and freedom of expression must've been one hell of a leap for your great-grandparents to digest?" I suggest. With up to a hundred-thousand young people flooding into the Haight-Ashbury district in the summer of 1967, I can only imagine how many made their way up the coast, a caravan following the charismatic musicians out into rustic West Marin.

"A fundamental shift in culture kicked in," Serena explains, her hands sweeping through the air as if outlining the very shift that she's describing. She leans forward slightly, her elbows resting on the table, eyes intense as she makes her point. "Big time." She pauses for a moment, letting the weight of the statement hang in the air.

Then, her posture shifts, becoming more rigid, as if bracing herself. "It has to be said, though, the pioneer ranch culture sure stood its ground. It clung on for dear life." She clenches her fists for emphasis, her fingers tight around her glass, before releasing the tension with a soft exhale. "And it's getting harder and harder by the year for the ranchers to survive out here, the few there are left."

"Tell us more," I urge, wishing for a time portal, a Scooby-Doo-mobile to transport us back to Northern California in the Swinging Sixties. If it's a sense of brotherhood and sisterhood we're

after, we could learn a thing or two from Marie's generation. These are fertile conditions for rapid social change.

"It's absurd how many ills plague our society today, especially when you consider the groundbreaking blood, sweat, and tears poured into the movements of half a century past."

Serena agrees. "The same struggles that spurred so many to march, to speak out, to sacrifice everything for progress—whether it was for civil rights, gender equality, or environmental justice—seem to me to have barely moved the needle at all."

We stand on the shoulders of giants, and yet we're still facing the same systemic injustices, the same deep divides, the same greed and inequality that those who fought before us hoped would be eradicated by now. It's as if, despite all the protests, all the rallies, all the tireless advocacy for change, those lessons were never truly learned, and the momentum for real transformation just slipped through our fingers. What should have been a catapult into a better, fairer world now feels like a slow crawl, with the same battles being fought over and over again—only now, they're dressed up in new, more insidious forms.

River's turn to interject. "I know it may feel like we're facing the same challenges over and over, but we have no choice but to be bold, to stick with it. Every generation of changemakers contributes to a larger, slow-moving wave of progress. Social justice movements, fueled by a sense of moral clarity and collective action, have transformed societies in ways that once seemed unimaginable. Each small victory, each act of resistance, builds momentum and with the rise of global connectivity, it should be easier than ever to galvanize support for justice and equality."

"In theory. As long as there are people who are willing to speak up, challenge injustice and fight for what's right, there's hope," Serena replies. "The key is to stay committed to the cause, even when the path ahead seems perilous and unclear. My grandmother's generation recognized that every step, no matter how small, can be part of creating a more just world."

She is as proud of her bohemian, counter culture heritage as she is of her pioneer blood. That much is clear. I guess they were all pioneers in their own way. As we all must continue to be. Her eyes dance as she describes her grandfather, a roving artist, a musician from the East Coast.

"He'd ditched a college teaching job in upstate New York, lured by the outdoor recreation and the back-to-the-land movement that was taking hold around the same time that Point Reyes National Seashore was formed."

Marie had been married-off initially in her early twenties to the son of a prominent local dairy rancher. Serena tells us how her spirited grandmother caused a major commotion in both families when she subsequently absconded with the artist/musician.

It was then that the nomadic Marie and her lover hooked up with the Grateful Dead and the band's early entourage out at the historic wood framed Burdell Mansion in Rancho Olompali.

Serena describes it as having been home to the Coast Miwok for thousands of years, the oak woodland site that was popularized during a brief skirmish during the state's Bear Flag Rebellion in 1846.

"It was a productive ranch in the 1860s and after subsequent ownerships, the house had become a hippie commune for the Deadheads and later, a haven for a group called the Chosen Family.

After years of all-day concerts and parties, fire severely damaged the mansion by the end of that same decade. There was a second, even more secluded Marin County spot. Out at Camp Lagunitas," she continues. "A four-acre former children's camp dotted with redwoods and surrounded by oak-studded hills. It was pretty much all paradise out here back then."

"As far as I can see, it's still pretty much paradise now," I reply. It's completely incomprehensible for me to imagine my proper English grandmother in her thirties, doing drugs beneath the oaks and dancing semi-naked in the sunshine. I express as much. Her idea of the Sixties-look, as captured in albums of old family photos, was a series of tailored herringbone skirts and matching, awkward boxy jackets, with big, brass buttons. Heels, a string of pearls and a jauntily-positioned pillbox hat.

Marie on the other hand: "She had quite the time of it, lucky girl," Serena says. "Did whatever she wanted on her spiritual quest, her dreams for a better world, except figure out a way to hang on to my grandfather. They were living in the Haight after all the hippies left. She had little choice but to come back to Marin, solo, in 1976, not long after Mom was born."

Marie raised her daughter, Serena's mother Veronica, back in Bolinas, in a small unit built on to her parent's modest Victorian, two blocks from the beach. While she didn't have to worry about a basic roof over their heads and though she worked part-time for the park service, money had been tight.

"Mom never knew anything much other than thrift store clothes and the free-spirit, non-conformist nature of her mother. My great-grandparents came around to the way things were, in time. They didn't have much more to offer other than their house, their love and acceptance, so I guess they all pitched in to make it work. And that was more than enough."

Billy and Nate stand side-by-side by the sink, seemingly attached-at-the-hip. The pair are intent on the shucking of three dozen fresh oysters as they listen on in on our history lesson. Rather them than me, I think, as this task takes expertise and is infamously tricky and laborious.

"How did Marie get the money together for this place?" Billy asks.

"She came into enough cash for a down payment, dealing and selling Summer of Love memorabilia. Stuff she collected that was left behind. Bought the beach house from friends when it was going cheap so she could get out from under her folks."

"Good job we're patient," Nate says. He's scrubbing at one shell after another, his hands continually under the cold water, removing any residual mud, sand, dirt and undesirable hanger-ons from the otherwise pristine waters of Tomales Bay. It's the cleanest water I know of for oyster farming, but it is the wild after all. So, I'm pleased to see that he's paying attention despite the two or three glasses of wine he's already put away. Good thing that Billy is the one with the shucking knife.

Cold and briny and beautiful, the scent of the oysters on a large, metal platter of ice is the essence of the brackish, salty-waters in which they were farmed. It's like the ocean air after a storm, a burst of cool, mineral-rich freshness. I sidle over to study Billy as he applies pressure and plies back the hinge of a shell with the dull-pointed, thick bladed knife. I inhale through my nose and the breeze of Tomales Bay dances before me.

"What do you think of our sweet little West Coast oysters?" I ask. "Be honest." Billy and Nate were both born and raised on the other side of the country, out by the Atlantic coastline. It hadn't taken them long to high-tail it back across-country after we graduated.

"Back home the oysters are saltier, brinier, crisp," Billy replies, shrugging his shoulders as he gives the matter some thought. "But honestly, I'm just as partial to the soft, creamy texture and mineral taste of these West Coast waters."

Eva's small, knowing smile tugs at the corner of her lips. "Nice for some," she remarks, her tone dripping with playful sarcasm. She crosses her arms, tilting her head slightly as she takes a step back, her stance confident, almost daring. "Oysters are a delicacy yet to frequent my kitchen sink," she adds with a casual flick of her wrist, the words rolling off her tongue with a slight edge.

"It's not like we're slurping a dozen a day," Billy replies.

"More like once every-other week, sweets," Nate says. "Don't suggest you've been depriving yourself when it comes to your elevated tastes."

Billy is quick with his response. "We all have our weaknesses."

"Dark chocolate," River admits. "Can't resist."

"Hence dessert," Serena adds. "Special-ingredient brownies await, homemade late last night by River's own expert hands."

It's been years. I'm not sure I'm up for edibles. Eva catches my reticence.

"Don't do it if you're on the fence, Tam," she says. "I for one will not be partaking this weekend."

"What happens here on the Sonoma Coast, stays on the Sonoma Coast," Jamie jokes. "Though, I gotta say, I'm more of a lightweight these days, if I'm honest."

"Well, don't be too much of a party-pooper, there are other delights in store," Nate adds. "River has more than enough mushrooms to share for whoever's in on it tomorrow."

I roll my eyes and cross my arms. I'm even less enthusiastic about the idea of a mushroom trip. It may do me good to let go, as Jamie had hinted at earlier, but I'd feel better by playing it safe, avoiding the need to rummage around in my emotional toolbox. If I were to volunteer, I could keep an eye on the others.

"The good-girl-gang," Serena says, reaching out to Eva and me. Condescending.

Eva is quick to explain that she's routinely substance-tested at work. "Could happen any time," she says. It's the perfect excuse to avoid being swept along with whatever shenanigans the others are getting themselves into over the next few days. As for me, I uncross my arms and keep quiet.

"Billy and Eva spent a long weekend together catching up this January,"

Nate announces, swiftly changing the subject. "Did you guys see that on the social?" He launches into what sounds to me like a passive-aggressive diatribe, highlighting his partner's prolific business travel and social life and how in-demand he is in general. Billy is in commercial loans.

"Forget about the carbon footprint. Client clicks their fingers, insists on meeting in person in the middle of nowhere, Texas and off Billy-The-Go-Getter jets with a nice little side-trip to San Antonio. Kind of Eva to put him up."

I can't figure out what he's getting at. Is he jealous of Billy's friendship with Eva? They date back as pals long before he and Nate hooked up in senior year. Billy and Eva played on an intermural soccer team throughout their college years. I would go watch them sometimes, scouting the field for cute guys. Not being the team-sporty-kind myself, it was surprisingly fun to support my friends from the sideline.

Billy and Eva appear to be avoiding making direct eye contact. Interesting. There's no way that they're up to anything untoward behind Nate's back. Not now, after all this time. I'd put money on it. Billy was known to be sexually curious, though, back in the day, when experimentation amongst us was rife. Wasn't there a thing with River for a time? It's interesting how that never became an issue and other trysts did. We all have our secrets, I guess, some shared in confidence with one or another of our friend group, others we've undoubtedly kept to ourselves. I wonder what this is about but I'm going to assume it's just Nate being overly-possessive. His fear of missing out has certainly been a thing.

"I'm off social media," I say, hoping to deflect the issue, whatever it is. "In case you haven't noticed."

"I guess you'd be at risk of being scrutinized for any questionable lifestyle choices by your patients," River says. "Kind of like teachers and their students."

"As if I have anything to hide," I reply.

Billy announces that Nate makes up in screen presence for all of us. "He's the prince of the media platform. Friends in high places."

"It's a major component in my business," Nate says, digging his husband in the ribs. "And what this one is not telling you is that he loves his social every bit as much as I do. Though he's more of a stalker, gay husbands and handsome, queer-lifestyle models more his thing. In case you couldn't guess. Never leaves a like or comment, however . . . the rascal."

"You're an icon yourself, Billy Sunshine, B-Dream," Eva says. "Fashionista, foodie, successful married man. What's not to brag about?"

Billy says he prefers a life of passive consumption. Observing trends.

"Well, I find it disingenuous not to engage," Nate replies. "It's not like I'm seeking the spotlight. I need to dive in in order to follow the zeitgeist, to understand the spirit of the time."

Eva is concentrating on removing soft orange yolks from two hard boiled eggs. She wears a look of concentration as she mashes the yolks in a bowl, along with honey, mustard and lemon juice.

"And what *is* the prevailing spirit, pray tell?"

I watch as she whisks in olive oil to the mix for a dressing. Next, she seasons it generously with salt and pepper, tasting every now and again with the tip of her pinky finger before she stirs in a half-handful of freshly chopped chives.

"Is this the dandelion salad?" I ask. I'm doubtful the citrus cattail salad I'm in the midst of concocting will be anywhere near as impressive.

"It's all about the bacon bits and the dandelion-flower garnish," Eva explains. I resign myself on my lack of finesse.

"Scene stealer," I reply, with a smile. It's my turn to dig her gently in the ribs with my elbow. I'm not out to take the limelight. Who cares? I'm not at all competitive in either the social media or culinary department. Or any department. Except for my desire for Jamie's affection. I do my own thing. I've no instinct for commandeering the popularity show. It's too bad I never learned to cook from Gran.

I picture her cottage garden on the windswept Norfolk coast, so English with its hollyhocks and rambling roses—its modest orchard with crab apple and pear trees and its small vegetable plot. Rows of asparagus and sprouts, parsnips, carrots and potatoes. Tomatoes, lettuce and string beans in summer. I wonder if Mum has kept the garden up? I wouldn't mind a garden like that someday.

Soil to soul. Isn't that what River is proposing? A plan to farm regeneratively? Dairy, chickens, fruit trees, beehives. Meadows of native wildflowers form the backdrop of this seductive scene.

Nate clears his throat and responds to Eva's question after having thought it through for a while.

"One thing is for sure, social media influencers, content producers, they've taken over from the media in driving popular culture. I don't think there's ever been a time where we depend more on our skills to ask questions, think critically. Saying nothing, simply observing isn't serving us well."

As for me, I can't be doing with it. Social media overload. There's only so much political polarization and dystopian fear I'm willing to absorb. My job has required me to set healthy boundaries, to prioritize self-care in my goal to find pockets of joy, to be able to do my work, day in, day out.

As the conversation swirls around me, their chatter mixes with the rhythmic chopping of vegetables and the scent of garlic sizzling in the pan. They're deep into their debate about toxic political divides, the overwhelming weight of climate change, the relentless march of technology.

Nate jokes about the "end time," and everyone laughs, but it doesn't feel like a joke to me. My fingers pause on the knife, the blade halting mid-air as I listen, my thoughts suddenly spinning. Is this really the end of normalcy, or have I simply failed to see the shift happening beneath my feet? I've seen it too often—patients arriving at my office with anxiety, depression and a thousand unspoken fears about the future. But it's not just in my patients, a little of this is in me too. A gnawing feeling that something is about to break.

Friday, Later That Evening

Seven bottles of wine, a dozen or more beer bottles and counting as I haul an armload of empties out to the recycling. I mutter under my breath that I've grossly underestimated the consumption capacity of a house-party that stretches over a long weekend. It's been so long. I'm out of practice. I should've known better, doubled the order of wine. It's not like I'm a stranger in their midst. As I toss one bottle after another into the recycling bin, I remind myself I'd be enabling if I'd purchased additional supplies. Aren't we supposed to be reaching a more moderate stage in life? I guess the pandemic put shot to that. This bunch, for the most part, is clearly not even close to sober-curious.

I left them lolling around the kitchen table, quietened at last by full stomachs and the dulcet tones of Nora Jones as they nibble on the last of the manzanita shortbread, which, by the way, is surprisingly good. I can taste the rich, buttery flavor, still, the tang of the crushed berries, sweet yet slightly tart. Minnie and Myrtle hoovered up the crumbs under the table and around the legs of our chairs.

"Leave the dishes 'til morning," River instructs. They're checking the dogs aren't eating anything else they shouldn't. "I'll deal with the clean-up when I wake up," they say.

Slowly, the bulk of the group meanders into the lounge.

"Here, let me help." Jamie springs up and joins me in swooping yet more empty bottles from the counter. He follows me outside, his arms full. His sleeves are rolled up, revealing a band of brown and green oak leaves inked around his left bicep. This is new, at least to me. It catches me off-guard, my eyes lingering with an underlying sense of loss of how we're no longer as intertwined as we once were.

"You okay with us sharin'?" he asks, bashfully. He's looking at me with that earnest, lopsided, sleepy expression of his. "It wasn't as if we were given much choice with the limited sleepin' arrangements."

"Thanks for not assuming," I reply. I shrug my shoulders, feigning indifference. "And no, it isn't like there's any other option other than a sleeping bag on the floor."

"Well, consider me the perfect gentleman," he says. He reaches out and shakes my now empty hand. This takes me by surprise. It's all too formal, in contrast to the warmth of our past. I'd rather just get on with it, avoid any embarrassment, crash out for the night without any further discussion.

What about me? Am I capable of that same polite courtesy? Now, as bedtime approaches, I'm not so sure. I thought I had mentally prepared for this weekend, for spending time together again. But the last time we shared a bed, it wasn't just sleep we were sharing—it was a passionate, unforgettable goodbye. A bittersweet end to the physical bond that once held us together.

I say nothing as I turn and walk back into the soft, flickering light of the open doorway. I'm not ready for him to detect my veiled yearning. I'm worried I'll mess things up between us for once and for all if I get carried away, coming on too strong and too soon.

There's a flurry of activity at the kitchen sink. Despite River's instructions to leave the dishes until morning, Billy and Nate are taking a turn at dishwashing duties. Their sleeves are rolled up to their elbows and Nate's hands are submerged in a basin of soapy bubbles. No electric dishwasher in this house. Billy stands close behind, dishcloth in hand, unaware of their audience, his lips brushing the side of Nate's neck. It's good to see them so affectionate and playful after their snippy jibes back and forth earlier.

"So . . . what's the verdict?" Serena calls out from the living room. I clear my throat, loudly, so that the guys know I am here. They turn just as I lean forward to blow out the flames on the beeswax candles that have burned half way down on a set of carved, wooden candle holders in the center of the table.

"I wanna know what everyone thinks. Which dish was the best?" Serena demands.

There had been so many candles throughout our student house. Scented candles in the bathroom, twinkling votives in the bedrooms, tapers and columns precariously balanced on stacks of text books, empty chairs, beeswax poured in jelly jars and saucers and wedged inside a motley collection of thrift store crystal. Multi-colored wicks burned throughout the night, at breakfast, at lunch, multiple, mis-matched unscented candles at dinner. And incense. No college digs are replete without an abundance of incense.

River is wafting a long, smoky stick of the patchouli-scented stuff as I walk into the living room, the heady fragrance of which transports me back to our forest walk earlier. They bend down to the coffee table and place it in an ornate wooden holder, decorated with gold leaf.

"Why must the amazing supper we've devoured become a contest?" they ask, throwing their hands up in mock exasperation, their fingers splayed as if to signal disbelief, a playful smirk tugging at the corner of their mouth, eyes flicking between Serena and the rest of the group.

Serena, not missing a beat, leans down, hands pressed lightly on the table for emphasis. Her eyes gleam with a mischievous spark, her lips curling into a confident, almost teasing smile. "It's not so much of a competition—it's an elevation, a celebration of all the wild bounty," she replies, a small shrug of her shoulders adding to the nonchalance of her justification. She lifts a hand as if to underline her point, then holds up an empty wine glass with a flick of her wrist. "It was a delicious meal, yes, but I would like to know which dish outdid the others, for future reference." Her gaze sweeps around the room, inviting an answer, but there's a challenge in her posture as if daring anyone to disagree.

Her long hair is casually braided on one side, and with a quick flick of her head, she tosses the braid over her shoulder before peeling off her apron.

It falls away revealing a long, flowing floral dress that sways gently in the candlelight. A fringe belt hangs low on her hips, adding a touch of boho flair. The dress, in my opinion, makes her look less like the Heidi-esque mountain dweller of this afternoon and more like a model straight out of a chic wine country boutique. Classic Serena.

"Each dish was spectacular, as are you, darling," Billy says, sweeping his hand in a grand gesture toward his host. "Exactly the same as always. Pure Serena." He flashes a grin toward Nate. "He'll back me up—he's heard me call it out every time I come across something that even *remotely* compares."

Nate nods in agreement. "It's not a natural look for an east-coaster to replicate," he says.

Eva lists her own fashion favorites from 2003. "Strapless dresses with a '50s vibe," she recalls as she curls and extends her curvaceous frame lengthways across the sofa, purring, like a well-fed cat. "I'm claiming this spot for the next half hour. Remember those purses we all bought, the ones with the wooden handles?"

"Yes. And I can still see you so clearly in those mesh tops, your zippered mini-skirt, obnoxious, hot-pink leg warmers to complete the look," I reply. We've laughed at our memories as they've taken shape during the course of the evening, images that dance around us, tease us, our youthful ghosts playing with the passage of time.

By contrast, Eva is currently kitted out in a fresh-looking set of crisp, white-on-white loungewear. The color scheme, or lack of, compliments her smooth, plump, olive skin.

"Eva was the ultimate pre-made punk princess," Nate adds, taking a measured bite over a napkin from one of the brownies that River is passing around. I reach for the last of Serena's shortbread instead. I'm not up for an edible this late in the evening. No thanks. Been there.

"Be careful around the dogs, guys," I remind them. Serena shoots me the kind of look an experienced mother gives to a well-meaning, childless friend.

I find an empty chair, settle into it comfortably my mind drifts back—way back—by a couple of decades and more. Serena had floated around in her bell-sleeved frocks, while I'd scoured magazines for new looks to better fit in as a newbie, not the stick-out-like-a-sore-thumb, deer-in-the-headlights

Brit, who'd landed, as if from a spaceship, in a Northern California beach-front campus.

Sandblasting denim was a thing back then. And we were into it in a big way. It was so popular, it became our number-one, do-it-yourself group fashion activity for a while.

"What about those wire scrubbing brushes we used to distress our denim jackets?" I ask. "You worked up quite the sweat on several occasions, Jamie, if my memory serves me well."

"And those god-awful, chunky highlights," Serena recalls, rather too gleefully, adding insult to injury with a disdainful recollection of my zealous, zig-zag part and face-framing bangs.

I still have the box of t-shirts with city names I'd worn excessively under a baggy, twill, thrift-store jacket. It's tucked away under my bed for posterity.

There was no such thing as loneliness back then, thankfully. Or cancel culture. For the first time in my life, I was truly not alone. We had free-run of an entire Victorian house-share with not a single lock on an inside door. Maybe the bathrooms locked, we did have some boundaries, but toileting was about it. Bath time generally involved long conversations with Serena or Eva balanced on the edge of the tub, smoking joints and cigarettes and talking until the water went cold.

I owe so much of who I am today to the time I lived and loved in that house with these people. I'd escaped the toxic wound that had festered after my parents' divorce and my dad's subsequent death. It was the first time in my life that I was able to look around a room and into the eyes of people who appeared to make sense, people who helped me figure out what was really going on, why I was here on this precious, imperiled, blue planet.

Yes, we were flawed, then and we still are. Each of us in our own unique way. And things were far from perfect. But as I look around the room tonight, a sense of hope stirs within me—a quiet, bubbling spring. It feels strong enough to fuel the perseverance I'll need to untangle the mess that is holding me back, preventing me from fully reconnecting.

Warm candlelight falls softly on each of our faces. The room holds an ethereal aura at this late hour. I'm feeling increasingly and uncharacteristically sentimental as the night wears on, in part, no doubt, due to the music, the convivial setting, a full stomach and the volume of wine I've consumed.

I sit back and absorb the room. The paneled walls smell freshly white-washed in contrast to an otherwise delicate, almost nostalgic scent of old books mingling with the faint, briny trace of seashells—whispering of the sea they once touched, now softened by time. The room is decked out with an assortment of leggy houseplants, eccentric folk art and a large, overflowing bookcase lined with dozens of old and eclectic hardback titles.

I'm happy to see that Marie's collection of cloudy, glass fishing-floats-in-rope have stood the test of time as well as an especially large, dusty-pink seashell which I instinctively lift and hold to the hollow of my ear. I listen to waves crash on shingle, though I know full well that it's only the echo of the noise that is trapped in space, playing tricks.

Serena lingers by the window, gazing out into the darkness. "Hear that?" she asks. As if we are in tune. "The waves. They sing to me at night you know."

"A swan song," River replies, stepping toward her and placing an arm affectionately around her waist. "This old house will become a part of that music someday, all too soon."

"Thanks for the reminder," Serena shoots them a look that makes them blush an uncomfortable shade. The atmosphere changes, instantly. "Way to ruin the mood. Mandatory evacuation is coming, sooner or later. I know. I'm on it. I don't need you to dig the knife in. The county won't get away with wrestling this place from me without some kind of a sale."

A government-subsidized deal to eradicate this imminently potential death trap would be what it takes to secure Serena's inheritance, she explains, her honeyed voice, now tense.

"It would at least free up some serious cash toward securing us a safer spot. On collective ground," she adds.

"Surely there's something that can be done to slow the rate of erosion?" Eva asks. "It's not like we haven't seen it coming out here as it has along most coastal zones."

"Yes, but not in this case. It's pretty dire," River explains. "As Serena says, best thing would be for the county to swoop in and buy her out. But that's not on the cards in the immediate future."

Serena glides across the room. Her body is fluid, malleable as she levers herself smoothly into an empty lounge chair, followed closely by Minnie and Myrtle. I watch as she drapes one leg over the side of the armchair, casually. She talks about the devastating winter we'd thought we'd be through with when we agreed to an April reunion. Winter had come on the heels of one of the worst droughts we've seen here in California for a hundred years or more. Those of us who live along the West Coast have managed to remain as stoic as humanly possible as we've endured the seemingly endless rain and floods.

"No chance of building a sea wall here for too few homes," River picks back up on the predominant issue of erosion. "Cliffs are crumbling into the ocean faster than they are in the south. Wind, rain, powerful winter storms, these old rocks are crumbling, all too rapidly. And the rising sea levels, they're no joke either."

Serena shrugs. "Hey, there's a saying and a song, something along the lines of if we're not living on the edge, then we're simply taking up too much space. Besides, it would be best case scenario if the government was to buy me out."

River says it's all about timing. They unabashedly launch into the clean-up costs of a beach house such as this, falling, calamitously into the sea. I imagine Serena's grandma, Marie, back in the day, happily beachcombing down below for shells and stones, watching the sun set over the ocean from within the sun porch in summer, snuggling up and reading her books by the fireside in winter. What would she make of our leveled hysteria?

"Isn't this why we're here?" Nate asks. "I'm as sorry as you are Serena, considering the prospect of this perfect place someday all-too-soon being reclaimed by the ocean. But we may as well be honest and face facts. It's what we set out to do with our idealistic pact. Figure out how to build an intentional community together."

Billy says he for one never imagined it would possibly happen so fast and so furiously. "Climate change. It's getting wackier by the season with far too many devastating and extreme weather events to count. Everywhere.

We assumed we we'd be dealing with this in our sixties, right? Our golden, retirement years. Now, here we are, getting real, bringing up our deadline by a good two decades."

"Fuck yeah," River says. "If I hear the terms bomb-cyclone, wildfire, or atmospheric river one more time this year. . ."

Nate asks: "So, are we in or are we out on fast-forwarding our plan?"

Jamie insists there's no need to get into any heavy-duty commitment tonight. I don't think he'd seen this amount of pressure coming our way. Besides, we have all weekend to talk. Jamie suggests the weed brownies Billy, Nate and River scarfed a half-hour earlier have another thirty minutes or more to kick in.

"I'll leave it to all you wise guys to solve the world's problems over the next couple of hours," he says, as he lays down and stretches out his long arms and legs on the surface of the rug. "Though it's doubtful you'll remember much of it in the mornin'."

"Since when did you get so sensible on us?" Nate asks. He tosses a cushion at Jamie.

"Since I agreed to take the boat out," Jamie replies, explaining how edibles can last as long as twelve hours in the system. "Not a good idea, man, 'specially if you don't know just how much you're ingestin'," he adds. "And River's brownies are legendary, practically a household name senior year."

Serena agrees. She says that River tends to make the mistake of preparing their brownies as overly potent for average consumption. "I've reminded you of this, how many times?" she asks.

"What, you're Team Mother now?" River snaps back. They're seated on the floor by her feet.

"Screw you," Serena replies, kicking River in the thigh a little too forcefully with the heel of a bare foot. She wears a silver toe ring on her second toe. It glistens in the low light. "I'm being a responsible host is all."

Jamie lounges on his side on the rug on the other side of where she is posted. I watch as he reaches out and takes hold of her ankle. He touches the bare skin of her foot, briefly before releasing his hold. "Hey, enough," he insists, gently. "Lighten up the two of you."

The gesture is too intimate for my liking. A stab of jealousy rears its pathetic head. They have history, the two of them. They were lovers before there was a Jamie and me. Though Jamie was the one to walk away from her in the end.

"We're all grown-ups," Jamie says, attempting to smooth things over. "There's no need to judge."

Well, I can't help myself on that score by my siding with River. If I was stuck out here alone with Serena for years on end, I'd be stoned by now.

"Anyway, the Good Doctor is here if we need her," Serena remarks. She swivels her feet to the ground, stands, saunters over and lands a big, old pantomime of a kiss on the top of my head. I wasn't expecting such an unnecessary show of theatrical affection. She's succeeded in shifting the attention from herself.

"I do love you for it, Tamsin," she declares. "One of us must take it for the team and maintain a level head, after all."

Jamie, casually grabbing his hand-built Santa Cruz acoustic guitar, its rich tone contrasting with River's more weathered Martin, a relic from a senior year find-pile. They're not aiming for perfection—especially not the sharp, iconic riff from Seven Nation Army—but for the sake of nostalgia and fun, they give it a go. Their audience is forgiving, focused more on the moment than technical precision. It's a fitting scene, a snapshot that pulls me back to those wild, never-ending nights in our student house, when the music was more about the vibe than the performance.

They stumble through the verses, their voices harmonizing in fits and starts, like an old, familiar tune they're too tired to take seriously but too nostalgic to abandon.

Serena's voice cuts through the air, tentative at first but growing bolder as she eases into the familiar melody of "I'm With You". The song feels oddly wistful now, a relic from a time when we were searching for anthems to capture the chaos of youth. Her rendition is imperfect, the edges a little rough, but there's a rawness to it that makes it feel more honest, more present than the glossy pop-punk original. Her voice dips into the familiar chorus, but there's something more reflective in it now, something quieter, as if she's not just singing the words, but thinking through them.

"It's all about friendship after all," Serena muses, her voice drifting between the chords. She looks up for a moment, catching my eye, as if she's sharing the thought directly with me, like we're both in on the unspoken truth of it. I nod, not just because I agree, but because I know exactly what she's doing. *Friendship*. The word comes out a little too easily, a little too shiny, and neither of us acknowledges the weight of the history behind it— the moments that are better left unspoken, the times we'd faltered, when the lines between friends and something more complicated had blurred.

Serena's smile is small and faintly apologetic, but she keeps on, pushing the music forward, as though it's somehow easier to gloss over what's not said when there's a song to fill in the gaps. Eva, standing beside her now, joins in, and her distinctive voice smooths over the roughness, harmonizing with Serena's in a way that softens the edges of the past. The two of them together create this strange, warm balance—like they've always known how to cover the flaws without saying a word.

Jamie and River, content to let the girls lead, keep the rhythm simple— just enough strumming to carry the song along without overthinking it. The guitars blend, almost casual, as if they're just along for the ride, adding to the intimacy of the moment without stealing focus.

We're nowhere near as carefree as we used to be, no matter how good the show that we're putting on tonight. Would we recognize the people we've become? A round of Dixie Chicks' "Landslide" wraps and I say my goodnights. I slip off to bed, the sound of music, laughter and the slow crashing and swelling of the night ocean blending into one.

Saturday, Early Morning

Sometime in the early hours I experience a sensation like I'm swimming upward into a slow, watery awakening, the sound of deep, rhythmic breathing. I wouldn't describe it as snoring as such. I recognize it after a moment, as Jamie in a comfortable rest. The cadence of his breathing tells me that I'm in the right place. I lay still, so still as to stop time, to experience the feel of his warm breath on the back of my neck, his body beside mine. No action or consequence required. A sense of peace floods my core, at least until he wakes up and there's an awkward pause before we reluctantly prize ourselves ever-so slightly apart.

He draws his thigh up into the hollow of my back. I hold my breath to prevent my quickening heartbeat from disturbing his slumber and waking him too soon. He stirs, draws away. It's all slightly absurd given that I am still married to the man.

I turn toward him. My arm reaches out on its own accord. My hand lingers on the surface of his warm skin beneath a layer of his crumpled t-shirt. In addition to the newer tree-tattoo, there's a more familiar one, the face of the Green Man in the space between his shoulder blades. It's been there since he was a teenager, apparently, inked during one of the seasons he worked a ceramics booth over spring weekends at the Renaissance Faire.

It's been a long time since I've traced the motif of leaves with my finger tip. Too long. A folklore symbol — the cycle of life, death, rebirth. A poignant reminder of the ties that bond, no matter the time apart. He'd liked that I knew about the Green Man the first time I'd seen him shirtless. My hand hovers and remains still as I savor the stillness and potency of the early hour.

Why did I not put up more of a fight back then? There had never been any drama between us. It was mostly her doing. Serena. Or at least that's the story I've told myself. He stirs and rolls closer, opens his eyes sleepily before reaching out and tucking my hair gently behind my right ear. A faint, metallic glow from the ocean illuminates his eyes caught between shadow and light, aligned now so close to my own.

Our lips meet and we kiss, softly at first, a surging tide of intensity deepening my need. I relinquish the last ounce of my reserve as I roll him, gently onto his back.

I no longer take birth control, I tell him. "Not much need for it," I confess as he rests the palm of his hand over my mouth. We sink into one another immediately, effortlessly and with near silent abandon. After, it's as if I've stumbled upon a core piece of my heart puzzle in a previously locked drawer, filling a space that has been glaringly empty, resignedly abandoned. I'm quietly exhilarated. I wish I could lay here with him by my side all day.

When I next awake, a second time, at dawn, I find a handwritten note on the pillow beside me nestled in the dent where his head had rested.

It's not a note. No. A rough outline of a song—clearly tongue-in-cheek, with smiley faces and hurriedly composed, but it's the thought that counts—I smile as I read the four verses, a chorus in between and a soppy bridge. I told him once, in our early days, if he ever wrote me the perfect love song, I'd know we were the real deal. This is admittedly maybe not the *perfect* love song as smash hits go, at least not at first draft, but it's endearing and sweet and more than enough of a spontaneous-effort, scribbled in pencil on the back of a used envelope.

He remembered. My heart skips the beat of a lovesick teen. I lounge a-while longer in the crumpled linens, resting Jamie's silly love song on my chest. I have no idea what to make of this other than it's all rendering me close to tears. I've never, ever, fully resigned myself to Jamie and me as mere platonic partners, but I never expected it to be this passionate between us again. Our parting had been so sudden, so painful, so complicated and, for all intents and purposes, final. I stare up at the ceiling in wonderment. If there's a higher force in play, this weekend. I need to get out of my own way and allow it some motion.

Intense. I am rarely so reckless. My mind paces and I clench my fists in a sudden panic. What if there was an accident? Why did we not use any protection? Slim chance, but you never know. How ironic that would be. I can hear my mother's pious response: "Well, that would certainly put the cat amongst the pigeons, my girl."

I roll out of bed and dash toward the confines of a tired, old, baby-blue and pink bathroom. I'm quick to wash away any evidence of my extra-curricular activities before the others are up and about. I feel my face flush with a warm glow. It feels like I'm flashing an overt neon sign announcing what we've been up to. It's hard to disguise.

I'm pretty sure nobody heard us—we exercised an impressive degree of sound restraint considering. I'd rather not hear any of them at it either. We're no longer in student digs with paper thin walls and revolving doors.

It was Serena who was infamous for her loud lovemaking. And, though it pains me to remind myself, it was Jamie she was screwing on-and-off on a regular basis and all the way up until a little more than a month before he and I were married. They'd bust up because of her wanderlust. It was at that time that I was getting ready to return, although reluctantly, back to the UK with my newly minted degree in hand.

I position the frosted vinyl shower curtain inside a petal-pink, narrow cast-iron tub before turning on the shower faucet. The soles of my bare feet cover rusty water stains around the stainless-steel drain as I stand beneath the shower's modest spray. I squint my eyes and check out the labels on a variety of shampoo and conditioner bottles in an attempt to match them to their owners. One of the best ways to piss off Serena, I recall, was to squeeze out the last drop of her precious, purple shampoo-for-blondes without her permission. Now the selection is distinctively more organic. I settle on a small, dark bottle of peppermint and tea tree shampoo with an invigorating scent, squirting a little into my hand and lathering my hair.

Warm water soothes my nerves as I cast my mind back to that morning, twenty years ago, the moment when Jamie came to me and casually, without any hint of a suggestion from me, or anyone else, or so I'd thought initially, offering out of the blue to marry me for the Green Card. I found out later that it was crafty Serena who had put the idea in his head. If she couldn't have him, then she'd figured out a way to bind him to the group. By talking him into tying the Green-Card-knot with me, because, that's what best friends do, he'd have trouble finding any woman better, or more accepting than her.

It was genius of her. She made him promise not to tell me prior to the wedding that it was her brainchild in the first place. Of course, I would find out soon enough, though she'd taken great pleasure in holding back this information. I'd thought his offer ridiculous at first, an afront to his freedom, newly graduating and ready to launch into the world. But there was no denying it, one of the quickest routes to Legal Permanent Residence in the U.S. was by marriage back then. Not now. Anything else was daunting in the extreme. I'd have had to have gone home and hunted for a job that would issue me a coveted H-1B work visa in order to return. It was sobering to have settled into the country during my four-year bio degree only to give it all up, my American life, my friends who had become my family in my big, solo adventure across the Atlantic.

Jamie had, unbeknown to me, broached the subject one evening with the rest of the roommate-gang after Serena had planted the seed of the Green Card marriage idea. They'd all jumped enthusiastically on board. To say we were clueless is an understatement. The city hall "wedding" took place a week before we graduated. It was basically an excuse for an all-night rave. Billy and Nate took photos. Serena prepared a wedding picnic with mismatched chintzy China, crystal and cheap bubbly on the beach at sundown. I should've been suspicious of her lack of push-back on the whole marriage plot even then but I naively assumed she was over him. She'd certainly not been shy in moving on and making her way into several other bedrooms in the house—wherever she was welcomed it appeared.

River and their then love-interest, a third-year philosophy student named Dakota had taken her in for a week as a potential throuple, I recall.

It didn't take long for Dakota to move out, claiming to have been unfairly sexiled by River and Serena when the novelty of a threesome wore off. That was the first of several times River and Serena shacked up together. It wasn't in the cards for them as a permanent couple until COVID hit.

There is only this one bathroom in the beach house, so I'm efficient in my showering and brief drying off with the most threadbare of towels. As for the youthful Jamie and me, we'd hesitated on talking through the physical implications of our prospective marriage initially. We'd each enjoyed the luxury our own rooms in the rambling student house—Jamie and Serena had doubled up for part of that year until they'd split and he'd taken the ill-fated Joshua's room. Josh had graduated six months earlier and was already off shedding his "student skin" backpacking in Asia.

The morning after the wedding, as the sun was rising, we'd fallen into my bed fully dressed. Nothing happened until we awoke. I'm seeing a pattern, here. I was suitably shy, thinking back, though neither of us had wanted for partners during our student days, we'd just not yet discovered each other that way.

To my surprise, a gallant, old-fashioned side to Jamie had blossomed into being. It was all so long ago but it feels like yesterday. That first morning he thanked me theatrically, on one knee, for marrying him and declared his commitment to seeing it through for as long as it took to get my papers.

"We'll need to make a go of it to convince 'em'," he'd urged as he'd laced his fingers gently through mine. As I said, we'd never come close to being intimate before. He'd kissed me tentatively as we laid together amongst the ruffled sheets of my student bed and I returned the favor. I wasn't about to question my good fortune. And we laughed at the craziness of it all as we self-consciously undressed and set about making it official.

It wasn't only not a bad thing, as we both agreed. It was lovely and surprising in a weird sort of accidental, clueless way.

My freshly-showered skin tingles, a gentle buzz beneath the surface as my body remembers that first time and again, more recently, this morning. There was and is an undeniable chemistry between us, something we may never have discovered if Serena hadn't pushed us together. It hadn't taken long back then to discover what a commitment we had made, whether or not we were "in-love" in the traditional way.

We'd naively assumed that the tedious application process would take around a year once we'd set about the tracking down of family documents on both sides and answering, literally, hundreds of questions.

His folks were furious when they found out. His mother told me to my face, after the fact, that she had been set on an outdoor wedding for Jamie at their family place. Someone who would bring him back to their community. And later, a couple of grandkids to roam their wooded property. I felt guilty for having shattered their illusion for the future of their only son. It freaked them out even more that I could've potentially absconded with him back to Britain at any point. They're good people and they came around eventually and softened to me. I actually think they were sorry when we finally split years later.

My mother, on the other hand, still enjoys this as one more example of my wanton neglect; my general parental disrespect. She considers the marriage my biggest mistake yet. It's not that she has an issue with Jamie. He's not the kind of guy for anyone to have an issue with. She distrusted our intentions from the start. And she certainly hasn't forgiven me for not producing a single grandchild in the process. As her only child, she figures she's all out of luck in the grandparenting department. I have wondered if she'd make a better grandmother than she was as a mother? I've heard of such things, though I'd be reluctant to subject any child of mine to her perpetual high expectations and rigid rules.

Jamie and I opened a joint bank account soon after we married with what little cash we'd scraped together in order to sign a lease for a small, airless studio apartment in San Francisco. It was our friends who'd generously chipped in for the cost of our application with the U.S Citizenship and Immigration Services as a wedding gift. We had to figure out how to do the paperwork ourselves as we couldn't afford a lawyer.

My towel is like a sheet of cardboard to the touch due to there being no clothes dryer in the beach house. Serena and River are staunch practitioners of line or air-drying laundry even if it does take several days at this time of year. I've spotted retractable laundry lines of varying lengths all over the place—on the porch, in the basement, even in the room I'm sleeping in. I should've listened to Eva's advice and brought a fluffy bath sheet from home.

I lean on the chipped, laminate countertop and peer into the cloudy mirror of a built-in medicine cabinet in order to apply a glob of sunscreen moisturizer to my face. The sunscreen cost me as much as what we used to spend on a week's worth of groceries in the early days in that first city apartment I shared with Jamie. We were clean out of ready cash by the end of each month but what we did have was a fountain of youthful ambition and hope and we made the dollars stretch remarkably well in order to satisfy our minimal needs.

After I throw some clothes on, I wander the still-sleeping house. I've no idea where Jamie is this early; walking the beach most likely. It appears we're the first two up and about. That's okay with me. My mind is racing with oxytocin-fueled possibilities. There's no instant formula to configure as to what comes next. I hope he's as happy as I am right now, floating in a space of shared potential.

I pause at the window, the soft light of dawn spilling over the sand, and then I spot him—Jamie, standing by the water's edge, his back to me. There's something different about the way he's holding himself today, something I can't quite place. The ocean stretches out before him, endless and wide, and for a moment it feels like everything is suspended in time. My heart stutters. I take a step closer, my fingers brushing against the cool glass. And then, without warning, he turns, locking eyes with mine from across the distance—and in that instant, I see it: a slight, unspoken tension, something unresolved, hanging in the air like a storm waiting to break.

Saturday Morning

Our first full day stretches ahead with a quiet sense of possibility. Those who stayed up late or early, depending on how you look at it, are awake and breathing, cradling earthen mugs of tea and coffee. They lounge in the soft morning light, scattered on any surface close to the warmth of the wood stove, limbs draped lazily in every direction. Jamie has returned, cheeks flushed from his walk on the beach, the salty breeze clinging to him. He brings with him not just the ocean air but also a weather update from another early riser he met on the shore.

I assume it was he who had stoked the embers of the fire from last night and built up a fresh stack of wood.

"Weather's not lookin' great, but nothin' too gnarly," he says, as he peels off his outer layers revealing a soft, plaid shirt in a color that sets off his eyes. "We're good to go down to the tidepools later this mornin'."

"What about your dive tomorrow?" Serena asks. I bristle. The sensible thing to do is to remain on shore in dubious conditions, if you were to ask me. Nobody does.

"Reckon it'll be okay," he replies, shrugging his shoulders as he stares out of the window. A thin, charcoal-grey thumb-line of the horizon is drawn over the rumbling Pacific.

"Don't go out on the water if it's dodgy, bud," Billy says—finally, someone else being sensible. He is rubbing his eyes. "We'll survive Sunday supper without the seafood."

Serena snaps; "Jamie knows what he's doing."

I've promised to make pastry for the wild mushroom tart we're to eat with a side of the last of the foraged salad greens for lunch. I'll leave them to battle it out. Nothing I say is going to make much difference. Jamie follows me into the kitchen where the stovetop tea kettle is humming toward a rolling boil.

He stands behind me as I search the refrigerator for the butter. I pause as he slowly but deliberately lifts my low pony tail and positions it gently to one side. His lips rest on the back of my neck. The skin there is rich with delicate nerve endings. His touch is intimate, sending a wave of warmth down my spine, rendering me vulnerable.

"We're good, right?" he asks. I turn, butter and eggs in my hands as I gaze directly into his freckled eyes. His thick, dark lashes are dewy from the morning fog.

"The fresh air suits you," I say. He gives me a playfully shy glance.

"I've been soaking up the fog with all of the other plant and animal life out here along the coast."

Fog being the last reserve out west when the long, dry months approach.

"It doesn't look as if we're in for much sunshine this weekend," I suggest, deflecting the intimacy of the moment. The privacy of the bedroom is one thing. Standing so close in the kitchen is another.

He leans forward and plants a single kiss on my forehead. Gentle and caring. Time slows down. I'm slightly uncomfortable with how comfortable this all is, if that makes any sense.

"I felt like I was walking through a huge cloud this morning," he says. We don't dive deeper into the topic of *us*. Instead, he follows my lead, sticking to safer ground, and starts explaining how fog is just a cloud that's close to the ground, made up of tiny water droplets. These droplets are about four times thinner than a human hair, he says, reaching up and tucking another runaway strand behind my ear.

"This thick fog we get here in Nor Cal," he adds thoughtfully, as he rubs his chin, "is, as you know, caused by a mix of weather and ocean conditions. The northern winds stirrin' up the ocean, pullin' cold water from deep down. It's when the warm air from the sun hits the cold water, that it turns into fog."

He shrugs and grins a little. "Look at us, getting all geeked out on the fog."

Jamie leans back, hands in his pockets, his voice picking up speed. "But the fact that it holds tons of water on a hot summer day. It's actually really important for a lot of species, especially the redwoods out here along the coast."

I nod, wiping my hands on a towel as I watch him pour coffee from the percolator, steam rising in a swirl. "I guess we should be grateful for the extra rain this late in the season," I say.

I walk over to the stove and turn off the tea kettle before making a start cutting butter into small chunks. The knife taps against the glass bowl with a rhythm.

"What worries me is that scientists say we've lost about thirty percent of the coastal fog we need around here," Jamie continues.

We both know that's bad news for the redwoods and the environment as a whole.

"What about the vineyards?" I ask. "They're still planting more vines."

Jamie thinks it's a bigger issue than just any one crop or plant. "Wildfires spread faster when there's less moisture in the air," he says. "It's all connected—like trying to fix the kelp forests."

He gets really passionate when he talks about kelp. His eyes light up. It's contagious.

"It's the plants in the ocean that could do the most to fight climate change," he says.

"Wait, am I right that seagrass absorbs carbon something like up to forty times faster than forests on land?" I ask, as I continue rubbing butter into flour with my fingers. I've learned more on this subject than he's aware of.

Jamie smiles, wiping a bit of flour from my nose. "Yeah, it's crazy," he says, sliding his hands back into his jean pockets to stop himself from messing with my dough. "But here's the thing: we don't have the luxury of time."

I listen carefully as he sips his coffee and explains how kelp can grow really quickly under the right conditions, pulling carbon out of the air before it dies and sinks to the ocean floor, locking that carbon away.

"So, what happens after that?" I ask, genuinely intrigued as I roll the dough into a ball.

"It helps restore ocean ecosystems, which in turn supports communities around the world," he says. "If we really want to bring the planet's climate back to pre-industrial levels—meaning less than 300 parts per million of CO_2—we've got to get rid of a trillion tons of excess CO_2 from the atmosphere. It's a huge task. We need a *lot* of kelp and microalgae to make it happen."

"Along with moving away from fossil fuels, I guess?" I add.

"Right," he says. "Not too heavy for you first thing? That's what I love about you, Tam. Always have. Good listener, smart and a quick study."

"That's why we're here, isn't it?" I ask, noting his use of the love word. We're playing a game within a more serious game here.

"One of the reasons," he replies. He smiles, resignedly and looks around for something to eat. "What's on the menu for breakfast? I'm starvin'."

Serena floats in, catching the tail end of our conversation.

"River and Eva's bakery haul is up for grabs, so get it while it's fresh, kiddos," she answers, unveiling a platter filled with an outrageous assortment of large and scrumptious-looking pastries, muffins and scones. "There's yogurt and berries too. Tomorrow we'll cook a brunch."

Eva is the last one up. There's a healthy glow to her face, almost the same dewy overlay that coated Jamie's eyelashes when he walked in. She brightens up the kitchen just by being here.

"What's with the radiant-morning look?" I ask. "Something's clearly suiting you."

"Mucha fruta y vedura as Mami says," she replies. "Eat your fruits and veggies. Keep a positive mindset and take every opportunity to sleep in."

She laughs, slightly nervous, I think, as she opens the refrigerator and pulls out a tub of Greek yogurt.

"Honey, honey?" she enquires of Serena, who points to the pantry.

"Help yourself to whatever you'd like. Don't wait to be invited."

Serena's all bare feet and ethereal robes, whereas Eva is lounge-wared-out again with a fresh ensemble of oatmeal-colored, cozy-flared pants, an oversize stretch organic cotton t-shirt and an adorable pair of tan sheepskin booties. I feel a little dowdy in my black leggings and simple, long sleeve top by comparison, padding around in my slipper socks with a sensible, hooded cardigan wrapped around my middle.

River makes an announcement that we're on schedule for tide-pooling in a half an hour.

"Whoever wants to shallow bathe or take a shower should get in line," they say. "After me, that is. I'm first."

"Best jump in together," Nate says. He winks at his partner who is biting into his second baked good, this one a large sticky bun.

"These are dangerous," Billy says, wiping his sugary hands on a dish towel. He hands the rest of the bun to his partner.

"Don't you know showering together is dangerous?" River asks. "Ask Serena. I don't remember the last time we took an outdoor tub together. We used to all the time during lockdown. Candles, music, the whole deal."

"Well, some of us have other things to occupy our time with," Serena says. She's snippy this morning. "Don't slip on the soap, boys."

Jamie, Serena and I have had a head start on the showering. Billy suggests Nate shower after River, then Eva and he's up to go last. "I could do with a minute or two to myself," he says.

"Okay captain," Nate replies with a mock-salute. "I guess I'll float my own boat this morning."

Billy and Eva offer to wash the breakfast dishes while the rest of us get out-fitted for our morning expedition.

First, I cover the pie dough in wrap to rest in the refrigerator for a couple of hours. Billy and Eva are standing with their backs to me. I'm sensing an air of conspiration between the two of them. Whatever they're plotting, they couldn't be kinder when I offer to dry the dishes, encouraging me to take a break from kitchen duties while they finish up.

Saturday Mid-Morning

"**B**illy's showing his social side this weekend but there's another, more secretive element to him, these days, one that he's intent on hiding from me," Nate confides as we make room on the porch to sit beside an iridescent line-up of blue and green abalone shells set amidst a driftwood collection. We're waiting for the others to join us.

Large boulders of neolithic rock anchor the hillside across from the house. I've heard said that a giant inadvertently dropped the heavy load from a tear in his sack while traversing the meadows a million light years ago.

"What kind of secrets?" I ask, studying a series of dotted holes in the pearlized undertone of a shell where air was taken in. Ocean waters have been closed to the taking of abalone for the past few years, so this assortment of shells must've been here a while.

"You two are the poster couple. Being secretive doesn't sound like Billy," I say.

"It started a year or so ago when we got serious about the adoption conversation," Nate explains. "It's put pressure on our relationship."

I ask him if they're both on board with an equal enthusiasm to become parents?

"It's not an undertaking to be launched lightly," I add. "I speak from a purely professional standpoint obviously."

Nate explains how the parenting subject has raised a bunch of cultural issues. "I want to adopt a kid," he says. "For me it centers around my concept of family, tradition. I never imagined how important it would be for me to ensure such a strong connection to my Jewish identity."

"And Billy has his own thoughts on that?" I ask. Billy was born and raised in an interracial Baptist family in South Carolina outside of Charleston. His twenty-plus-year relationship and subsequent marriage to a white, Brooklyn-born Jew appears, on the outside at least, to have melded their two, very different cultures remarkably well.

"He wants us to engage a surrogate," Nate replies. "He's changed his tune on adoption entirely. It's basically to do with him being the end of his line. His parents both passed a few years back if you remember? His sister never had kids and doesn't intend to and he insists the pandemic changed the way he feels about the future, how we go about building our own family."

"And you're not into this option?" I ask. "Surrogacy? Even though it sounds like Billy's set his heart on it?"

"I'm the one who set my heart on adoption," Nate replies. He's jostling around, he can't sit still as he pulls a pre-rolled joint from his pack and lights it. He extends the joint to me in offering. I shake my head.

I begin to say that it's maybe a little early in the day to get high, but I close my mouth before the words spill out.

"Maybe one of each?" I ask, circling back around to the topic in question. "A surrogate birth and a subsequent adoption?"

Nate turns his face from me, takes a hit. "All this smoking and drinking—I know what you're thinking," he says. The air between us smells skunky with a tell-tale hint of diesel fuel. "That I don't have what it takes to make a good dad, but you see, it's the stress of the adoption situation that has me all riled up."

"Well, it's probably not helping you reason with Billy," I reply. "Maybe after this weekend you might think about some counselling? Go talk to someone together, separately, both?"

"If it worked out with his plan for a surrogate, I suppose we could compromise and maybe think about adopting another kid, after," he says, stubbing the end of the roach on a rock by his feet. He's changing his tune, slightly. "I'm not being unreasonable, Tam, I'm just so anxious about the surrogate route."

"Can you tell me why?" I ask. I'm genuinely interested in hearing more of Nate's own personal stakes within one of the most important decisions of any partnership. The girl-meets-boy, falls in love, marries, has babies, lives happily-ever-after trope is as antiquated as the old fairy-tale princess stories my grandmother read me as a child. Today's options for becoming a parent are unlimited by one's imagination and determination.

Nate scratches his head. He's taking his time to think it through. There's a palpable delay in his reaction which doesn't surprise me. His eyes are red and there's a distinct shift in his mood from tense to relaxed. "In part, it's ethics," he says, mulling it over in his mind. "If we can offer a loving home to a child who already exists but isn't wanted, isn't that more meaningful than creating a baby who never asked to be born?"

He never took Billy's last name or Billy his, he explains. "If I agreed to a baby with a surrogate and it's his baby, it'll share his name and I'll be left out. That's one thing that bothers me. But my main issue is that I'm afraid the kid won't love me as much as him. And what if it is forever missing its biological mom?"

"Well, that could be the case with adoption, too, if you don't deal sensitively with reality early on," I reply. "And as for the given last name, why not use both of your names, all three of you?"

He remains adamant that with adoption, Billy and he would both be on equal footing with the child. "Billy, however, insists adoption will take too long".

"What if you were to bank your sperm and have a second child by surrogate, afterwards? Then you'd have a child from each lineage?" I suggest, digging deeper into the possibilities.

"We're not A listers," he replies, his humor restored. "People pay up to a hundred thousand for surrogacy these days. Imagine what we could do for an adopted child through the state system with that kind of money? College won't be any more affordable in eighteen-years-time, for sure."

I ask him if he's heard about the news of warnings from scientists regarding the apparent decline in sperm count and the potential reproductive challenges we might face in the future.

"I think we, as a society, should start thinking of generations down the line, not just the next to be born. Maybe you could bank your genetic material sooner rather than later?"

Nate is well-read. He says he's aware that of the political implications of the birth rate being down around the world. "Am I right in assuming that your interest in my and Billy's sperm means that you'd rank it super high quality as a medical professional?" he asks, smiling now despite the seriousness of the subject. "This is a new take on the *I Donated* sticker."

I explain, trying to keep it calm and measured, that his and Billy's genetic diversity is actually kind of crucial for the future of humanity.

"I wasn't intending to get so heavy this morning," I say, "but imagine the beautiful babies you could make with surrogates from different racial backgrounds."

Thinking out of the box, I urge; "All I'm saying is, don't be unwilling to explore different avenues toward becoming a parent."

Nate thanks me for the frank discussion. "But to be fair," he says, looking me in the eye. "You've hardly contributed to the global population yourself, have you?"

He presses on and asks if I've given up on the idea of parenting. "Have you considered, maybe adopting some day?" he enquires, eyebrows raised, turning the tables on me.

I experience a jolt in my core. What he says hits home. Truth is I've never considered myself as someone who would not have a child of my own someday. It's just that my medical studies and professional life have swallowed up the bulk of my reproductive years. I've thrown myself into my vocation as a doctor, continuously putting others before myself.

At forty-two, am I viable? I'm the one who should have banked my eggs. How many times have I told my patients that women have a far lower chance of conceiving naturally after turning forty and at forty-two percentages pretty much fall off a cliff.

It's a touchy subject. I'm past my reproductive prime, I know that. And, as I said, I should've followed my own advice and opted for fertility preservation before my mid-thirties. Would I be prepared to adopt? To single parent? By now, my chances of getting pregnant in any single ovulation cycle are around five percent or less. I rest a hand on my belly instinctively thinking back to last night. Better odds than winning the lottery at least.

"Honestly, back when we were in our 20s, I guess egg freezing just wasn't something we really thought about. We were all so focused on building our careers, traveling and living life in the moment. It felt like something that other people did if they were struggling with infertility or if they had a serious reason to delay having kids."

I remember hearing about it here and there, but it seemed like such a big, expensive thing to commit to and I didn't feel like it was for me. Now, looking back, I wish I'd taken it more seriously. If I'd known how much more accessible and common it would become, maybe I would've thought differently.

"My mother would be more shocked than anyone if I showed up with a kid in tow," I add.

I think of Mum in this moment with a typical lack of tenderness. How she hijacked anything good that came to me with her own suffering which she cultivated to new heights after the split. When Dad died, during my junior year of high school, I vowed to get as far away from her as possible. I didn't plan on spending the rest of my life here when I first arrived as a foreign student. If we'd had a better relationship things may have turned out differently.

She'd tell you some other version of my tale. That my emotional development was interrupted by my father's actions. Or something along those lines. And because of that, I've deprived her of a normal mother/daughter relationship, of grandchildren. Selfish Tamsin. Wallowing in my own grief of our fractured family. Whereas in actual fact, Mum had long before created a household that was so dogmatic and with so many rules and regulations, all I could do to survive my teenage years was to steer as clear of her as possible. The scars don't disappear. They fade, but they're still with me.

I link arms with Nate, rest my head on his shoulder.

The surprising network of support that surrounded me by my senior year at Santa Cruz, was unlike anything I'd experienced before. It was like I'd landed on a different planet. One with an entirely new set of customs, cultures and an easy acceptance that felt good and made sense.

Spending this weekend here at the beach, exploring ideas for the future, sitting here like this, hits me that this is my surrogate family after all. And the imperfection of it is a universal part of the human experience, I guess. Growth and healing are possible even within these complex, imperfect dynamics, surely?

"How is your dear mother?" Nate asks, shifting position and bringing me back into focus with his note of sarcasm. "Been back lately?"

I briefly recount my last visit. It was in the midst of the Track-and-Trace system nightmare the UK government enforced on visitors in 2021, to manage the spread of COVID. Travelers, including dual nationals such as myself, were required to complete an in-depth passenger location form before arrival.

"I took government mandated, super expensive tests before departure from the States and within two days of arrival in the UK and pleased my mother no-end as her captive audience, being required to quarantine in place for the first ten days."

I don't go into too many details but the daily telephone calls from the UK Track and Trace team were intense. Two weeks later they scrapped the whole program.

"Sounds worth all the aggravation, though, after your professional ordeal," Nate says. "Maybe not the intense time with mother-dear, but hanging out at your grandma's cute little cottage must've been nice. And at least it's not about to fall off a cliff."

Gran was my role model as far as mothering goes. Spending time with Mum in the seaside cottage where I had so many fond memories is another story— more transactional than tender. It doesn't mean she doesn't care, but her approach to motherhood is more shaped by her own personal limitations and emotional distance.

"She'd modernized the place," I say, on a positive note. "Restored the thatch, thankfully. I barely recognize it aside from the bluebell woods down the lane and the seafront view. The location can't be beat as long as the flooding holds off."

I explain how North Norfolk may be among the worst hit regions in England with the ever-pressing issue of rising sea levels.

"The outlook is pretty bleak. I hate to say this, but climate scientists predict parts of The Norfolk Broads, Great Yarmouth and surrounding areas as under threat of being wiped-out and potentially underwater in the next few years."

"That's terrible," Nate remarks, his eyes wide like searchlights. "Kinda like conditions along the New Jersey and Florida flatlands?"

"As well as some of the low laying areas in New York and Los Angeles," I add. "And the land around San Pablo Bay, to the east of where we are now. The UK powers that be, well, they're rapidly increasing flood defenses with more land drainage pumping stations than ever," I explain, "but the risk of coastal flooding is way higher than previously thought."

"So, you won't be ditching us and retiring to your grandmother's cottage any time soon?" Nate asks. "A life of charming, waterside simplicity."

"I fear by the time I'm of retirement age there may not be much habitable land left along that stretch of the coast. Besides, I don't look good in cottagecore."

Mum would simply not talk about it, the potential for flooding. Frustratingly, I was not allowed to discuss anything unpleasant with her on that last trip. She dominated our conversations with petty issues, likewise refusing to acknowledge any advancing weakness in her own physical or mental defenses. I get it. Nobody wants to confront this stuff. But I'm a doctor. I am pragmatic. Trained to remain objective and focus on the facts. This does not do much to bridge our divide.

"Forget the past," I declare jumping up from the porch step. I reach out and pull him up to stand beside me. I turn to him, ready to shift the conversation back to something more hopeful. "It's the future we're interested in."

A flash of light, too quick to be anything natural—just beyond the horizon, where the sea meets the sky. My stomach drops. Nate notices too, his brow furrowing.

"What was that?" he asks, his voice low, as if afraid to say it out loud.

I hesitate, trying to convince myself it's nothing. But then another flash—longer this time, brighter—cuts through the growing dusk. My pulse quickens, and suddenly the weight of everything I've been trying to ignore crashes into me. The weather is intensifying. And something tells me that this is just the beginning.

Saturday Late Morning

"**S**eaweed is incredible," Jamie says, his eyes lighting up with that spark only a true enthusiast can have. "It doesn't need soil, fresh water, or fertilizer to thrive. It grows fast, full of nutrients, and supports all kinds of life. Fish find shelter in it, and it even helps absorb carbon dioxide," he adds, his arms moving in wide, dramatic sweeps as he dives into his favorite topic: marine algae and coastal ecosystems. "It gets everything it needs from the ocean, and in return, it gives oxygen back to the atmosphere," he continues, planting his feet firmly in the wet sand, his rain boots sinking a little with each word.

We stand in a semi-circle around him, buckets in hand, casting nets. The tide pools before us are a chaotic patchwork of shapes and colors. Jamie, holding up an enormous piece of bullwhip kelp he's just pulled from the shore, looks every bit like a circus ringleader, grinning as if he's showing off a rare treasure. The top of the kelp is a shiny, softball-sized float, with two flattened, leaf-like blades extending from it, shimmering in the sunlight as they sway gently in his grip.

"These fresh, salty blades are the tastiest when eaten raw," he says, looking at Billy and Nate, who seem skeptical. I stifle a laugh.

"Steaming or drying them works too, if you want to bring out their flavor," River chimes in, always quick to defend Jamie's enthusiasm.

A flock of western gulls swoops down from a sky bruised in purple hues. My gaze drifts to the surf, and I catch sight of a pair of seals darting through the foam near the shore, their playful dives pulling my attention away from Jamie's lecture.

"Cutting the blades a couple of inches above the float, while it's still attached to the ocean bed, lets the kelp survive," Jamie continues, his voice steady as he turns back to me. "If you cut the float or the stipe, it's done for," he adds, making sure I'm following. The stipe, he explains, isn't the nutrient-packed stem you'd expect from a land plant. In kelp, it's what anchors the blades to the seafloor. The piece Jamie's holding looks like it's been washed ashore, likely after a storm. But it's fresh—when he bends it, it snaps cleanly.

"Leave the rubbery kelp alone," he warns. "Same goes for the leathery, shriveled stuff. Or anything with white spots. It's past its prime."

Billy, like me, seems easily distracted this morning. He's fiddling with his water shoes, which seem to be giving him trouble. But Jamie doesn't miss a beat, pressing on with his lesson about marine algae, which are classified into three groups: green, red, and brown. Kelp, including the giant and bullwhip types, falls into the brown category, and that's where Jamie really starts to shine.

Earlier, before we headed out, Jamie showed us his California sport fishing license. River has one too. It's illegal to forage for seaweed without one, so we're following their lead this morning. Funny how much things change when you start caring about the planet and the rules that keep it in check.

River pulls a sharp knife from a leather pouch on their belt, stepping forward to cut off a foot-long section of kelp from the stipe Jamie is holding. I'm not sure if it's light rain or just the ocean spray misting over us, but it's enough to make me want to lick my hand to check. Instead, I pull my focus back to the lesson.

"We'll cut this into half circles back at the kitchen," River says, holding the section of kelp carefully. "When it's fresh like this, I prefer to eat it with the skin on, but if you want, we can peel it off with a carrot peeler."

Jamie explains how kelp is a seasonal alternative to overfishing in coastal communities around the world.

"It's better for both the environment and the local economy when kelp is harvested by hand, seasonally, and sustainably," River adds.

A dubious look settles on Nate's face. He's hard to impress. "So, other than eating it raw, what else do you do with it?" he asks, clearly not sold.

Eva, ever the creative, pipes up, "Personally, I love me some pickled kelp in a glass jar, layered with onions and a little garlic."

She pauses, then adds, "Or you can use this one"—she scoops up a sheet of maroon-colored seaweed—"for a refreshing Turkish towel face wash."

I raise an eyebrow. "Is it edible?"

"Nope," she laughs. "But it's used in thalassotherapy, a treatment using seawater and sea-derived products for skin rejuvenation. The rough texture contains potassium, sodium, calcium, and magnesium—good for the skin."

Jamie chimes in, his favorite use for edible seaweed: "Basil sea pesto. Just throw a bunch of kelp blades into a food processor with fresh basil, egg, garlic, parmesan, pine nuts, olive oil, salt, and pepper. Boom—next-level pesto in minutes."

"Isn't that what they call a Chef's kiss?" Serena teases, expertly dodging sea foam with her waterproof boots.

She grins, recalling the kelp-crust pizza she and River made just last week. "And a soup, too. Kelp makes an amazing zuppa toscana in the winter—hits you with a savory umami punch from the start. The pizza crust has a delicate seaweed flavor—like the ocean, but not overwhelming. Crispy edges, a subtle saltiness."

I take mental notes—kelp is low in carbs and calories, high in fiber and antioxidants. A reminder to myself to at least attempt to incorporate some kelp into my diet when I get home.

As I feel the chill of the wind and ocean spray, I zip up my lightweight jacket, wishing I'd dressed in something warmer. The others, though, seem to be in a kind of trance, absorbed in Jamie and River's lyrical lesson on foraging.

We weave, like a school of shore-bound fish, closer into the tide pools.

I tread carefully so as not to slip on any hard, slimy surface. I'm enjoying being a spectator, watching Jamie in his element, surrounded by his admirers. Everyone loves Jamie. I know this. I've always known this. It's part of why I never really allowed myself to accept his permanent commitment to our unorthodox union. I've never believed I'm enough for him, is what I'm saying. Our coming together was a curious and delicate blend of youthful naivety, friendship and circumstance. Growing up together was a test: one I flunked instead of doing the hard work and seeing it through.

On the flip side, I might just burst from unexpected joy today if I allow myself to fully embrace it. Looking back, I was weak to have left him when I did; I can see that now. To be close again, the two of us, regardless of what strange twist of fate has brought us here—it feels best not to question it. We used to laugh about how we'd waited until marriage to be intimate, and now, here we are, mysteriously drawn back together after all this time. Estranged partners, tentatively dipping our toes back into the waters, unsure but somehow pulled to each other once more.

Jamie turns toward me. He reaches out his hand and guides me through the narrow space between a cluster of large, dark, shell-encrusted rocks.

I watch her closely as Serena reaches out in turn and holds on to him just a little longer than necessary. I've convinced myself that I've forgiven her for her part in all of it. It's not like I'm blameless here. I created the distance between Jamie and me and she stepped right in to fill the gap. It feels like ancient history now, honestly—it's almost tedious to revisit. We've all moved on, each of us in other relationships at different points since. Serena's with River now, as I keep reminding myself. It would be petty to let jealousy continue to sneak its way back in.

Still, a familiar urge creeps up from deep inside—like self-sabotage, though maybe more like self-protection. It's hard to tell, but it feels like both. I consider turning around, heading straight back to the house, packing up, and walking away. Save myself the trouble of any potential heartache. But what good would that really do? All it would accomplish is leaving me even more alone, maybe for good. No. I can't run this time. I have to stick it out, face whatever demons are waiting. It's time to deal with the truth, once and for all.

Billy and Eva have wandered off a ways, out of earshot. The wind picks up and stings my face. I see Billy reach out and wipe a spray of sand, gently from the corner of Eva's eye. Nate darts over to the two of them, cutting off his conversation with River. He's spotted this display of tenderness too. Billy lingers, close to Eva, unaware of his partner's approach. Whatever they're talking about, it's more than a friendly confiding. Body language gives us away no matter how hard we try to disguise what we're feeling. As I've said, Billy and Eva have been close since freshman year. Her brother from another mother, she says. They're both such strong, kind-hearted characters, drawn to one another as friends by their compassionate natures and steady temperament. Only this is something else, something I haven't seen before.

"What are those two doing?" Serena asks, her tone sharp. "Lollygagging when we've got work to do."

River steps in between us, their voice calm but firm. "Give them some space for a private conversation," they say. "Stop trying to control everything, Serena."

Serena shoots them a venomous look. "Fuck off, River," she snaps, then stomps off toward Jamie.

I can't help but feel uncomfortable with the way she snaps at her partner—demeaning, unnecessary. It stings in a way that doesn't sit right with me.

"Oh dear," I say, looping my arm through River's. "I can't imagine how much work it must have been, organizing this whole weekend," I add with a gentle smile. "We're all a little hungover, but a good meal will set us right."

The topic of lunch—and whether anyone's up for mushrooms later—hadn't come up yet. Serena, almost on cue, offers a quick, somewhat awkward apology, then propels herself toward River, planting a long, purposeful kiss on their unsuspecting lips. River looks surprised, but the tension melts from their face, and they pull Serena close, hands settling on her waist. I can't tell if this is for our benefit—some kind of public show to settle the air—or if it's a genuine attempt at mending things. The push and pull between them has been so evident since we arrived, that much is clear. There's a certain intensity between them, but it doesn't always feel easy to be caught in the middle of it. I'm not picking sides, but if I had to guess, I'd say River's been the one to broaden their emotional range in the past couple of years, trying to find solid ground on shifting terrain.

Jamie waits patiently until we've all shifted our focus. He crouches beside a deep tide pool, pointing out a vibrant orange and purple sea star clinging to a rock.

"What we really need to do is reconnect more with nature," he says, his voice calm and content. He's not bothered by the tension between the others—he's fully in his element now. "There's no better place than this when the tide's out."

He gestures toward a thick cluster of mussels covering the rocks. "See these? They secrete something called byssal threads—strong, fibrous filaments that anchor the mussels to the rocks. Pretty incredible stuff," he adds, his excitement rising as he explains. "This intertidal zone is home to algae and all sorts of invertebrates, specially adapted to survive the harshest extremes, both underwater and above."

He pauses, letting the weight of his words land. "All while getting pummeled by the surf."

He goes on to explain the Pacific coast's tidal rhythm—two low and two high tides each day, with one being lower and the other higher. "Tides being caused as you know by the gravitational pull between the Earth, the moon, and the sun," he explains. "It's the moon's pull that drags the Earth—and its water—toward it."

By the time he finishes, I have a new appreciation for mussels, and for the relentless power of the tide.

"What's the rule for eating shellfish in California again?" Bobby asks. "Remind me."

Jamie nods, shifting into teacher mode. "It's always good to check the current advisories before harvesting mussels or any bivalve shellfish for sport," he explains. "The Department of Public Health issues a quarantine for sport-harvested mussels every year—usually from May through October. That's your safest bet."

He pauses, looking around, then adds, "And watch where you step," he says, pointing to the jagged rocks. "Also, for anyone who's been away from the coast for a while, remember never, ever turn your back on the Pacific—not even for a second."

He lowers his voice as he encourages us to slow down, look closely, exercise patience in our observation of tide pool life, much of which is camouflaged. "They'll emerge in time, if they feel safe," he says, though he could be talking about any living being on earth, including me.

Nate picks up a small rock and turns it over in his hand. River takes it from him and immediately, with a swift correction, puts it back where he found it: "It needs to go back exactly where it was," River says. "It blows my mind, but it's a fact. Many salt water creatures stay in the same spot their entire life."

Bobby hones in on the subject. "Imagine that? Never finding your way home after some clueless and marauding troll lifts your house up and drops it in a whole new country."

Nate mocks a gesture of horror with his hands to his mouth. "I know something else you don't," he says to his partner. "Take the anemone for instance. River told me on the way down here that the clever sea anemone has figured out how to clone itself. Asexual reproduction. And although it prefers to stick around, hanging out with its offspring on the rocks and all, it's not opposed to the occasional sluggish glide around the water."

"That would solve a bunch of problems," Nate adds. "I mean, who wouldn't want to clone themselves?"

"Not me," River says. "It took me long enough to figure myself out. Why do that to the next generation?"

"Well, I would," Serena says. "Mini me—super cute."

River laughs. "I'm not sure I could deal with two of you. One's more than enough. There's only one Serena, only room enough in my pack for one queen of hearts."

I can't help but think this on-going, on-and-off-exaggerated show of antagonism and affection is some kind of learned method, buying time so as not to be snapped at again.

"If we were to look under this mussel-bed we might well find ourselves a giant green anemone," Jamie instructs. "Otherwise known as old man of the sea."

"They can live for as long as a hundred and fifty years in the wild," River says. Jamie nods. "At least eighty in captivity."

A hermit crab scurries under a rock followed by a larger crab which zips across the tide pool. It's not a Dungeness and not nearly big enough for us to consider as a catch. We point to sea stars and a purple sea urchin which has used its jaws and spine to carve out a cubbyhole in a softer rock.

"Tide pool fish are masters at camouflage," Jamie explains as he points to a young prickleback which has made a move back into its special spot under a rock after hovering almost perfectly still. Tide pool fish, he says, are able to survive out of water for several hours if conditions are moist enough.

Eva knows all of this and more, but I'm learning more than I ever knew I needed to about marine algae growing on rocks. And we see for ourselves how many intertidal invertebrates are tucked between blades and stipes of small, subtidal species, with tantalizing names such as green sea lettuce and pin cushion algae, olive-brown rockweed, smooth and shiny, one blade laminaria. Sea palm, Turkish towel, stony pink encrusting coralline algae.

"This is all well and good," Nate announces, hands on hips. "An abundance of greens. But so far all *we* have to eat is kelp."

"Apparently," Eva replies, pointing to a thick covering of olive-brown. "The rockweed that's so prolific in these parts is super good for the thyroid. You knew that, Tam?" she asks.

I didn't, but I'm interested to hear more. The small, gas-filled bulbs on the end of each blade are fun to pop.

"Raw, or steamed, rockweed tastes kinda like okra," Jamie says. "Best sampled raw if you ask me. Best to start with the tender young shoots"

"Native American foragers called it Indian popcorn. They figured out how good it is for us."

River gathers a small bunch of rockweed into their bucket.

"Next we're gonna forage a little of this lovely, bright green sea lettuce to add to our haul," Jamie says, pointing out a translucent green algae that looks similar to a leafy lettuce.

I'd no idea of the diversity.

"It's a bad idea to forage in a harbor or back bay, however," Jamie instructs, his tone serious now. "The intertidal zone is best for healthy seaweed."

This is all rather hard core in my opinion, plus my hands and feet are tingling. Needless to say, I nod my head approvingly.

"What about the mussels?" Billy asks.

"They must be gathered by hand, or with a hook or line—nothin' else," Jamie says, handing him a pair of gloves. "Stick to the rules. Start by pryin' a couple off the rock with your hands. Give it a go. And if you see anyone using a crowbar, screwdriver, trowel, or rake, that's a big no. Mussel beds are heavily protected—those tools can wipe them out."

"Are they safe to eat, though?" Billy asks.

"Usually, yeah—between November and around mid-April, based on the shellfish safety guidelines. Technically, the season stays open 'til May first, but we're already pushin' it. I'd play it safe this time and leave 'em be. If you do pull any off, just put 'em right back," Jamie says. "In winter, I go for the smaller to medium ones. Let 'em soak overnight in clean ocean water to get the sand out, then scrub 'em down good and pull off that tough beard before steamin'. And remember—if they don't open after steamin', toss 'em. They're no good."

"Fascinating as this morning's instruction is, I'm headed back to the house," Nate announces. "I'll brew a fresh pot of coffee and wait for you all up there."

Before I can join him, Nate is already out of earshot. Billy catches my eye. "For all his eco-event expertise, he's a lazy-ass when it comes to the greater outdoors," he says. "I'm sure it's not coffee he's after."

We walk side by side, a little ahead of the others. Overhead, a brown pelican glides by—its wide, prehistoric wings slicing through the air with surprising grace, belying its size. I ask Billy how he's holding up. Then, after a pause, I mention that something's been weighing on Nate, though I stop short of explaining.

"He's worried about you," I say.

"Well, I'm worried about *him*," Billy replies. "He should be concerned about his own well-being, not mine. He's drinking too much."

"What do you think is stressing him out?" I ask. "You two are my poster couple for marriage, you know."

Billy says no marriage is perfect. "Sorry to burst your bubble, Tam.

Especially when it comes to the subject of starting a family. It's not as easy as all that."

"You're both on board then?" I ask, not giving any more insight away. "A baby?"

"The issue is how to go about it," Billy replies. "That's where we disagree. But it'll work out. He'll see. You'll see."

I hope so. "Sounds like it's a long and bumpy road you're headed down," I say.

"Not as long as you'd think," he replies. He smiles to himself and looks upwards to where Nate is headed. "And you, Tam? If my instincts are correct, any lack of enforcement in your top-to-toe arrangement last night?"

I blush. I'm not ready to talk about Jamie and me. I'm enjoying the private rush for now. And it's nobody's business but ours.

Jamie bounds up, on cue, wedging himself in between the two of us, his arms encircling our shoulders.

"Godparents someday?" Billy asks. "The two of you?"

"Are you expectin'?" Jamie asks. He's joking, but given that it's a tricky subject with Nate, I wait to see how Billy will respond.

"A little early to announce," he answers. "Hold that thought." He has our attention. Now I'm intrigued.

Saturday around Noon

va is in the bathroom. I'm bursting for a pee. I dance around outside the door for a couple of minutes before giving up and heading outside to relieve myself alfresco. Jamie sees me as I dart out of the front door and makes to follow. I hold my hand up.

"Nature calls," I warn. "One bathroom, seven people. The math does not compute." It's easy for the guys to piss up a tree but another thing altogether for a woman to relieve herself discreetly, especially when its blustery and she's wearing pants.

I head downhill and circle around the house on a staircase of wooden rail pilings where I find myself a suitable spot beyond a pile of old crab pots and old rope stored beneath the deck.

I'm crouched down, pants around my ankles, breeze on my backside when I hear Eva and Billy step out on the deck. They're talking quietly but the way the sound travels on the wind, I can hear them clearly.

"Tell him today." Eva urges. "It's time."

"I'd rather wait until Monday," Billy replies. "It's not fair on everyone else if he doesn't take it well."

My ears perk up. I hadn't intended to eavesdrop but I can hardly prevent myself from hearing. Surely, they're not having an affair. Neither of them is the sneaky type.

"This is not just Nate, it's about to impact us all," Eva says. She's calm but assertive. "Best get it out in the open."

Billy pauses before he responds: "It's the greatest thing ever. It's so perfect! I want to keep it to myself a little longer."

I hear the screen door open above as I shake myself dry and stand, hurriedly pulling up my undies and pants.

It's Nate's voice I hear next. "You two again. If I didn't know better, I'd say you are conspiring."

"Darling husband," Billy says. "Whatever I do, I do for you. Come, give me a hug."

I scuttle back up the path and into the house. The bathroom is free and I head in to wash my hands, checking my flushed reflection in the clouded mirror.

"Keep out of other people's business," I warn myself. I'm not getting paid to figure this one out. So often a patient comes to me with one thing and it's something else entirely. I've no idea for sure what's going on with Eva and Billy and Nate. It's not my problem though I love them each equally and dearly. But then there's Nate and his sensitivities. I know what it feels like to be thwarted. I don't wish that on anyone.

Jamie knocks on the door, gently. I open it and let him in. There's a smell of sea salt. He shuts the door softly behind him. His expression softens as he stands beside me at the mirror, washing his hands. His lips are chapped from the cool wind.

"I wish we were somewhere else, anywhere, away from them all, just you and me for a few hours," he says. "This charade—you and me actin' all nice and polite and hands-off with each another when all I want to do is be alone with you."

"They'll know soon enough," I reply. I'm pretty sure they've guessed what's going on between us by now. We're radaring all the give-away signals. "It's hardly top secret anyway. Let's just say we're happy to be here together."

Jamie asks, one eyebrow raised. "Tell me, Tam, what's your interpretation of happy together?"

Serena nudges the door open before I have time to formulate my answer. "Don't mind me," she says as she squeezes past the two of us, avoiding my eye as she heads toward the loo. I follow Jamie out of the tight confines just as she's unzipping her pants.

"Bloody hell, the woman has no shame," I say. "Never had, never will." It's not lost on me that Jamie has seen it all anyway and plenty of times.

"Don't mind her," he replies, raising his eyebrows and tipping his head. "I've sand in my socks," he deflects, as he heads back outside. We were undoubtedly thinking the same thing. It's all in the past and it's silly, I know, but I'd let him go, largely because of her and I'm loathe to make the same mistake again. Serena is always on the sideline, somehow, waiting to pounce.

Eva calls me from the kitchen. My wild mushroom tart has turned out to be more than passable for a first attempt. I'd rolled my pastry the length of a small cookie sheet earlier and made it large enough to feed all seven of us heartily. It was easy enough to put together with a medley of wild mushrooms sauteed with shallots and garlic in olive oil. I tossed it all with a pile of shredded Gruyère cheese, seasoned it with fresh thyme, salt and pepper. Eva and I taste-test a sneaky, warm slither and it's rich and delicious.

"Yum. Thought you claimed you're still not much of a cook," Eva says, rubbing her tummy. "Living solo through lockdown must've upped your skills." I guess there's hope for me yet.

"It's encouraging that we all know our way around a kitchen, these days," River says, overhearing our conversation. "If we're gonna broach the subject of communal life, the heart of living together will be involve some serious meal scheduling and rotations."

It's about time we talk about it. The pact. The seven of us. Our plan to set up an intentional community. I more or less assumed we'd ditched this idealistic dream after going our own ways for so long. But the pandemic and the rate of climate change have fast-forwarded everything and it appears that the pact really is back on the table. Not as a distant vision in another twenty plus years, but, hypothetically at least, sooner rather than later.

"And if we farm and source and purchase all of our weekly food supply as a cooperative then it'll cut down individual grocery expenses significantly," River adds.

"Shush now, River. Let's talk logistics on Monday," Serena joins the fray. "Right now, let's concentrate on getting today's lunch on the table."

She bustles about, assembling a large salad with the left-over greens from the fridge, throwing in a generous amount of raw kelp that River has cut into rounds. She tosses in handfuls of dried persimmons and walnuts and drizzles her concoction with a generous glug of olive oil, salt and pepper and a magic squeeze of lemon juice.

Billy asks if he's allowed a glass of wine. "I know we suggested we should hold off until evening, Tam, but it *is* the weekend."

"Restriction would be tiresome," Serena agrees, deftly pulling the cork from a bottle of white she holds between her knees.

"We're cutting back when we get home, Nate and me," Billy adds, as he shrugs his shoulders in concession and holds out his wine glass for a pour.

"Speak for yourself," Nate replies. "I'll be the one to decide when personal austerity measures are called for thank you very much."

These are the moments that make me wonder how we'd manage to set any reasonable ground rules in a communal kitchen. We're historically a party crowd when we're together. How would we adapt to austerity measures realistically? I let it go for now. It's not my job to police other people's drinking habits. Serena clearly thinks she's the one to literally call and pour the shots this weekend, given that this is her house, her kitchen. It's her territory for now, not mine. But if we're to discuss the pact in the next few days, best to be entirely upfront and honest in our expectations. I can hardly believe I'm truly entertaining the idea.

Mum spent a good deal of my childhood directing me not to speak my mind. She claimed I had no power to make any real changes. I resolve on the spot to speak my truth going forward with this lot or I'll run the risk of finding myself back where I started, backed into a corner without so much as a say so. It's clear that there's so much we haven't thought about as far as a workable plan. It's a test, this weekend. I see that now. I, for one, am aware of my allies and frenemies both and in order to progress, personally, to be heard, I will stand my ground from the start.

The group is gathered at the kitchen table. We're noisy and hungry and animated as we pass an assortment of hand thrown plates, platters and bowls around, anti-clockwise. Billy, Nate, River and Serena are already on their second or third glass of wine; the rest of us, more moderate, alternating or substituting with refreshing, hydrating ice water.

"Music, maestro," Nate commands, gesturing with comic-like conductor arms. I lean over to the counter and pick out a compilation 2003 CD from my murky stack. Avril Lavigne, Johnny Cash, Good Charlotte, Sean Paul, Pink, Madonna, Beyonce and Jay-Z—hits from our senior year.

"The last year of mainstream embracing all of the genres," River remarks, drumming the table with their knuckles.

Eva says the music takes her back to evening meals and endless bowls of pasta. "And too much cheap vodka," she adds, tapping her forehead gently with the inside of her wrist. A tiny butterfly tattoo surfaces beneath a stack of silver bangles.

"Rounds of buttered toast and gallons of rum and cola," I recall. "Back when butter didn't cost a fortune and soda had yet to become a four-let-ter word."

Jamie remembers the giant Dutch oven—a different, dubious left-over stew on the stovetop daily in the colder months. "Bay leaves, unidentified legumes and assorted veggies with mushrooms doused in the cheapest red wine," he says. "Serena's specialty."

"At least I shared," Serena says. "Unlike some." She looks at me.

I'd been raised an only child, as I've said. And my mother was a fro-zen-food convert. It had come as a shock to me as a newbie in student housing as to how much food my roommates consumed, especially when stoned, which was most of the time. They'd teased me unmercifully at first for hoarding my meagre supplies of canned foods and bread for toasting. My British staples—PG Tips tea bags, Weetabix, Cadbury's chocolate, digestive biscuits, Heinz beans, Colman's mustard, HP sauce. I couldn't bear to live without these familiar comforts of home those first few years.

The pleasures of communal dining emerged once I figured out the general equity as well as the spontaneity and fun of it all. Shared meals with this bunch remain a revelation—celebratory, unprocessed, delicious and festive, no matter how lavish or modest.

Undercurrents of the old, younger us swirl around the table as we dine:

love, acceptance, resentment, admiration, competition, shards of unresolved conflict. I tune out the conversation to better absorb the scene. I'm good at this. My stomach is a direct route to my heart and I focus on refilling it with good-spirited camaraderie. Good food when shared, I discovered is sensual, seductive.

I've eaten so many meals alone over the past few years I've forgotten how great it is to sit around a table with these people. It's not that I consider a table for one a stigma. There's an art to appreciating a nourishing meal, alone or otherwise. Lockdown exacerbated this, my living outside of the family dinner concept for so long. Housemates, I reminded myself in my toughest moments, would have labeled their own food items in the fridge anyway, keeping to different meal schedules around work shifts. Still, it's not been easy coming up with fresh and novel ideas every day of the week when catering for oneself solo.

"Your idea of a meal was quintessential ex-pat, Tam. Remember?" Serena asks, poking a bejeweled finger in my rib. "Neat vodka, cheese or beans on toast. Happy to see there's been some element of evolution in that department."

I shuffle my chair, so as to create some distance from her. It stings to be reminded of how she used to tease me unmercifully for my simple needs and my fresh-off-the-boat vernacular.

I cave and reach for an unopened bottle. It too is mocking me for my restraint. Another glass will do. I need a buffer from her digging. If it's not River, it's me she's after.

"That's enough, Serena," Jamie is swift to come to my rescue. "Let's chill on the memes for now."

Serena leans back in her chair. "Oh, come on, admit it," she continues, regardless, balancing the heels of her hands against the table top. "Tamsin is the least inclined to make herself at home in the kitchen."

Eva speaks up. "Ay, please! Just because she's not throwing dinner parties every weekend, it doesn't mean she can't cater nutritiously for herself and others. We all have our own ways of doing things. Working from home affords you more time for all these foodie fixings."

Nate reaches for a thick slice of bread to mop up his lunch and as he does so, he knocks his half-filled glass of wine onto a cream-colored cotton tablecloth embroidered with orange poppies. "Oops, sorry, my bad. Good thing it's like— one of a pile of these old linens," he says, blotting the puddle with his napkin.

Billy jumps up from his chair, nudging it into the lower cabinet door behind him. "Damn, Nate," he says giving him a side-eye. "You're getting sloppy. How much have you been sippin'?"

Nate leans back, giving his accuser a long, measured look. He pauses, letting the silence hang for a beat before responding, his tone cool and composed. "How many times do I have to tell you? It's my business and mine alone how much I choose to drink. Since when did you become my keeper?"

Billy's not about to back down. He crosses his arms, tilts his head slightly and with a raised eyebrow, asks:

"Always thinking of number one, a true bon vivant. Do you seriously think you're ready to parent?"

Nate's expression falters, a mix of frustration and defiance. "Actually, I'm having one last hurrah with day drinking and . . . everything else this weekend," he says, his voice tinged with annoyance. "Since when did you become so righteous?"

Billy tilts his head, a wry smile tugging his lips. "When I found out that I'm gonna be a dad," he replies, his voice soft but firm. The moment the words leave his mouth he brings his hands together, palms pressed in prayer, holding them up in front of his face like he's making a silent vow.

The room is suddenly dead quiet, like someone just pressed pause. Our eyes lock on Billy and Nate, waiting for either of them to break the tension with whatever comes next.

"What the hell?" Nate almost chokes on his wine. He shoots out of his chair, awkwardly pushing it aside, and stumbles toward Billy. "Is this some twisted joke?"

Eva sits frozen, not moving a muscle. We all turn to her as she slowly lifts one hand to her face, her other hand gripping her water glass. After a beat, she lowers her hand from her eyes, then delicately brings the glass to her lips. She takes a long, slow sip, swallows and then coughs into her fist, her shoulders trembling slightly.

"I think it's time we tell Nate, Billy," she says.

Saturday, After Lunch

Jamie, River and Serena slip out of the kitchen, sweeping me along with them. No-one says a word as we hike back down to the beach. The dirty dishes are still on the table. Clean-up can wait. The sky is darkening in color as the afternoon progresses. I didn't think to grab a jacket. Jamie wraps his arm around my waist and holds me close, a warm contrast to the cool, damp edge in the air.

"Any other bombshells while we're at it?" Serena asks, breaking the silence. "Damn."

River pauses. "Look," they say. "It's complicated."

"You *knew?*" Serena asks, her posture tense, jaw set, waiting for an answer.

"Kinda," River replies, shifting, slightly. Their gaze flickers between Serena and the ground, not meeting anyone's eyes. "Sorta."

"What do you mean, *sorta?*" Serena demands. She swivels River around forcefully to face her.

River hesitates for a moment before responding, their voice low. "I confronted Eva after I heard her throwing up in the bathroom earlier," they admit. "I knew she hadn't had a drop of booze last night, unlike the rest of us. It was pretty clear something was up. She made me promise not to say anything."

"But Billy, for fuck's sake," Serena says. "I mean, how?"

Jamie and I stand glued to the spot. We're at the half way point down to the shore. It's not like me to miss a pregnancy. I guess I've been preoccupied with my own stuff.

River takes a breath before they explain: "IVF. His sperm. Her egg. They didn't

"do" do it. But the business trip guise back in January. It was their discreet plan of action for the initial process of placing the embryo, their first fertilized egg, into Eva's uterine wall."

"And it took? First try?" I ask, raising an eyebrow. "That's pretty impressive, considering Eva's age."

"Excuse me. She's not *that* old," Serena says, pursing her lips. "We're none of us *that* old."

By statistical standards it's a slim chance any of the women in our group would be so lucky as to fall pregnant so fast.

"I'm a little insulted he didn't ask me," Serena confesses. She crosses her arms across her chest and stares up at the house.

"Would you have said yes?" River asks.

"Bit late to respond to that question now," she replies, shaking her head slowly, a small, almost exasperated sigh escaping her lips.

"We all need to be there for Nate," I suggest. "After the three of them have hashed it out."

Jamie places a hand on my shoulder. He asks me how I think Nate will handle this. "I mean, it's way out of left field, isn't it?"

"Not entirely." I share the general theme of our conversation that morning. "Billy and Nate were figuring out how best to start a family—one way or another."

"Nate's little drinking problem needs to be dealt with first," Serena says, leaning in to our huddle.

We're all equally taken aback by Billy and Eva's revelation. Serena kicks sand with her sneaker.

"I *wish* it were me," she says.

"Well, that's news to me," River remarks. "I thought you didn't like kids."

Serena is quick to reply. Though she doesn't much care for other people's children, she confesses how she's warmed to the idea of one of her own, recently.

"I don't mean to be pushy," I say, as I reach a hand out to Serena. It's my turn to intervene. "But you shouldn't wait too long if you're serious about this."

"Maybe I'll hit Nate up tonight," she replies, stepping back, a glint in her eye. "That would even things out, no?"

"Serena . . ." River says, more offended than hurt. "There are such things as boundaries, you know? Other people's feelings to consider for once. Mine included."

"Well, I'm never been opposed to mixing things up," Serena replies.

Given Serena's past tendency for embracing the concept of free love, this really shouldn't be a shock to any of us.

River wags a finger at her. "And you?" they ask Serena. "Have you finally figured yourself out? Enough to handle parenting, a long-term commitment? Because if you have, we should be having this conversation privately, just the two of us."

Jamie chuckles softly, breaking the tension, the laugh lines at the corner of his eyes crinkling. "We do need to talk about the subject of the next generation," he says. I'm all ears. "With the world the way it is, finding a safe, stable place for starters is about as good a foundation as any for the possibility of any of us bringing new life into the world."

Wow. I'm not sure what to make of this as a group discussion. I suggest that Serena save such a sensitive subject for a later hour—after Nate's had a chance to process Billy's revelation.

This only encourages her to persist. She turns her focus to Jamie. "Maybe you then?" she asks, posturing suggestively. "How about it, Jamie? I'm surprised it didn't happen when we were back together. We gave it a good go."

I freeze, locking my gaze on her, my frustration boiling over. This is too much— way too much for me. And for River. She knows it. Jamie grits his teeth, jaw tight with annoyance. He's not thrilled to be dragged into this, either. But what can he do? Without a word, he turns and walks away, avoiding the confrontation, his back to this whole mess.

River steps in, voice firm. "Jamie and Tam are working things out, Serena, so cut it out. This isn't the time to reopen old wounds."

"Whose wounds?" Serena needles. "We're all good aren't we, Tam?"

It's my moment. "You know very well whose wounds cut the deepest," I reply. "Sneaking in that summer, grasping your opportunity the minute my gran passed. If I hadn't been stuck in England nothing would've happened."

"Takes two," Serena retorts, her blue eyes sharp and challenging as they lock onto mine.

Jamie has turned back toward us, his voice cutting through the wind. "Serena, enough," he insists, his tone serious, making it clear that he's not granting her the last word. He strides towards us, standing his ground. "We were both at fault. There's history, sure—always will be, but it's done. It's been over for a while. And if we can't find closure, then this whole thing, this revisitin' our pact, our little community, our cozy dream for the future, it's never gonna work."

"Look," I step forward, arms stretched before me, hands open. "The skeletons are out of the closet. At least I hope we've heard everything. If there's anything else anyone needs to say, now's the time."

River shoots Serena an enquiring glance, awaiting her response.

"What?" she asks.

"You know," River replies.

"I think what River's getting at is that shortly after we graduated, I chose to terminate a pregnancy. It was my decision and mine only. And to be honest, I probably can't have kids now anyway given the complications I had."

"And you're just tellin' me this now?" Jamie asks, his voice tight with frustration. He's tugging at his hair, his mind racing a mile-a-minute.

"Because it might not have been yours, Jamie," she answers, coolly. "It could've been any one of a handful. I didn't know and honestly, it would've been messy and impractical to try to figure it out."

Jamie stands there, mouth agape. At that time, he and I had just entered our clumsy marriage. Serena's pregnancy would've definitely thrown a wrench in the works. But there's no way I would've stood in her way if she'd wanted to keep the baby. If it was his.

"I couldn't put you through it at the time," Serena says, softening her stance as she her places her hand on Jamie's arm. "I've had a hard time forgiving myself, to be honest. And later, well, I never told you I was off my birth control that summer when Tamsin was in the UK, because I convinced myself if I fell pregnant, I'd redeem myself somehow."

"We were in it for real you know, Jamie and me?" I step in between the two of them. "Ten years, all through medical school, rotations and all."

"But it was you who left him here, indefinitely," she replies.

"And you took it upon yourself to tell him that I wasn't coming back," I remind her. "You told him I had taken my nice, new, shiny California medical training with plans to disappear into the NHS. It was a lie. I had no intention of staying in the UK permanently and you knew that."

"That's as may be," Serena says. "But you have to admit, there was always that concern in the back of your mind that he would leave you for me some day."

River has had enough of this back and forth between us. "Focus on the facts, Serena."

She stands firm, hands on her hips like the world owes her something.

Jamie's turn to speak. "I confessed my mistake the minute you returned, Tam," he says, shaking his head, avoiding my gaze. "I had no choice. I felt so damn guilty for not trustin' you. I blamed myself for you packin' up, after and leavin' without a fight. Figured you were after a clean break once you'd cleared your student debt with the money your grandmother left you."

By then, Serena had been desperately unhappy in the city. "She asked me to move with her to Bolinas, back to her roots," he said. "But it didn't feel right. In fact, it was all wrong. I declined."

He faced me, directly. "Truth is, Tam, it was then that I realized how much I'd grown to love you. I now know I'm *in love* with you still. After all that's happened between us. I'll always love you."

"And what about me?" River asks Serena. "How do I factor into all of this?"

Serena shifts her feet in the sand, then lifts her head, meets River's curious gaze. "Well, you came back into my life after enough time had passed for me to get Jamie out of my system for the most part." She reaches for River's hand. "I didn't realize it at the time, but it's true. You've been the one sure and steady thing in my whole adult life. Finally, someone who's non-judgmental and open. You're the only one who isn't freaked out by my . . . need to be close. I didn't want to ruin it by unloading all my baggage on you."

River's furrowed brow softens, their expression easing. "I've been around you long enough," they say. "Your baggage is yours, just like mine is mine. And that's alright. It's part of our journey, of what makes us who we are."

It's an intimate confession to be a party to. I'm not good at this. I prefer to be on the other side of a desk, impartial.

Serena's voice waivers. She says she's done piling on to her cart. "Pushing it around, all that baggage, from one point to another, it's been exhausting," she confesses. "This house, it's precarious position. It's always in the back of my mind. We're not settled. We're not safe here."

Jamie asks if it's mainly the beach house that's driving the rush to find a property. The fast-forwarding of the pact. We've barely broached the subject until now.

"Your situation out here, it's heavy," he says. "I get it."

"It's part and parcel," River replies. The tension lifts as they lead us down to the water's edge. The tide is coming in and the pools we'd wandered around this morning are filled with salt water. There's a calmness to be found within the swirling surf. It's as if the whole world's problems are flowing into the ocean.

Jamie sets his gaze far into the distant horizon. There's a navy-blue line that divides the sky from the turbulent Pacific. Is he thinking of the child that might have been? I picture a towheaded, blue-eyed toddler. I recalculate the years. He or she would be turning twenty.

I can't help but imagine Eva and Billy's baby. All that potential for a beautiful, kind hearted creature. A smart and sporty new human. Who could've planned this creation any better? And the fact that both of them will play equal roles in raising their child is undoubtedly a gift. But then there's Nate. How the hell are they going to convince him that jumping on board this surprise parenting train is in his best interest? And the real kicker, the destination of where to raise the child is still a complete mystery.

Saturday Afternoon

I watch the three of them from a distance as they gesture frantically on the deck. We're nearing the house, climbing uphill. It's obvious from their quick, jerky movements that they're interrupting each other, attempting to sort through Billy's bombshell about the baby. Eva keeps her distance from the two men, wisely so. She's been through enough with the men in her life. But this? This is something different entirely. Billy holds his ground while Nate shifts from foot to foot like he's ready to throw punches, only instead, he's hurling accusations. Eva wraps her arms protectively around her belly, as if bracing herself for whatever comes next.

We can't avoid them much longer. Eva's pregnancy is, in many ways, a small miracle. Realizing that, I find myself feeling surprisingly invested in what's to come. But at the same time, I can't help thinking that Nate should've been part of this monumental decision from the very beginning. He has every right to be angry, to feel betrayed.

"You go first," Serena says, propelling me through the door. "You of all people should know what to say in such a difficult situation."

Should I? I suppose the last few years have taught me more about compassion and diplomacy than I ever expected to learn. I never had a choice but to confront the unimaginable horrors—hospital wards overflowing with patients, the grim reality of temporary morgues packed with bodies. It was a period of absolute despair— one I desperately hope not to experience again though I know it is likely in all probability.

A face appears in my memory. A woman in her late sixties named Sandy. She reminded me of my mother, only a more gracious version of the parent that I'd wished for when I was younger. I watched Sandy die in a triage ward, slowly, over the period of several days. Her daughter was not allowed in. The humility of it all was crushing. Sandy's face had somehow melded into my mother's during that period of isolation and pain.

Sometimes it is hard to believe it is over. But what *is* coming next? That's the trillion-dollar question. It's certainly brave for my friends to bring a new life into the world. They will need all the help and support I can offer.

The other three kick-off their sandy boots and follow me into the house. River shuts the door with gusto, announcing our return.

"Remake the fire in the woodburning stove, would you?" Serena asks Jamie. "Take the chill out of the air," she adds, in a whisper.

"How's this going to go?" River asks in an equally lowered voice. We gather around the woodburning stove. Drama is best discussed around a fireplace, don't you think?

"We need to come together, reunite the tribe, let them know we're here for the three of them," I suggest. "Actually, the four of them."

Nate opens the door and propels himself into the open space before we have a chance to come up with a plan. The room is super-charged. It hums with energy, every inch of space vibrating with intensity. The air feels thick, almost as if it's alive, crackling with the kind of electric buzz that makes your skin tingle. His mind and body are evidently working in fight or flight unison, working a mile-a-minute.

"Let's not add to the level of drama," he suggests as he runs his hands through his hair. "At least I know what my Halloween costume's gonna be this year."

Nobody asks him to elaborate, but he does so anyway. Self-deprecating humor being his way to diffuse the situation.

"A cuckold," he explains, flapping his arms. "Giant fucking Cuckoo, that's me."

"We pushed the limits," Billy says, glancing downwards, as if the weight of regret is too much to hold in his gaze. "We felt sure you'd be accepting, delighted, once you had time to get used to the idea."

"It's veering into the sordid," Nate replies, shaking off Billy's hands on his shoulders. "Even if you didn't sleep with her. Going behind my back. The calculated deception-part."

Eva speaks up tentatively. "Truth is, I didn't dare think it would work," she says, her voice wavering, soft and slow. "At least not without multiple attempts. It was a long shot and we didn't want to raise any expectations. We would've told you this weekend, Nate, when the moment was right, truly we would."

"Then why not clue me in in the first place?" he asks, his voice louder, more forceful as he leans forward, eyes narrowed accusingly. "I would've handled it way better than this."

"Because, we've been truly selfish, acting on a wild impulse," Eva replies. "I'm not proud of keeping it a secret. Truth is, though, I wanted this as much as Billy. I want a baby every bit as much as you do, Nate."

"But I'm the poor Schmo who's been drinking himself into denial every day. How am I gonna be accepted as a parent?"

"Because I pick you, Nate," Eva says, standing tall, her posture open but not aggressive. "Billy and you. This lucky little duckling's gonna have two dads and a mom. And several awesome aunties and uncles. What could be better?"

Nate is crying now. His chest rises and falls with shallow breaths, as if each inhale is a struggle against the overwhelming weight of the moment. Eva continues to tear up, her eyes glistening with unshed emotion and, for a moment, she seems caught between wanting to hold herself together and the overwhelming pull to reach out to him. Her breath catches in her throat. The tears well up quickly but she blinks them away, determined not to let them fall—at least not yet. But it's clear she's struggling to keep control of her emotions as her face softens, the resolve she's been holding onto faltering in the face of Nate's reaction to their news.

He rebuffs her attempt to embrace him, stepping back and wiping his nose on his sleeve. It's Billy's turn to step toward his husband. He lifts his hands, gently cupping each side of his partner's tear-streaked face. With a tenderness that feels almost reverent, he presses the lightest kiss to his forehead. This time, Nate does not pull back. I don't know where to look. None of us do.

"Nothing was working between us," Billy admits, his voice heavy with regret. "The whole baby thing—it was tearing us apart. When Eva confided that she so desperately wanted a baby, I felt like it was now or never. She's the one who is the least complicated. The one who doesn't have all those personality quirks and flaws. It felt like a blessing, honestly. We've been waiting, just trying to get through the first trimester in peace, and now that it's almost over, we were finally ready to tell you."

Nate shoves Billy back, his hands pressing hard against his chest. Without a word, he curls up on the couch, drawing his knees to his chest. "Just… leave me alone for a bit," he murmurs, his voice low and broken. "I wanna punch you so bad right now it hurts."

"I get it, and I deserve it," Billy says, his voice tight. "But this isn't how we should be starting our journey into parenthood. I'll give you the space you need, I promise. Just . . . know that I did this for us, above everything else, no matter what you think."

Serena takes Billy's hand and steers him into the kitchen.

"Stay," Nate asks, patting the seat cushion. I sit down beside him. The others have all left the room.

"This is bad. What do I do? How did you get past what happened with Serena and Jamie?"

"I let it go, eventually—mainly to keep the group together," I answer. "But honestly, I played a role in it falling apart. I never really believed in myself, or in being Jamie's wife the way I should've. Things don't just fall apart without a lot of backstory, you know? I've learned that the hard way."

Nate's opening up to me, and I can feel myself doing the same. "I've been such a dick," he says, his voice breaking as he sobs. "The drinking . . . refusing to back Billy's dreams, his whole way of wanting so damn badly to be a dad."

He claims this is the first major stumbling block they've encountered in all the years they've been together. "I don't want this to be the end," he says, a tremor in his voice. His hands loosely clenched at his sides. "But I see how easily it could be."

"It's more like the beginning," I assure him. "If you choose to see it that way." I pause, then add, "The alternative is that you walk away and end up ruining not just your own life, but Billy's too." I take a breath. "And the baby—think about how devastated Billy would be and how his mental state could affect this child's most formative years."

"I guess this shmuck's gonna have to accept it," Nate concedes, his voice thick with resolve, wiping his nose with the cuff of his sweater. "I'm gonna be a dad." He pauses, his eyes locking with mine and, for a moment, the air between us feels like it's holding its breath. "But... what if I'm not ready?" The question hangs there unanswered, the weight of it settling into the silence like a firework just waiting to explode.

Saturday Evening

We're huddled around the crackling firepit, beers in hand as the light fades. Some of us pass around joints, the smoke rising into the cool evening air. Dinner's over and for now, the rain holds off. Wrapped in thick layers, we're sprawled out on a bunch of makeshift cushions—old sleeping bags pulled from the depths of the basement by Serena and River, their frayed edges a reminder of countless wild weekends, long-past.

Don't ask me why, but I've decided to just go for it. I haven't revisited the world of shrooms in years, but I've been intrigued by what I've heard—friends and patients experimenting with microdosing psilocybin, especially in the wake of the pandemic.

Despite the government recognizing psilocybin as a breakthrough therapy for issues like smoking cessation, alcohol addiction, treatment-resistant depression, and cancer-related anxiety (the list goes on), it's still illegal to possess it. That makes this situation a lot more serious than it might seem, even though it's just a private gathering.

What complicates things even further is how tricky it is to measure a microdose, since the potency of mushrooms can vary so much. I know that one fifteenth or twentieth of a mushroom could be way stronger than another, so it really feels like playing a risky game.

With Jamie and Eva right here to look out for me, it honestly feels like the safest time to dip my toes back into this, so to speak. There's a part of me—my curious side—that's itching to break free from this self-imposed cage of playing it safe. I've spent way too many years trapped in my own head.

"Who'll ever know?" Nate asks, sensing my hesitation. "Your secret's safe with us. Secrets being kind of our thing." He can't resist throwing in a jab but, honestly, I can't blame him. He's still here, after all, going along with it all.

"Anyway," Serena says, "it's already been decriminalized in Oakland and Denver. Hell, even the entire country of Australia has accepted its merits. Magic mushrooms have been around for thousands of years—it's kind of absurd that we're only just now starting to recognize their potential."

I'm taking Serena's advice for once and opting to imbibe my portion in a tea. She says it'll be a milder trip that way.

"I'm really only looking for a micro-dose," I insist, my fingers fidgeting as I twist my bracelet in circles around my wrist. A strained attempt to sound casual-but-confident comes off a little forced. "You all do it your own way, but I am not planning on freaking out on anyone."

The truth is, occasional night terrors have haunted me on and off since I was a teenager, after Dad left, and they've only gotten worse since he died. I guess it's the fear of being abandoned that lingers. Over the years, since Jamie and I split, I've learned to live with this but they've never fully gone away.

Eva and Jamie have volunteered to keep an eye on each of us, assuring me, especially, they'll be on alert for any sign of fear or confusion that could lead to reckless or disturbing behavior. I can't help but picture myself floundering in the ocean, lost in the dark of the night. My mind is spinning, turning in circles—clockwise, then anticlockwise, a dizzying rhythm. At the very least, I hope to experience what Serena promised—the sensation of togetherness for once, of being at one with everyone around me. I need to feel that unity, the connection we all came here seeking.

First things first, though, I pull River aside. "Before I abandon all prudence, let's talk about where you source your supply."

They're quick to reassure. "I promise you, Tam, my supplier, Bridget—she's solid. She gets her stuff straight from the Pacific Northwest—Washington State. Psilocybe azurescens. The most potent shroom on the planet."

River knows what they're doing. I guess I will trust them well enough when it comes to sourcing—as much as I'd trust anyone in this arena, but the idea of taking the most powerful variety—even in a small dose—does little to qualm my hesitation. I feel slightly sick at the prospect of wading so willingly out of my comfort zone.

But River is quick to address my lingering doubts. "Since we're all about dissecting society this weekend," they say, "figuring out how to build our own ideal community, let's view this as a chance to gain a deeper understanding of each other."

After all, as Serena mentioned earlier, the idea of shifting how we see ourselves individually within the group dynamic—it would be a powerful tool.

"Come on, the worst thing that could happen with Eva and Jamie watching out for us is a little stomach cramping," Serena urges, attempting to lighten the mood.

Now that she brings it up, I can't help but think of the other potential side effects of this "flying saucer" shaped mushroom—muscle weakness, nausea, vomiting, headaches . . . I am a doctor, after all. But even so, there's something incredibly tempting about the idea of sparking parts of my brain that have been shut off for so long. Maybe, just maybe, they'll reconnect and start communicating again.

I don't remember the last time I did anything this daring. Or dumb.

Those of us who are partaking anticipate hallucinogenic effects to begin around twenty to forty-minutes after ingestion according to River, but it may take longer for some than others.

"Less for you, Tamsin, as you're micro-dosing. Be prepared to give your trip upwards from three to six hours," they say.

"So, I'm calculating, if all goes well, we'll all be sound asleep in our beds by one in the morning, correct?" Billy asks, his tone playful. "Once we've finished dancing around, carefree and naked, and frolicking on the beach?"

I cringe at the prospect of making a complete fool of myself.

Billy confesses he's not interested in a full-blown hallucinatory encounter either. "I'm hoping for more of a bump of spiritual insight," he says. "If you're in, Tamsin, then so am I."

Nate on the other hand, looks a bit overwhelmed. And for good reason. He and Serena are taking their doses encased in honey and eaten off a spoon.

I attempt to make diversionary small talk with regards to his post-pandemic wedding business while I wait for my magic tea to brew.

"Are your couples still as all-out-green on their big day since restrictions were lifted?" It's not just polite chit-chat to take the emphasis off our present recreational activity, I'm genuinely interested.

Nate launches into an enthusiastic diatribe of how the environmental impact of *just one day* has become such a huge thing.

"My couples are all about the carbon footprint calculator," he says, beaming now he's back on his own territory.

"It's not that you can't invite a hundred guests if you were to renew your vows with Jamie, Tam," Billy jumps into the conversation, all too presumptively. "But if you hire your buddy Nate, here, you'll basically be defying an industry known for its excess and extravagance."

Joking aside, I have fantasized about the prospect of Jamie and me re-tying the knot for real this time.

Nate thanks Billy for the validation and promptly shushes him. This is his area of expertise and he's owning it.

"Studies show you'd need to plant almost three thousand trees to offset the average American wedding," Nate explains, his eyes brightening. "Imagine?" His posture is more open now, shoulders squared and there's a sense of authority in the way he speaks, as if he's been waiting for the right moment to share his knowledge. "COVID restrictions reduced that travesty by over ninety percent. What the pandemic did was show us that weddings can be done differently. And it's stuck."

I ask him which other elements of a wedding are most detrimental to the environment?

"Number of guests, air travel, imported flowers. Meat," Nate replies. He leans back slightly, arms crossed over his chest, a small smirk tugging at the corner of his lips as he delivers his next

remark. "Not like you did any of that when you and Jamie got hitched. You've banked some serious carbon offset capital in your past."

"So," Serena is next to join in. "If River and I were to get hitched, we'd be seriously foraging for the kind of forest-themed feast I'd have in mind. Meadow flowers and natural foliage for decor. I'm picturing my bouquet now."

"You and your upcycled clothing, your vintage plates, Serena, let me tell you, you'd be my dream bride," Nate replies.

"Don't hold your breath," River quips. "Serena talks a good talk but she'll never agree to getting hitched."

Serena raises her arms, jingling her stack of bangles in response. "Never say never," she says. "A zero-waste wedding while I still have my looks. Sounds like a fun time."

"I've said it before but with all this flurry of interest, maybe you *should* look into getting ordained, Nate," Billy suggests, patting his partner's arm. "Once we've found the compound, you could marry them all off. About time Tam and Jamie decide to take their commitment seriously. A double wedding in a wildflower garden would be ideal for planting trees and offsetting any carbon emissions involved. Multiple birds with one stone."

I can't tell if he's serious or messing with me. "Thanks, Rev. Moon," I say, "but a mass wedding-cult initiation wasn't exactly in the fine print of our intentional-living agreement."

River jumps in, a smug expression on their face. "Besides, Serena and I've already sorted our wills. We've left everything to each other. We're basically married already."

Serena shrugs and then reaches down to pet Minnie and Myrtle. "It's all about the dogs, in truth. Gotta be sure these two cuties are taken care of. As for the rest, who needs the fairy-tale expectations?"

River gives a small, dismissive wave, as if brushing the conversation aside. They unfold their sleeping bag with deliberate slowness. Their shoulders are a little stiff, like they're trying to keep some distance from the subject of marriage and when they finally lie down, they don't look back at anyone. Their gaze is fixed on the cloudy night sky, eyes scanning the dark expanse, avoiding the group. It's a subtle but clear signal that they're not in the mood for any more talk about weddings and they'd rather get lost in the stars than keep the conversation going.

I roll onto my side, close my eyes and wait for the world to tilt just slightly on its axis. A shift happens—subtle, but unmistakable. I'm aware enough to notice it, still conscious of the neurobiology at play as my mind begins to wander. The first wave hits and suddenly the sand beneath me feels like sugar, soft and pliable. Within minutes, there's this release—a kind of emotional purging that feels almost physical. I feel myself floating, drifting above a vast sea of warm, brown tea, the same liquid used to brew the mushrooms that started it all.

"Time to reconnect," Serena says, her voice soft as a marshmallow as she reaches out toward us. "With each other. With nature."

I roll my eyes, but only Jamie notices. He flashes a quick smile. I'm not far enough gone to lose my grip on reality completely—still, I'm ready to place some trust in her, maybe more than I should.

"You're okay," he whispers as I float around in my head. "I'm not going anywhere."

A large trunk of driftwood appears before me, twisting into the shape of a ladder. It's redwood, ancient and weathered and for a moment, I'm convinced it leads straight into the core of the Earth. I don't move, though, caught in a kind of trance. The firepit flames leap and swirl, performing a slow, hypnotic dance. As they flicker higher, they part, revealing the unmistakable figures of my grandparents—silver hair, familiar bodies, now glowing faintly in the firelight.

Then, through the shifting shadows, I see him again. The Raven—just there, standing by the edge of the trees, watching silently. His presence feels like it's woven into the air itself, like he's always been there, just beyond the firelight. His eyes meet mine and the world feels both bigger and smaller in that moment.

Other visions emerge, more unsettling at first but I allow myself to drift, shedding my body, releasing the fear that tries to anchor me. The moment I let go, he reappears. The Raven. This time he's draped in robes of oceanic blue, flowing like the tides themselves, carried by an invisible wave rising from the Pacific. Brown pelicans, ravens, and gulls circle him, a kind of bird-choreographed procession, ushering him ashore.

There's a rush—a powerful sense of my own fragility, the weight of mortality pressing gently on my chest. But as I watch, the Raven transforms into my father and the negative energy, the old rifts my mother wove between us, start to dissolve. They weaken, fade, until they're nothing but whispers. A warmth blooms from deep within, pulling me closer to it, like I'm slipping into the soft core of my own being. Peace settles over me and before I know it, I'm lifted—hovering, weightless, suspended in that serene calm.

I drift gently back to earth, feeling a tender touch to my head. It's Eva, her features delicate and enchanting. She has grown a pair elfin ears which give her an ethereal charm. "You're alright, my little one," she whispers, her voice like a soft melody. "Just keep going—you're completely safe."

I'm starting to see everyone for who they truly are, like I'm embracing humanity in a broader sense, beginning with those around me on our journey to the galactic center. As I look up at the sky, a geomagnetic storm gathers, unleashing a cascade of cosmic rays in hues I've never encountered before.

The energy pulses around me, enveloping me completely. Suddenly, I find myself floating again, suspended in the midst of a swirling whirlpool, its currents shifting endlessly. I sense the water rushing toward me from two opposing directions, colliding with a powerful force. Yet, I feel no fear. The turbulent currents don't intimidate me even as I drift toward the outer edge, I remain calm and untroubled, embracing my place in this magnificent chaos.

I'm connecting deeply with the kelp forest below. It shares its secret: for centuries it has been trapping carbon and storing it deep in the ocean floor's sediment. For the first time, I truly grasp its significance—a powerful carbon sink, absorbing far more from the atmosphere than it releases, far surpassing the carbon capture of forests above sea level.

I lean into the wind and it guides me toward the shore, flooding me with the realization that I am an integral part of this beautiful planet.

I'm the first to awaken from what can only be described as the wildest, most technicolor of a dream. My forehead feels cool to the touch and a wet washcloth slips from my grasp as it falls to the ground. My legs feel rubbery, like a cartoon character as I clumsily try to stand, only to drop to my knees on the floor.

~

We're in the living room and I have no idea how I ended up here. Eva is resting on the couch, radiant and peaceful, exuding a sense of hope. Suddenly I'm overwhelmed with gratitude and love—it's intoxicating. I stand, glance out the window; the fire in the pit has died down and it's pitch dark outside. The only sounds are the soft snores of Minnie and Myrtle, the gentle breathing of my fellow travelers and the rhythmic crash of the ocean waves.

The others gradually return to their senses and join me, talking over one another, excitedly sharing their vivid, colorful experiences. Billy describes, vividly, how he felt he had come close to extinction, finding comfort in the realization of his small role within the mysteries of the natural world, all its glorious textures, meanings, and hues.

A cooling washcloth rests over Nate's eyes. Jamie sits me down and positions himself beside me with a shallow bowl containing more of the cool, damp cloths.

"You were totally in it for like three-and-a-half hours," he says. "How'd it feel? Nobody freaked out, but you sure kept Eva and me on our toes."

"So much for the micro-dose," I reply. "I remember walking to the shore with the others. I don't know how much of it was real but we danced around and splashed about, draping each another in giant kelp fronds. And we laughed hysterically for what seemed like a really long time."

He nods, taking my hand. "Somethin' along those lines," he replies with a wink.

It's all coming back to me. How the night sky and the sand had teemed with life, a sense of wonder unlike anything I could have imagined. It was funny really, as if I'd been reduced to the size of a tiny hermit crab, at one with the ecosystem. At the same time, I was transfixed as I'd watched myself quite literally floating in the middle—for once no longer mentally and physically drained as I'd undoubtedly been since the outset of COVID, but light and carefree, cradled in the center of the swirling ocean.

The Raven, steadily hovering overhead.

Sunday Morning First Thing

J amie rouses me from sleep. His parting of the batik curtains reveals a dramatic sky painted in shades of silver and black, like a negative from a vintage film reel. The pink-on-white pattern of the faded fabric is a throw-back to Veronica's tenure. Beneath it, there's a lingering hint of incense, probably from when the batik was first brought in, adding a layer of nostalgia to the air. The scent of the sea is faint but present, a reminder of the beach just outside the poorly insulated window.

Veronica financed her adventures in Indonesia with buying trips for batik and other unique decorations, much of which found its way into the beach house. Though the fabric retains its beauty, it's showing signs of wear due to years of exposure to the sunlight.

Minnie and Myrtle's unclipped nails tap along the hardwood floor. I listen to their morning patrol as I slide over into the warm space next to where Jamie is resting on his side. I notice a dusky-colored three-inch scar, visible in the low light between his t-shirt and boxers on his exposed left hip.

"What's this?" I ask, gently tracing the scar with my finger. I used to know every inch of him. Jamie's narrow waist and hips, his long, muscular legs, as familiar to me as the well-toned sinews of his chest, shoulders, and arms.

"Shrapnel fell on a work site," he explains, raising himself on one elbow in my direction. "I slipped on the scaffoldin', sliced myself on my own utility knife."

I trace the scar with my finger.

Our bodies fit together effortlessly. Jamie is lean, and I'm on the curvier side, so there's no harshness between us—just soft, seamless lines. Is it possible that I'm more attracted to him now than I was back in the early days of our relationship? Or have I simply become more aware of his magic?

"I've got an ancient condom in my bag," I say, holding up my hand before things go any further.

"Little late for that now," he says, smiling a second time as he lifts my sleep shirt and circles my belly button with his pinkie finger.

I clear my throat to make myself clear. I haven't been on the pill for three years.

"So, you haven't slept with anyone since?" he asks, his expression amused, no apparent trace of jealousy.

"I didn't say that," I reply. "But I don't go in for unprotected intimacy as a rule."

He knows and I know that we've each had several other short to medium-term relationships over the past decade since we last slept together.

"And you?" I ask, raising an eyebrow. "Mr. Popular. Am I putting myself at risk of anything unwanted?"

"No," he replies. "I'm careful."

I decide to take his word for it. As he says, it's a bit late now.

"No little Jamie's out there after all?"

"Not that I know of," he says. "Anyway, what's stoppin' us from hoppin' on the trend and spontaneously addin' to our little community?"

As in . . . procreate. The two of us? "Are you serious?" I ask. "Is this just a random suggestion, or have you actually thought about it?

He muses, the blonde hairs on his knuckles tickling his chin. "I guess I have given it some thought, yeah."

And? I roll him over onto his back and press for more.

He looks me in the eyes. "Well, the way I see it, if we truly are talkin' about creatin' a self-sustainin' community after all, one that's capable of thrivin' into the future, then we'd best get to work on that second generation. Make it even more of a worthwhile endeavor."

"You're worried that after the last of us dies, Eva and Billy's child will be left solo, holding the fort?" I ask.

"It sounds a little post-apocalyptical put that way, but you have to agree, it'd be a dreary deal for any kid to be raised up in an otherwise childless community? Fun as we think we are, we're in our forties," he reasons, his expression earnest. "What'll we do? Make a schedule to build forts and dress up, play hide-and-go-seek with Eva's kid?"

He strokes my underarm, which elicits a mix of ticklishness and warmth. "Which is why it would be wise for the two of us to address this while it's still an option."

He leans back slightly, adopting a more casual stance, as if he's throwing the idea out there without any pressure. It's the last thing I had expected from him to be honest. He's clearly been considering our reunion more seriously than I had imagined.

"Sounds a bit formal," I reply, steadying and positioning myself so as to better look him in the eyes.

I explain again, carefully, how it's not exactly prime fertility time for those of us who'd be called to carry these future members of our little commune. I'm not exactly a prime baby-making machine these days.

"When we came up with the pact twenty years ago," I add, "it's fair to say we assumed we'd have raised all our babies by the time we were ready to shack-up as merry retirees and all."

"Yeah, well, things sure took a different path for the two of us than the traditional set-up," Jamie replies with a grin. "If we'd known then what we know now, we should've gone for it and had kids after you finished medical school."

I raise myself up on my hands and ask him what he means by 'gone for it'. I tilt my head, intrigued now but cautious. How would we have managed to raise children with our schedules?

"Parentin'. We should've, Tam. You and me. I'd have made a decent primary-caregiver for the kid, or kids. Just think, we could've had a hormonal pre-teen or two mopin' around this weekend."

"Kids were the last thing on our minds," I reply. It was true. I for one, thought I had all the time in the world. "It's no use looking back."

"We're different people now," he says, rolling me over and resting his body on mine. "What would be better than one or two of our own to contribute to the world's last generation?"

"Are we better people now?" I ask, gently levering his t-shirt up and over his head. "That's the question."

"You bet," he replies, his tone, playful. "But to be sure, best investigate further."

Sunday Breakfast

Delicious huckleberry pancakes tease my taste buds as Serena transfers a batch of fluffy breakfast circles from griddle to plate. A gentle breeze drifts in from the open kitchen window, dispersing the lingering scents of her cooking—the rich scent of butter mingling with the toasty, comforting smell of the pancakes. A hint of vanilla and nutmeg.

Despite our rebellious night by the firepit, Serena appears unfazed, tackling her morning duties with ease.

"Man, that trip was something," River remarks as they clutch their plate to their chest like a shield in their advance towards the front line.

Nate and Billy appear surprisingly affable after yesterday's revelations. Last night, I felt a definite sense of collective harmony that has persisted into the morning. They're very much together, it seems, Billy with one arm slung casually over Nate's shoulder.

Eva is the first to eat as she tucks enthusiastically into a pile of pancakes with extra berries and a pool of maple syrup.

"Where'd you find the huckleberries?" she asks. "This sweet-tart flavor, so succulent."

"One of our secret spots in the hills above Tomales Bay," River replies. "Early fall. They're fantastic to freeze, taste as good as fresh."

Serena bemoans the difficulties of harvesting huckleberries, noting their tendency to cluster on stems closer to the center or crown of the bush. During their last harvest, she says, she and River had to navigate through the prickly undergrowth, making every effort to steer clear of poison oak.

"And they're a favorite with all kinds of wildlife," she adds. "If the bluebirds, bear and mice don't get to them first, then we consider it a win."

"Bears?" Nate asks, lightly tapping a finger against his lips. "I don't think we went into this in sufficient detail."

"Oh, don't get all paranoid on us. They're shy and elusive for the most part," River replies. "Black bears are way more interested in nuts and berries than you."

Nate says he wouldn't bet on it, implying he's had enough surprises for one weekend.

And Jamie warns that a black bear sighting is not out of the question.

"Spring is when the young bears disperse. They typically follow rivers and creeks into new territory." He mentions there have been increasing urban sightings in the North Bay that have typically caused little alarm. "They're smart, they generally figure out their own way back into the wild."

"Well, I for one am most grateful to the convivial black bear population for sparing us at least one huckleberry bush," Billy declares, as he licks an excess of syrup from his thumb. "Yum. Heaven on a plate in its purest form."

Nate leans in and wipes his partner's sticky lips with the edge of a napkin.

"All good in the Daddy department?" Serena asks, direct as ever.

"I'm wrapping my head around it, yes," Nate replies. He pauses before reaching, diplomatically, for Eva's hand. "Don't think less of me for throwing such a total hissy-fit,' he says. "Now I have had time to think it through, at least for starters, the last thing I want is to mess this up."

Eva wraps her arms around him as we watch her draw him to her and kiss him gently on each cheek. "It's going to be an amazing journey," she offers. Her face shows her genuine adoration. "I promise you, Nate. Co-parenting with two of the men I love most in the world. It's the best gift I could ask for."

Nate blushes. He reaches out tentatively and lays his hands on Eva's tummy. "Don't go getting sappy on me," he says. "I'd rather we all move on from any mention of my melt down."

We'd lost regular contact with Eva for a few years while she'd grappled with her turbulent marriage. We're all aware of how important she is to us, individually and as a whole. No more so than now.

The tea kettle whistles. Billy appears to be slightly wary still of this fast-paced turn of events. Nate's apparent show of acceptance of the baby news after his initial reaction.

"Take all the time you need," he says, adjusting his posture by shifting his feet. "This was major news. And its delivery should've been thought out with far more tact."

Nate looks around the room at all of us, taking in each of our faces, our concern in turn as he opens up in more detail.

"My brain," he says, "the best way I can put it is that it just stopped fighting during last night's trip. I don't really get how, but I'm not nearly as freaked out this morning. Especially with Eva around. I know she wouldn't just bail on us, leaving us with a crying baby and no idea what the hell to do."

"How will it work?" Jamie asks. "I mean, with you guys livin' in New York and Eva in San Antonio?

"I'll relocate—for a while," Billy replies. "Nate will travel back and forth to start with. He's said as much this morning."

"I'm not missing out on the birth," Nate says.

This seems as good a moment as any for me to bring up a documentary I've watched in which a gay father's brain was shown to develop like a mother's after adopting a baby.

"The brain is brilliant, it simply produces more oxytocin, the hormone that creates bonding," I explain, hoping it helps puts Nate a little more at ease.

"You'll be amazed when your hearing heightens to alert you to your baby's cries."

Jamie says that he too hopes to experience all of this himself in the not-too-distant future. Serena jumps on his declaration like a like a surfer catching a wave, effortlessly riding the momentum of the idea, gliding with it until it crashes at my feet.

"I'd totally volunteer to be your baby mama given the chance," she replies with a broad, splashy grin. "But it looks like the good doctor might have beaten me to it."

"Overstepping again, Serena," River joins in the fray. How many times do we have to watch their feelings being stomped on? I'm learning to deal with her obsession with Jamie, but it's a whole different thing for her partner to accept.

"Just throwing it out there," Serena responds, sitting down and stabbing her fork into a slice of pancake. "But honestly, it's not looking likely for me anymore."

"Why's that?" Eva asks, clearly curious. She wasn't there when Serena had made her own confession down at the beach.

Serena responds directly to her: "Because I'm having a procedure in a couple of weeks. The results of which will be the deciding factor in the motherhood stakes."

"What kind of procedure?" It's my turn to probe. She's the one who has brought it up.

Serena takes a deep breath before answering, her tone, having lost its sweetness, is blunt. "If you really want to know, my fallopian tubes were scarred and narrowed after an infection following the abortion. It's made it hard for my eggs to move from my ovaries to my womb apparently. I need to figure out what I'm working with—whether my eggs are even viable or if I'd be risking an ectopic pregnancy. Or, I'll need to decide if I want to go ahead and have my tubes tied."

In my experience, most women treated for pelvic inflammatory disease are still able to get pregnant. I tell her as much, hoping to offer some reassurance despite her imminent challenge. I've seen plenty of patients in my follow-up care who've managed to navigate this as a fairly common issue.

The irony isn't lost on me. Serena is finally in the best place of her life to become a mother—physically, mentally and nutritionally. Logistics aside, River is a devoted and loving partner and would make a great coparent.

"You're in great shape otherwise," I note. "So don't count yourself out just yet when it comes to conceiving and carrying." What I don't say is—just absolutely not with Jamie.

I look back at him after I've said my piece. Jamie glances at the time on his water-resistant diver's watch. There's a silence for a moment. Nobody wishes to make things any more uncomfortable.

"Once I'm back from the boat, we should start to brainstorm' the different regions we'd be interested in lookin' at for the future," Jamie says, adeptly changing the subject.

The sky rumbles ominously, making me aware of how anxious I am about him heading out on the water today of all days. He picks up on my unease right away. Tilting his head in that endearing way of his, he tries to ease my worry with what he construes as an innocent remark.

"Serena was in on this afternoon's excursion at first," he says. "She was gonna stay in the boat while I dive, but all things considered, I've decided it's best I handle this one alone."

Best for who? I'm unsure if his announcement of leaving her on land is to appease me or because he's wary of the changeable conditions after all.

Serena extends her hands, palms out, bangles jangling.

"Much as I'd love to make good on my expedition with you," she replies, reaching out to Jamie, "my sea legs are none too solid these days."

Serena suggests we'd maybe somehow manage without the sea urchin haul, but then quickly shifts gears, launching into a dramatic lament over the thought of missing out on the creamy pasta dish she'd clearly been craving as the perfect finale to our weekend gathering.

"Garlic, anchovies, chili flakes, fresh sea urchin… delicious," she sighs, giving me a knowing look—her subtle way of letting on she's tasted this dish before.

Jamie chimes in, explaining how the urchins he's after feed on algae and seaweed, especially the giant kelp he's so committed to protecting. His diving trip this weekend, it's obvious, is more than just a hunt—it's his way of giving back. To the ocean. To the environment. To his friends. The idea of him leaving the ocean behind for an inland home suddenly feels unimaginable.

"And hey," he adds with a trademark grin, "since we're on the subject of reproduction—you all are gonna love the best part of the urchin: the creamy roe. The Japanese claim it's an aphrodisiac."

"Sexy," Billy replies, with a whistle. "Tell us more. Like, what's it like down there in the ocean when you dive?" he asks.

"It's like being surrounded by a bunch of massive, super flexible green giants," Jamie says, his eyes lighting up with excitement. "Spring's when the growin' season kicks off. Kelp fronds can shoot up by two feet a day when the sunlight hits just right."

He says the best way to picture diving into a forest of bull kelp is for us to close our eyes and imagine swimming through a shadowy underwater filled with dense, rubbery trees.

"Reachin' all the way to the surface, their every movement dictated by the wind, swells and tides."

"Legend," River declares. "Sign me up for any other planet-saving mission, but not this one. I'll be your ride to the boat, but there's no way you're catching me out there in the depths."

Serena deals River a playful jab. "Yeah, well, that's not gonna happen," she says. "I'd stick to the monthly coastal cleanups with the kids if I were you."

"Someone has to take care of the shoreline," River replies, quick off the mark from all the training she's put them through. They reach by her and grab their truck keys from a hanger by the refrigerator.

"Don't worry about me—I'll be fine out there," Jamie says, trying to reassure. "It's just a light rain, nothing serious. I should be done in under a couple of hours. Still early yet."

"So, back to business," River says, as they prepare to leave. "As Jamie just pointed out, it's time to start marking out potential relocation zones. The sooner we lock something down, the better—if we're gonna dodge the heat, the drought, the wildfires, the power and water outages, the rising sea levels and all."

I look around the room. Once we accept the harsh reality of the future, climate-wise, it feels less overwhelming and hopeless in a way. It's just science. And taking proactive steps, together, feels pretty empowering. We're not talking about some isolated bunker scenario, shutting out the rest of humanity, after all. Who'd want to emerge into a desolate world, right?

What we're envisioning as a group of old friends is building a community that not only thrives where we settle but also actively improves the land and connects with the surrounding community.

Sounds great, doesn't it? Yet, in all honesty, this spirit of selfless collaboration is not coming easily to me. I've been flying solo for so long aside from my work. And even then, that core part of my life has been tested to the extreme these past few years.

River hands out a pack of rainbow-colored index cards and pencils, instructing each of us to jot down five essential elements of a place we'd consider home given its relevant climate change criteria.

"Then grab a second card and write down five ways we can boost our collective social, mental, and spiritual resilience within our community," they add.

This is getting a little too "woo-woo" for my taste.

Trouble is, it requires such a leap. The whole touchy-feely, hand-holding vibe, the idea of this idealistic unity—it's unsettling. Who am I? Who have I become? What am I doing? I wasn't raised like this, certainly never exposed to the bohemian concept of communal living. That wasn't ever a part of my upbringing aside from my experience of student housing. Even now it takes me several glasses of wine and a full-on Joan Baez album to start loosening my grip on my ingrained cultural hang-ups.

"Take your time," River adds, looking directly at me. "You've all morning. Jamie and I will complete our cards later."

"As long as there's no mandatory howling at dusk," I remark. I can't help myself. I was never comfortable with all that business. Polite applauses for the NHS back in the UK, now that's more my style. Banging of pots and pans in Italy I could manage at a push. Opera on the balcony is alright. Plenty people embraced the primal, full-throated howl, Jamie included and he'd tried his best to recruit me at the tail end of our lockdown cocktail calls, but sorry, it was not happening with me, however hard he tried. Stick-in-the-mud maybe but I'm way too restrained to abandon the degree of inbred decorum I was raised on. It's non-negotiable. Even if I did agree to the mushroom trip last night. I can't believe I did that, though I made it through without any negative effects.

"Consider it a call to adventure," Eva says, resting one hand on her stomach. "Each of us brings our own unique experiences, strengths, and skills to the table."

"Yes, we do. Now, take a third card," River seconds Eva's suggestion. "And make a short list of what you're good at, what we might not know about each other as we've matured. Ask yourself what do I do that nobody else in this room does, no matter how trivial?"

"I make a mean Manhattan," Billy offers with a wink. "And aside from giving a decent manicure, I set tile like a pro."

"As for me, well, I'm a natural with a chain saw and wallpaper," Nate replies. "And I've a hankering for taking up pottery."

As the guys joke around, it hits me—I haven't really thought through the practical side of our plan, the whole pact, as much as I should have. But somehow, this weekend, it's all starting to feel more real—and more urgent. What once seemed like a dreamy vision of communal living, all Kumbaya around the firepit, now has me seriously wondering if the entire idea might just be completely absurd.

"Before you take off, it'd be helpful to hear what kind of timeline you're thinking for actually packing up and moving—as a squad," Billy says, shifting the conversation toward the practical details with River and Jamie. The talk is getting real now. "I just want to know so we can start the search seriously."

Jamie scratches his head, clearly more tuned in to his upcoming dive than logistics. "Here's how I see it," he says. "We've got to make our move before there's a big wave of people fleein' areas hardest hit—or about to be hit—by the most extreme of climate change. Once we've picked a safer spot, we'd be smart to get things movin' right away."

"Like, in six months? A year?" Eva asks. Upending her world with a baby or toddler in tow is a significant ask.

"However long it takes to raise the funds to secure a property and set up the basics of our living quarters," River replies. "If we're all in, that is . . . ."

Serena leans in slightly, her arms crossed loosely but her posture open, as if gauging everyone's reaction. Her eyes flicker between each person, a small smile tugging at the corner of her mouth, though there's a hint of tension in the way she holds herself—like she's waiting for someone to push back or speak up. "So. Are we really all okay with the idea of shacking up together?" she asks.

I don't know why but I nod anyway. "As long as I've got my own space at night, even if it's modest." I know deep down, though, I'll probably have to compromise at first. A few months of living under one roof, max.

Billy says he imagines it taking us several years to create what we've envisioned once we've settled on a destination and property with good air quality and natural resources, not too far from a city.

"We shouldn't expect it to be all picture-perfect at first," he adds. "We'll take the best we can get and make it better. The reality is, there's no escaping the climate crisis entirely. So many parts of the world are becoming uninhabitable. Any place that's less risky is going to get crowded real fast."

"And the longer we wait, the more we'll be made to pay later," River adds. "Half of Florida will be on the move pretty soon."

"I'm concerned that some of our favorite spots may be underwater before long," Nate says. "Unfathomable though it seems."

Jamie suggests Denver, Raleigh, Salt Lake City—cities that are ranking well for climate readiness. He briefly touches on their high scores for economic, social and government engagement, their adaptability to more extreme weather. Then, ever-so stealthily, he casually throws out the idea that maybe we shouldn't rule out staying somewhere in the general Bay Area after all.

"Karl the Fog as he's known fondly, online. Our natural and benevolent air-conditioner — he's a pretty big plus," he says. "There are plenty of lower-risk geographical zones around the Bay we might consider takin' a look at. Earthquakes and wildfires aside."

"Seattle ranks pretty high for preparedness too," he adds. But he says the higher risk of earthquakes and rising sea levels really turns him off the idea of making a move to the Pacific Northwest.

Leaving California is a tough decision for me, also. The prospect is not something I'm taking lightly and I communicate as much. Coastal California has won my heart over the past twenty-plus years.

Jamie is quick to agree as I knew he would. "But securing a large compound in the Bay Area is probably going to be cost prohibitive," he reasons.

"Anyone got any Canadian connections?" Eva asks, half-joking. "I hear Ottawa's on the least-risky list globally, right up there with Glasgow, Scotland!"

"Billy in a kilt sounds good to me," Nate says. "Not to mention there'd be an abundant availability of Scotch."

"I think you have a photo of that somewhere in your archives," Billy replies. Nate started scanning print photos he took during senior year but he ran out of time to complete the project by this weekend. He was the only one who made an effort to haul a camera around with him that year and it's bound to be a fascinating trip down memory lane when we do finally get to review all that he captured during our last hurrah to our student days.

"Wherever we do end up, we're definitely gonna have to make compromises and adapt," Jamie says, slinging his pack over his shoulder. "And for some of us, that's gonna be a much bigger challenge than for others."

"Yeah, each of our respective ways of life as we've known it . . ." River adds.

"Time to look at the bigger picture, step off the grid, secure our own food source," Jamie adds.

And in saying so, off he goes, intent on showing us how his idea of foraging is done with his intended uni haul. But as he walks away, I can't shake the worry creeping up—what if he's not as prepared as he thinks?

Sunday Late Morning

River reverses the van out of its tight confines of the narrow garage, tires scraping against gravel. The space is impossibly small, the walls on either side too close for comfort. Yet they maneuver the vehicle with precision, their eyes flicking between the side mirrors and the looming edge of the driveway. I follow Jamie out onto the covered front porch. Pillows of gravel-grey clouds spit tiny raindrops on the driveway.

"I wish you wouldn't go," I say, slipping my arm through his. "No-one will be too disappointed if you take a rain check. It's not like we're at risk of running out of food."

He shoots me the look. I remember it well. His way of reminding me what it is to be a free spirit, regardless of our most recent intimacies.

Diving is his deal. I console myself that he knows what he's doing. I must put my trust in him if this is going to work. He pulls me closer and kisses me tenderly on the forehead.

"I've handled way worse than this," he says, his eyes crinkling at the corners as he plants one last kiss on the back of my hand and jumps into the passenger seat. "Later," he promises, rolling down the window and flashing me a grin broad enough to help settle the nerves still buzzing in my chest.

I watch the van back up the driveway, make a sharp turn and then disappear over the rise in the highway to the south.

There's work to be done filling out the flashcards River assigned. My mind continues to flip-flop. How am I supposed to rebuild my career in a place I don't even know exists yet? This is madness.

Something tells me, with all the Type A personalities involved, there's going to be plenty of debate about our destination before we come anywhere close to settling on a place. Jamie's not about to give up his access to the coast without solid reasoning. His passion for restoring the kelp forests is a huge part of who he is. How does anyone walk away from the ocean once it's in their soul? Aside from myself, Serena, in particular, will be tough to sell on such an idea.

Eva and Serena are standing close together, their shoulders almost touching, a subtle closeness that suggests a quiet camaraderie. I watch as their heads lean slightly toward each other, speaking in hushed tones, their eyes darting around as if to make sure they're not overheard. There's a tension in their posture, a shared secrecy, as though whatever they're discussing is important—and private. Serena's arms are crossed loosely, both of them lost in their conversation, unaware of my approach.

"What *are* you going to do about it?" Eva asks.

Serena sighs, glancing out the window. "I could sit here like a princess in my ivory tower, but it won't stop this old house from sliding into the sand and surf sooner or later. I'm pretty screwed once the insurance comes up for renewal."

"When is that?" Eva asks.

"July first."

"Like, no more than a couple of months?"

"Yep."

"Could you sell it to someone else other than the government?"

"Who the hell wants to buy a house that's falling off a cliff?"

"I dunno, someone clueless. A start-up bro with a stash of cash and beach front aspirations?"

"No," Serena says. "I could never do that. But I am gonna have to come up with a solid game plan soon."

"What does River say?"

"River knows the deal. It's such a touchy subject, they're reluctant to bring it up."

Eva says it must be adding extra stress on their relationship.

"You think?" Serena responds with a sharp, almost dismissive tone. She turns off the gas just as the tea kettle begins to whistle, keeping her back slightly turned as if ignoring the question.

Eva moves in a little, her tone softer but direct. "I've noticed that River seems to trigger you a lot more these days. Do you think you two will be okay moving forward with this plan if things are still tense?"

"It's not River's issue, it's mine," Serena replies. It's time to let them know I am here. But not quite yet. I'm curious to hear more as I step back into the shadows of the entryway. Minnie and Myrtle make no move to give me away.

"All this baby business. No offence, Eva, but it's difficult for me. I'm most likely *not* ever gonna have a biological child of my own. I'm coming to terms with that but it's something else to face it as a finality when I've always thought I'd figure out a way."

Eva shuffles closer. Her touch is tender, as if silently offering support without saying a word. Serena, still standing rigid for a moment, gradually melts into the embrace, her body relaxing in this quiet, intimate moment. Eva's hold appears to ground Serena as she lets out a breath that she most likely didn't realize she was holding.

"This little one's going to need all hands-on deck to raise," she says, gently taking Serena's hands and placing them on her belly. The air shifts, the moment feeling more fragile. It's my turn to take a breath, letting the weight of it settle.

"I know, babe, and I'm really stoked," Serena replies, her voice tinged with a heaviness. "But seeing Jamie and Tamsin together . . . it's like being stabbed in the stomach with a knife. All I can think about is how I made the biggest mistake of my life when I toyed with the pair of them and that damn Green Card marriage . . ."

"I've heard more than enough," I declare, striding in with my hands firmly on my hips, cutting her off mid-sentence. "It's you who is disrespecting *my* life, Serena," I shout, stepping forward and jabbing a finger toward her turned-away face. "I wouldn't even be here, invading your space, if it weren't for the fact, I have forgiven you and Jamie. But of course, you have to waltz back into the center of the picture."

I grab her by the shoulders and pull her toward me, the force of it making her stumble slightly. She's caught off guard, her mouth dropping open in shock. I'm steaming mad and she knows it.

"If you're not over him, then you need to tell him. Be clear. Give him the opportunity to make his own choice. Take care of your unfinished business so I can take care of mine. And I think you owe your partner an explanation while you're at it."

"Keep River out of this," Serena warns, stepping back defensively. "There's nothing wrong with River, it's me who's the fuck-up."

Eva intervenes. "Okay, slow down Serena. From what I see, River is about as loving and loyal as could be. It'd be a shame to wreck their trust and your relationship by telling them you're still a little in love with Jamie, especially if Jamie's no longer in love with you."

"It's been a long road," I admit, trying my hardest to gain some perspective, to ease up on her a bit. "It's been years since you last pushed for another round with Jamie's affections. He might've been your puppet back then, but no more."

"And it's all turning out for the best," Eva says, softly. "Let's give this some air. How about the three of us leash the dogs and take a breather before the heavier rain comes in?"

We grab our jackets, two of us walking with our shoulders hunched, heads low, clearly sulking as we step outside. The air feels heavy between us as we meander up and down the narrow stretch of grass and sand, the dogs trailing behind us. Eva, ever the politician, positions herself between us, her posture open but purposeful. She moves smoothly, trying to bridge the gap and with a calm, almost practiced gesture, hooks her arms around ours. She hands each of us a leash, her eyes flicking back and forth between us, silently urging some kind of reconciliation.

"Come on, let's face it. What we have here is a classic triangle," she says with a sigh. "But the facts don't change. Let's break it down: Tamsin is still legally married to Jamie. They're husband and wife. Neither of them has pushed for a divorce, right?"

I nod, my throat tightening as tears threaten to well up.

"But why not?" Serena presses, her voice laced with confusion. "That's what I've never wrapped my head around. You made it clear you were done playing house when you came back from England."

"Because you slept with my husband, Serena. It was you who couldn't keep your hands to yourself."

"He's just as guilty," she shoots back. "Don't fall into that same old trap, blaming it all on the woman."

I stifle an urge to slap her. Good thing Eva's in the middle. Sweet, loving, motherly Eva. No wonder Billy picked Eva as a birth partner. He was smart to steer clear of Serena and me and our tangled web. Things are complicated enough.

We've been over this. My patience is stretched to the full. This woman never gives up. It's her passive aggressive desire to dominate. It took Serena a decade to make a play to reclaim Jamie. And now another. Talk about persistence. She, like me, is clearly adept at playing the long game.

"Can't you see what you did?" I ask, one more attempt at reasoning. "You set me up with Jamie in the first place so that you could keep him on the back burner for yourself, for later. Trouble is, even though we discovered we were surprisingly good together after all, for me there was always that element of doubt that he'd simply settled."

"And now?" Eva asks. "Since you've been apart for so long? Do you still have those concerns?"

"It's finally our choice," I explain, muting the inner critic that is lurking in the shadows. "We've figured this much. I'm enough. He's enough. We're more than enough for each other. It's our time to call the shots in our relationship now—Jamie and me."

"And here I am to screw it all up again," Serena says, her voice tinged with self-mockery. Her face twists into a sharp grimace and she sniffs, like she's caught a whiff of something unpleasant. For once, there's a flicker of genuine regret in her eyes, something she doesn't usually show.

"In a nutshell, yes."

"Though it's all completely different this time around and in small part thanks to you, if I'm honest, Serena," I say. "For bringing us all back together. Jamie and I now have a fighting chance."

"So, what's to do?" Eva says, steering us around and back toward the house. Still only a light rain.

"We tackle the subject together?" I suggest. "You, me and Jamie, in private. Clear the air. When he gets back."

"And River?" Eva asks.

"No. Leave River out of it," Serena replies. "I'd rather not fuck up another good thing if I can help it."

"Wise," Eva replies. "'Coz if you did decide to break your commitment, then they deserve way more respect."

Serena sighs. "I'm sorry, Tam," she says, her voice heavy with resignation. Her gaze drops, avoiding direct eye contact. "I'm a jerk. But maybe all of this heartache was necessary for you to learn to believe in yourself."

Only Serena could say such a thing. That she was with me all along so that I would be forced to travel the long and arduous road to prove my worthiness. She opens up, however and blames her overbearing-need for love and attention on her mother. Veronica was married three times and was needily single during the final years of her life.

"My mother . . . she just never gave a damn about anyone else," she admits, her voice tinged with a mix of frustration and self-awareness. "I'm really trying not to end up like her, but it feels like I'm just wired that way."

"Try harder," my words are firm as I kick off my shoes in the covered porch, the motion almost punctuating my point. "There's a good deal more than you, me and Jamie riding on your breaking the cycle."

My posture is straight by now but there's an underlying weight in my shoulders, a mix of determination and something softer. I tell her that I forgive her.

"We've carried our familial burdens for too long. We're both enough as we are right now."

The silence hangs heavy between us, thick with the weight of what's been said—and what's still unspoken. Serena looks at me, her eyes searching mine as if trying to gauge whether I truly mean it, whether my forgiveness is something she can believe. For a moment, it feels like everything's teetering on the edge, fragile and raw.

Then, just as I think the moment might pass, her face shifts and she opens her mouth to speak. A sharp knock at the door cuts through the moment making us jump. My heart skips a beat. My eyes flick toward Serena who's already tense, her body language shifting, something unreadable flashing in her expression.

Early Sunday Afternoon

The rat-a-tat-tat echoes through the house, sharp and urgent. I move toward the door, an unsettling feeling in my stomach intensifying with every step. When I open it, I'm met by the sight of two figures. The Raven, his face set in quiet determination, standing alongside a heavy-set older woman whom I assume is his mother, her long hair, silvered with age, tied in a knot at the back of her head. She's wearing a muted, deep olive-green weatherproof jacket over a thick woolen sweater and flannel pants. Her weathered hands and features are marked by her years of coastal living. She's beautiful.

"We didn't mean to disrupt," the Raven says, his voice low, with an edge of concern. He doesn't flinch at the sight of me, but lingers, patient and poised, like he's reading the shape of my thoughts. He's not surprised to find me here and I'm not surprised to see him either. He's dressed in the exact same way as when I first met him and in each real or imagined scenario since.

His eyes flicker briefly to Serena, as if measuring her reaction. He tilts his head, slowly, thoughtfully. One obsidian eye comes into clearer view, fixed and unblinking, studying me with unnerving calm as he speaks.

"There's a storm brewing, and we're picking up something unusual on the ham radio frequencies. Thought we should check in, see if you're prepared . . . might be worse than it looks."

His mother, standing silently beside him, clasps her hands together tightly, her sharp gaze fixed on the horizon beyond the porch. Her face, lined with age, tells a story of a life lived well within the rhythms of the ocean and the natural world.

There's something in her silence that speaks volumes, like she knows something we don't.

I hesitate, wondering not that they had come to us but why. There's no reason for it to be anything but a passing storm later this evening, right?

"Unusual how?" I ask, my words cutting through the rising wind. This time I know he's for real.

The Raven looks back at his mother, his expression unreadable, before he turns his attention back to me. The tilt toward me isn't sharp or aggressive, but deliberate, the way someone might lean in closer when a story takes a darker turn.

"We—my mother, Kaya, and me, we suspect the storm's a cover for something else," he says, his tone calmer than before. "Something you might want to be ready for."

The air grows colder as I try to decipher the look in his eyes. The storm is coming, but now something else is on its way? Something we aren't prepared for. This is the Raven, I remind myself. Prone to alarm.

Serena steps towards them. She reaches for Kaya's clasped hands and holds them in hers.

"Kaya's family has lived on the Sonoma Coast for generations," Serena says. "Her Miwok ancestors and the coastal landscape combined make her especially in tune to the elements."

Serena asks them if they'd like to step inside. "Come into the warm, won't you?"

"No thank you," Kaya replies, her voice, low and steady as she stands her ground. Her practical boots are made for rainy winter wear—built to last, like her. "No time to intrude."

"She's insistent," the Raven says, his arms by his side. "My mother's a woman of deep resilience, but others out here are not so prepared."

"What are you trying to tell us?" Serena gets to the point. "Please—go ahead. We're all ears. I have nothing but respect for you and your mother," she says to the Raven. "What have you picked up on the radio, Kaya?"

Serena reiterates how the Raven and his mother are part of a network of weather spotters who communicate real-time conditions to agencies such as the National Weather Service.

"We heard about an approaching flash storm from others in our network," he replies—on his mother's behalf. "It's my mother's belief that storms are messages from the spirits, our ancestors, of an imbalance, a call to pay attention to something or someone within our community."

Kaya speaks now. "Something important must be addressed," she says. "It's the voice of nature telling me so."

"So, what do we do about it?" Serena asks.

"Prepare for nature's way. A cleansing of the land," Kaya replies. "A force to clear the way. You should leave now. You are not meant to stay."

"The time has come for you to leave," the Raven adds. Calm and purposeful.

Kaya's presence, her unmistakable dignity continues to command our attention as she and her son turn to leave.

"Wait . . ." I call. I can hardly let them walk out without another word. He's clearly still on my case. This information is all a little too abrupt to know what to do with.

Serena steps in front of me. "Let them go," she says. "There's a delicate dance between the human world and the spirit world. Whatever she's picked up on the Ham network is upsetting her balance. A shift in things."

"Where do we go from here?" I ask. "And what about River and Jamie?"

"I didn't sense that immediate a fear in her eyes," Serena replies. "I doubt we're in any imminent danger. Let's talk about it as soon as Jamie gets back."

Eva asks who was at the door.

"The Raven of all people," Serena replies. "Tamsin's run-in at the winery on the way up here, remember? With his mother."

"What did they want?" Eva is curious.

They let us know that we may be in for more of a storm than we were led to believe."

"And she said to leave, now." I add. "Which we're hardly about to do with River and Jamie gone."

Serena reminds Eva of the Ham Radio connection.

"And Kaya, the mother, she's an environmental activist like her son. And an artist. Carves intricate patterns into wood. People consider her mixed-race identity a bridge between cultures out here along the coast."

"Then maybe we should listen to her?" Eva asks. "What if things do get hairy out here?"

"It's a little late. I think she's being superstitious is all," Serena replies, running her fingers through her hair. "For whatever reason, maybe the Raven has more of a problem with my having a house party this weekend than any of us realized."

I want to believe that Serena is right about the overreaction. Maybe this warning didn't come from a recognized source after all. But then again, who am I to question the intuition of someone so connected to this land and the ocean?

～

Yoga or watercolor painting? Our options after we finish up with the flash cards, our wish lists for creating our tree-lined oasis, a dream-future in the midst of what we're all aware is a bit of a pipedream, in truth. Something like ten percent of intentional communities actually succeed. Basically, we'll each be required to commit to being mature and responsible human beings for the rest of our lives if we're to make it work.

You'd think that wouldn't be too much of an ask, but most anyone who has ever shacked up in any manner of speaking, communication and money conflicts are inevitable, egos, disagreements as to how domestic duties are distributed, annoying guests who stay too long . . .

Eva supplies the watercolor paints, brushes and paper. She's gifted each of us as inspiration, a small, original watercolor of her own, rolled and tied with a blue satin ribbon. I open mine. It depicts a turtle, slow moving on earth, fast and agile in water. Is that how she sees me?

I understand how Eva's art connects the natural world and the ancient cultures just as Kaya's strong connection between her Miwok heritage and the coastal landscape binds the two together. It's something to witness—these rare intersections in our fast-pace, modern world.

And I can easily imagine how Eva's art brings her much-needed stress relief from the rigors of her job. Me, on the other hand, well I'm embarrassed to admit how long it's been since I picked up a paintbrush, or even a colored pencil for that matter. Not since the early days of lockdown when I took an uncharacteristic notion one time to sketch a still life of the fruit bowl in my kitchen in the middle of a sleepless night. I didn't know it at the time, but waking in a panic-pattern after working fourteen-to-fifteen-hour days would become the norm. There'd been little room for art. Or play.

We gather by the living room window—Serena, Eva, Billy, Nate and myself—casually observing the waves and chatting away, delaying the start of Eva's art activity.

My thoughts return to the Raven and his mother and her direct, no-nonsense warning. River has yet to return. We're all watching, attentively as a giant cumulus cloud pushes upward over the Pacific in a rising column of air. Flashes on the horizon. A thin streak of electric lightning out of nowhere strikes at a point that appears to be close to shore.

The room darkens, the walls shake and the lightning renders us silent as we witness the display of an electric storm play out through the safety of the glass pane.

"Jamie's smart, he'll have ditched the diving expedition and turned back with River for sure." Billy is the first to speak his mind, voicing what we're all hoping. "There wasn't any mention of this, even a short-lived disturbance in this weekend's forecast."

The lightning heats the air as it passes through in a rapid and intense fork, producing shockwaves as the violent energy reverberates indoors. Claps and rolls of thunder rattle the window panes as they cling to their old and inadequate casings.

I'm awash with a mix of fear and awe. The atmosphere is charged, almost palpable, as though the house itself is vibrating with energy. The window panes appear all the more fragile in the face of nature's fury.

"Christ Almighty," River yells, bursting into the house with an almost frantic energy, their body tense with urgency. "Where in god's name did this come from?"

Rain hits hard against the glass. The ocean is heavy and the wind has changed direction.

"Where's Jamie?" The words fly out of my mouth though I already know the answer.

"Out there," River replies, hunched forward, as if bracing against the force of the ocean as they point to the Pacific. Their chest heaves as they try to catch their breath, the sudden panic in their movements palpable. "I waited 'til he got his gear on before I headed back from the harbor. Damn it, guys, it wasn't even raining then."

We stand there, the six of us, frozen to the spot. Minnie and Myrtle cock their ears alert to our concern. Minnie's low growl sets my goosebumps on edge. If circumstances were different, with Jamie by my side, this may have been exhilarating, being drawn to the power and raw beauty of the storm.

"He'd have turned back, surely?" Serena asks. "Best not panic, yet. The minute Jamie clapped eyes on those towering clouds he'd have made the judgement call."

"I hope you're right, Serena," I reply, on edge, as she knows that I know, we all know, that it's entirely possible that the isolated lightning wasn't visible from where his boat had made its initial way out.

A dense, sinking feeling closes into the pit of my stomach. These are forces beyond human control. I reach for the back of a chair and steady myself.

"Take a seat, Tam," Nate says, soothingly as he reaches for my arm. I detect a quiet edge to his tone, a subtle tension beneath his calm reassurance. "He'll be fine. No one knows the ocean in inclement weather like Jamie."

I loathe the sickening weight of helplessness that creeps up on me, a poisonous residue rising from the deep well of my past. There's no way to control what's beyond my reach. When Dad died, this ugly emotion swelled up inside of me, growing uncontrollably, until it spilled over and turned me into a blubbering wreck for months. I convinced myself that I wasn't enough of a daughter—that if I had been, I could've stopped him from cheating on my mum, from dying. Then, after Gran passed, when I found out not long after that Jamie and Serena had hooked up, that toxic residue I'd buried deep inside resurfaced. In response, I packed up and ran the moment Jamie confessed, taking refuge in my work.

For years, I've been living with only half of myself, shutting down my love and in doing so I've thrown away an entire decade of my life.

Part of me is ready to drive down to the harbor and search for Jamie myself but I already know he's not there. He's out on the water, for sure.

"I can't just stand here like a lump," I say, twisting my hands together.

River suggests we set up a couple of search parties along the coast. "We have two vehicles," they reason, their face a mixture of concern and determination, brows furrowed slightly. "I'll take the van back to the harbor and start from there. Tamsin, you drive your car, stop by each of the various vista points."

"What about emergency services, coastal rescue?" Billy asks, more than a flicker of concern in his voice as though he doesn't want any of us to sense how frightened he is. "First things first."

It's Serena who questions an actual emergency. She suggests we act on River's suggestion and go look for him first. "Jamie will be pissed if we activate a rescue team too soon."

We're in various stages of grabbing shoes and jackets when the air is ripped apart by the most vicious, violent rumble—something like a freight train, but louder, sharper and with a monstrous momentum. It builds quickly, roaring through the house, an ominous sound that makes the walls feel like they might cave in. Our hearts pound in sync with it, a primal, sinking feeling of dread. Whatever it is, it feels like it's coming straight for us—an earthquake, a flash flood, or something even worse, something gigantic and devastating, barreling our way. Fear tightens our chests and, for a moment, all we can do is listen, frozen, half expecting the earth to crack open.

I snap into survival mode, tearing myself away from my chair and rush to the kitchen window. Through the glass, I catch sight of the hillside down the road where the land is slipping away, tumbling in a terrifying cascade. A massive chunk of earth—mud, rock and debris—slides down the slope, a stretch of land where nothing but bare dirt and stone holds it in place. I grip the windowsill, my mouth falling open as I watch in stunned silence. The weight of it crashes onto the asphalt below, a relentless, fast-moving force that's swallowed the highway to the south, leaving nothing but chaos in its wake.

My mind races. If this landslide was centered directly across from the house, we would've been washed clear off the cliff in a matter of minutes.

We're each in a state of shock, speechless. All we can do is listen, mesmerized, as the haunting sound of large boulders knock together, a series of low growls or the gurgling of a deep, swollen river, as if the ground itself is groaning under the weight of its own collapse.

Time stands still until gradually the noise begins to decrease in volume. The ground beneath the house feels treacherous in its wake. We stand, frozen, our bodies tense and still as we absorb the overwhelming sound and sensation of the earth shifting, each of us caught in a shared, paralyzed moment of disbelief. The air itself is thick with moisture, heavy as I slowly begin to exhale.

I unclench my fist and check my cell phone frantically for coverage. Nothing. Why Serena let her landline go during these past few years of wildfire evacuations I have no idea. Not smart. Too late.

"Stay away from the door!" Serena yells, her hand raised in front of her, palm out, cautious, hesitant movements like she's trying to ward off the chaos. "Wait—there could be flooding or more slides coming."

"We need to evacuate," River says, their voice tight, in a move toward the door.

Serena disagrees. Her body language is strong and assertive, leaning slightly forward as she issues her orders, making it clear she's in control of the situation despite her nervous shifts of weight: "There are likely more slides further along the highway. And it's too dangerous at the waterfront right now. You go down to the basement, River, turn off the electric and the propane line and grab the first aid kit."

Even a small gas leak could be lethal. We all know that. I offer to help. The heaviness of the moment is reflected in every small action, from our shallow breathing, to slow, tentative steps.

"I know the drill," River replies, furtively. Their voice is low but firm and their hands gesture in a calming manner, almost like a way of signaling that they know what needs to be done and don't need anyone else to intervene. "You all stay here."

"Tamsin. Eva, help me gather the valuables, documents and such—the Grateful Dead posters," Serena points to the cabinet under the kitchen sink. "Stick whatever you think is important into trash bags."

She instructs Bobby and Nate to throw our clothing into the various duffels we'd traveled here with.

"Best to get it all outside, under the cover of tarps, away from the house," Serena says. "Should we need to get out fast."

By the time we've grabbed whatever she deems essential, the loud, rumbling noise has dissipated. Though in the distance, I hear what may be more movement in the opposite direction. I'm shaking, though my adrenaline is definitely kicking in, displacing the sick, sinking sensation in my stomach. I desperately want to be out searching for Jamie instead of offloading Serena's faded memorabilia, but we're stranded here now.

The lid slides off the top of a heavy box filled with old photo albums I'm hauling out to the front porch. The others are outside helping River assemble a canopy they've unearthed in the basement. I spot a stack of journals tucked in alongside the albums. I rifle through and hurriedly read Serena's name on the covers. Seeing as nobody's looking, I shuffle purposefully through the chronological stack until I find her 2013 journal.

It's all here. In writing. I rapidly scan her entries from what was basically, in my mind, Operation Jamie Seduction. My hands tremble nervously as I flick through the pages to the week before I returned to California from the UK. It started a couple of days after Mum and I had buried Gran on a bittersweet sunny day in the small graveyard of the pebbled church overlooking the North Sea. My posture is tense, shoulders tight. I don't have time to torture myself with the graphic details, so I skim forward, my breath shallow as I focus on what she'd written after she discovered my imminent return.

My expression flickers with a mixture of pain and disbelief, my lips pressed together. I pause for a moment, my body stiffening as I try to steady myself, gripping the journal more tightly.

"There's nothing more to it," Serena had written in her perfect, cursive penmanship. *"He's beating himself up for what he has to do now to confess. It's not as if I forced him into it. Cheating takes two. So, what if I did embellish the*

idea that Tam was done with it, with him—this whole scam of a Green Card marriage that I had concocted in the first place? My last chance and I took it."

It's astonishingly simple how she'd dismantled everything we'd shared. I'm torn—both furious with myself for needing to absorb the information and yet oddly comforted by the fact that Serena's lie about me abandoning Jamie for good was her own mistake, her own undoing.

"If I can't have him then neither will she," she'd underlined, twice. *"I gave it one last try, and I guess it's clear he's more into his wife-of-convenience than I thought. The moment she catches wind of what we've been up to she'll bolt—quick as hell. If I know Tamsin, she won't put up much of a fight. She's way too conflict adverse and polite for all that."*

My eyes sting in their sockets. A deception laid out, fully confessed. And I'd walked straight into the trapdoor she'd left open.

"If he'd adored me even half as much as he claims he does her, then I'd be content," Serena had added at the bottom of her entry. *"Even if he loves her as he swears that he does, then he's going to have one hell of a time attempting to win her back."*

And what had I done? Played into her hands. My stomach churns as I realize it—I walked out on him just like she'd predicted, no fight, no resistance. What a fool! Serena had nailed it. My breath comes in sharp, uneven gasps as I fold the journal in half, my hands trembling violently as I slip it into a deep pocket inside of my jacket. I can feel the heat rising in my chest, a tightness gripping my throat. I know exactly what I have to do. I'll rip out those pages—tear them to shreds—and burn every last word in the back of the woodburning stove. The thought of watching them ignite, curl, and turn to ash, makes my pulse race. When it's done, it'll be over. All of it. I can feel the weight lifting, clarity settling in like a heavy fog clearing.

Had I really been that easy to manipulate? Jamie and me both. We were so easy to play—but that ended the day I left. We each paid the price, but apart.

River, who has headed back up the path in a near torrential downpour, takes the box from my arms as we rush to ferry more paraphernalia down to the canopied area. I hold my arms to my sides to hold the journal in place.

"Won't the wind whip through this flimsy thing?" I ask, pointing to the canopy. My voice is barely audible over the roar of the storm.

River claims it can be anchored more securely: "though it may tear into shreds which is why we need to weigh down the tarp covers."

I help pull the edges of the tarp taut, my fingers slippery with rainwater as we struggle to tie the knots. The downpour soaks through my clothes, making each movement heavier, more difficult. My hands are cold and the ropes slip between my fingers with every attempt but I grit my teeth and tighten them as best I can. The wind is picking up, howling through the trees and I can feel the strain in the tarp, already fluttering like a flag caught in a storm.

River pulls at a corner of the tarp, securing it to a nearby post with a bit more force than necessary, eyes squinting through the downpour.

"The landslide closest to us seems to have settled," Nate declares, his voice tinged with weariness as he wipes rain from his brow. He and Billy have cautiously made their way across the blocked highway, their figures barely visible through the sheets of rain, drenched from head to toe despite full rain gear. The ground beneath them is slick and unstable and their movements have been slow, deliberate, as they've navigated the few hundred yards of treacherous terrain.

"We can't get through from the south. It's a mess down there." Nate pauses, shifting his weight and glancing northward, his face grim. "And the bad news is, there's been another, a second, smaller slide further up to the north."

Billy nods, his jaw clenched, his eyes scanning the horizon, his body tense as if he can still feel the pull of the earth's instability beneath his feet. The rain continues to fall in relentless torrents, soaking us to the bone, adding to our growing sense of urgency and frustration. The two of them exchange a brief, silent look, knowing the severity of the situation now.

"Jamie?" I snap, my voice raw with urgency. "We have to figure out where he is, now!"

My cell phone bars remain at zero as my mind floods with horrific images of him in the ocean, fighting against the cold, choppy water. I turn my back on the others and race down to the beach, my eyes desperately searching for any trace of his boat.

"He did say he'd dive near the house," Serena calls out, breathless, as she catches up with me. Her hair has come loose, streaming behind her like a pale-yellow, rain-soaked kite. "Though I doubt he had enough time to motor all the way up here, anchor, set up his fins and gear."

It stings that she knows his routine.

"The dude is fearless. Experienced," River says, catching up to her side, their breath coming in sharp gasps as they keep pace. We're stumbling down the slippery rock path, my feet sliding, the cold rain drenching us with each step. Behind us, debris rushes downhill, crashing into a swirling mass of driftwood and weathered logs the size of utility poles. The sound of the water is deafening, pulling at my focus. "He's a big advocate for safe diving," River adds, their voice strained, muscles working hard against the wet, uneven terrain. "As soon as the storm hit, I'm sure he would've turned back for the harbor right away."

But Serena doesn't seem reassured. Her face is taut, her eyes fixed on the roiling horizon, brow furrowed in deep concern. The wind howls in her ears but she presses on, voice low and laced with worry. "Trouble is," she says, her gaze never leaving the horizon, her body rigid as if bracing for something more, "thunder and lightning together are a diver's worst nightmare. The wind and waves can turn dangerous in an instant." She exhales sharply, her hand clenched into a fist at her side, the cold sinking into her bones. "I hate to say it, but if lightning hits his boat, it could be disastrous. There's no cabin to take cover in." Her words hang in the air like a heavy fog, suffocating all other thoughts. We all know the risk, but none of us can shake the growing pit of dread in our stomachs.

"Okay, let's take it easy," River says, as they grip my arm. "He's gonna stay as low as he can in the boat given the situation. If only we'd left fifteen minutes later, we could've waited it out in the harbor instead of dealing with this on the open water."

None of this is doing anything to ease the terrible doom-knot raveling within my stomach. "You think a life jacket would help in a storm like this?" I ask. "And what about a signaling device if his radio's shot?"

We desperately weigh the possibility of there being other sport fishermen and divers out there on the ocean equally unaware of what was about to hit.

"Surely at least one marine radio will alert the Coast Guard with a distress call?" River suggests.

Serena gasps. "The Raven. And his mother. They'll for sure be watching this play out. They warned us after all. If they see anything at all they're our best bet to be onto emergency services."

I one thousand percent take back anything negative I said earlier with regards to the Raven. A hundred thousand percent. Suddenly he and his mother are my closest allies in the slim possibility of bringing Jamie back alive.

"He's gonna need to find a narrow stretch of water to anchor the boat," River says. "Otherwise, he risks being pushed ashore. He's mentioned once or twice how he anchors from the bow to keep the boat facing the waves just in case conditions are bad enough to lose visibility during a dive."

Billy and Nate burst back onto the scene, their breaths ragged and heavy from sprinting downhill, their rain-soaked faces flushed with exertion. Each of them is gripping a wetsuit, the fabric heavy in their hands, water dripping from them like a soaked sponge. They skid to a halt, mud splashing beneath their feet as Eva comes up just behind them, her movements swift and urgent. Her hair sticks to her forehead, a few strands tangled with the rain.

"I found these," Nate says, panting, holding the wetsuits out toward us. His arms tremble slightly from the run, but his eyes are sharp, focused. The fabric of the suits looks wrinkled and damp, as if they've been shoved into a corner for years but they're still usable. "Whoever's the strongest swimmer should suit up just in case we have to go in after him." His voice carries the weight of both hope and dread. We all know what he's suggesting—someone may have to dive into the churning water to search for Jamie. There's no denying the urgency, the cold fear settling over us like a thick blanket.

"Jesus, Nate," Eva snaps. "None of us are qualified for ocean rescue. You know that."

"It's as treacherous as it gets out there right now," Serena adds, gesturing to a patch of foam. "The areas where the waves aren't breaking, where you see foam and sediment being pulled back into the ocean—that's where the worst of the rip currents are. Stay clear of them. The last thing we need is a sleeper wave coming in and catching us off guard."

I'm no diver, as previously established with my recounting of my pathetic record of issues with buoyancy, but I am a fairly strong open water swimmer. I learned the basics as a child and teen, spending summers with Gran, swimming alongside her in the summer waters of the North Sea. And my years of living in close proximity to the coast in the UK and in the safer stretches of water in California have taught me a lot.

The gentle stretch of soft, golden sand in the East of England, lined with vibrant beach huts and dotted with mud flats, salt marshes, shingle, and pebbles, feels suddenly even more of a world apart from the rugged, wind-swept cliffs and crashing waves of Northern California's Pacific coastline.

We all know that the Sonoma Coast is one of the most treacherous places to swim even on the calmest days with some of the strongest rip currents around. Add the heavy storm surf and unpredictable ground currents and it becomes a deadly mix.

But none of that matters to me right now. I don't hesitate for even a second. I grab one of the wetsuits, tearing off my sodden clothes and leaving myself in nothing but my underwear. My heart is racing, my breath coming in shallow bursts, but I don't feel fear—just a raw, desperate need to get to him. It's like my body's taken over, my sympathetic nervous system surging with adrenaline, pushing me into motion, ignoring the cold wind and rain pounding against my skin. My mind barely keeps up, just trying to focus on the one thing that matters—getting to Jamie before it's too late.

"Serena, grab the first aid kit," I order, enunciating as clearly as I can. "And a rope. Who's coming with me?"

It's River who suits up alongside me. "If we're going in, we stay calm," they urge. "Do not attempt to swim directly to shore, move sideways across the rip current."

I whip my head to the south, my eyes catching a glint of metal, shimmering faintly in the choppy distance. A surge of hope explodes within me and before I can fully process it, I'm launching myself into the air, my body moving on pure instinct. I scream instructions at the top of my lungs, my voice raw and desperate, as I wave my arms frantically above my head. In that moment, everything feels like it's happening in slow motion.

Serena is back, charging down the shore like a force of nature, her whistle piercing the chaos of the storm. She's got a flashlight, and Eva's right beside her. It's a blur of motion and sound, but there's a flicker of hope burning brighter now, like a beacon cutting through the darkness.

A partially capsized boat, 300 meters from shore comes into sharper view. We watch helplessly as it flips before our eyes.

A wet-suited figure—Jamie, it must be—appears, barely visible through the chaos of the savage waves, struggling dangerously close to the boat. There's no sign of a life jacket and as he shifts with the pull of the rip current his body seems to stall between the crests. Panic grips me—*he's tangled in kelp,* I know it. My heart races but I can see enough to know he's not giving up. He's strong, resilient, and fit enough that, for now, he's holding on—fighting the cold and the violent surf. But I can't shake the terror that, any second, the waves could take him under.

"It's not safe!" Serena yells, yanking River back by the arm. "Are you out of your mind?" The boat sinks into the churning water and vanishes, leaving the figure we think is Jamie frozen in the same spot, helpless. "You'll drown, both of you!" she shouts, her voice raw with panic.

I wade into the cold surf, the icy water biting at my hands and feet and attacking the thin layer of adrenaline coursing through me. Every step forward feels like I'm pushing through a thick, invisible wall. As soon as I'm past the shallows, the heavy waves crash down on me, each one slamming into my chest, flipping me over and pulling me under. My mouth fills with saltwater that burns and stings as I choke, coughing violently, the taste of brine thick on my tongue. My lungs burn for air, but it's impossible to get a full breath as the waves keep pounding me, dragging me deeper into the tumult.

I'm only a few feet from the sandbar, but it feels like miles. The ground beneath me shifts, the winter storms having reshaped the sea bed, the sand like quicksand, pulling at my legs and threatening to drag me under. The air smells of salt and seaweed, sharp and heavy, mixing with the scent of wet earth as the tide shifts. The cold wind cuts at my face, a sharp contrast to the heat rising in my chest.

I can't stop, though. I force myself to stay composed even as panic claws at the edges of my mind. River's somewhere out here with me but I don't know where. I focus on the water, the dark, murky depths, trusting only my instincts to guide me through the waves as I fight my way toward Jamie.

Each wave is a battle. I angle my head into the chop, bracing against the force, breathing in short, desperate gasps, the air thin and salty as I tuck my nose and mouth under my armpit, trying to shield it from the constant spray. The wetsuit feels restrictive, tight around my chest, but it's the only thing keeping me from freezing in the icy water—probably no warmer than fifty degrees, the cold seeping into my bones. My skin tingles where it's exposed, the biting chill burning through the wet fabric like needles.

I reach Jamie, by some extreme miracle. It's him as I knew it was with every fiber of my soul. He catches my arm and holds me close to his body as I attempt to tread water. No sooner have I caught my breath when a huge wave smacks into us and takes us under. My heart beats like a drum. The air is being dragged from my lungs. My ears are filled with the sound and sensation of thunder. Everything happens in slow motion. I'm not sure which way is up or down. Absolute lack of control. I let go and all I can do is submit to a rhythmic force that is far more powerful than me. In doing so it shoots me with some strange, magnetic strength up toward the glimmer of light.

River's head pops up beside us as we gasp for air. At first, I think they're a seal. They raise an arm and brandish the knife we used yesterday for foraging seaweed. They disappear in several attempts of free diving for what feels like forever, submerging and taking a series of rapid breaks in between waves.

As River finally breaks the surface, gasping for more air, Jamie rises up like a buoy. "Float!" he yells, his hands reaching out for mine and River's. He's freed from the tangle of kelp and there's no time to waste. We need to get back to shore.

"Float!" Jamie repeats, more urgently this time. "Hold onto my hand and float. Don't fight the current, it'll take you under."

I swallow another mouthful of saltwater, the sting of it burning my throat. Panic surges in my chest as I imagine me getting tangled in the kelp next, my limbs caught and dragged down. Floating is all I can hope for now. It's my only choice. I must believe I can do it.

"Face the waves and follow them back to shore at an angle," River calls, their voice strained, but firm. They point an arm, directing us toward the path we need to take.

I grip Jamie's hand, holding my body as still as I can, desperately trying to remain as calm as possible, despite the beating of my heart and the roar of the surf around us. The water tugs relentlessly but I follow River's instructions, angling my body just enough to ride the waves, praying they'll carry us back to safety.

Jamie tries to lever my body upward, urging me toward the surface but the force of the surf rips my hand from his grasp and he vanishes into the undertow. I'm thrown into a tumble, spinning, diving, desperately fumbling through the dark, cold water for what feels like an eternity. My heart continues to pound in my chest as I finally make contact—his shoulder, the wetsuit slick with seawater. I grab it with everything I've got and yank him upward, pulling him toward the dim, angry light of the sky above. With a quick, desperate move, I cradle his head against the crook of my arm, keeping him afloat, struggling to stay above water myself.

For once in my life, I float, belly button upwards toward heaven, head back, pulling the water with my free arm, regulating my breathing as best I can. The trouble is, it's all the same color, the ocean, the sky . . . I'm not sure I can do this much longer.

The intense current weakens about a hundred yards from shore and I swim out of it, sideways, diagonally, through the breaking waves, floating again to catch my breath and somehow, miraculously, still managing to tow Jamie in along with me.

River is already ashore, their feet planted firmly in the sand. They step back into the surf, hauling Jamie's limp body toward the shore, dragging him onto the beach. I collapse beside them, my body like a beached whale and I just let go—sobbing uncontrollably, overwhelmed by a wave of relief so intense it hurts. It's over. I can barely wrap my head around it. We're safe.

Late Sunday Afternoon

Wet sand beneath is gritty and cold as I drop to my knees, my hands trembling as I check Jamie's neck for a pulse. My heart skips more than a beat but I don't have time to panic. The air is thick with salt and damp, the ocean behind me churning violently, a broken line of white foam crashing onto the shore. The smell of seaweed and brine hangs heavy in the cold April air. I quickly assess his airway—it's clear—and I snap into action. My fingers are numb, but I work quickly, pressing one hand against his cold, damp forehead while my other slides beneath his chin to tilt his head back.

Pinching his nose shut with my thumb and forefinger, I let his mouth fall open, the sharp tang of salt still lingering in the back of my throat. The ocean's roar feels like it's miles away as I inhale deeply, steadying myself, before sealing my lips over his. I blow into his mouth, watching closely as his chest rises with the first breath, praying it's enough, praying the sea hasn't taken him from me.

I force myself to stay calm, focusing on the task at hand. With the heel of one hand, I press firmly into the center of his chest, my other hand stacked on top. I interlock my fingers, hoping to avoid the probability of breaking any ribs. My heart pounds in my chest, echoing in my ears like a war drum, the frantic rhythm of each beat matching my urgency. I press down hard, keeping my arms straight as I lean over him, counting the compressions in my head—thirty before I give him two more breaths. The minutes stretch on, every second feeling like an eternity but I don't stop. I repeat the cycle again and again, each compression, each breath, until finally, his body jerks under my hands. He stirs. I roll him onto his side and within seconds, he coughs up what feels like half the ocean. Saltwater spills from his mouth in thick, choking waves.

Goosebumps rise under the fabric of my wetsuit. Jamie's physical conditioning—combined with the way he kept his cool when he saw us in the water—likely saved his life. A weaker person wouldn't have lasted as long out there, the relentless pull of the ocean dragging them toward an underwater grave.

A helicopter suddenly swoops into view, its rotors chopping through the air with a deafening roar. For a brief moment, it feels like something out of a ridiculous action movie I've scripted in my head—an instant rescue, too perfectly timed to be real. I stand there, speechless, as it hovers overhead, then lands in a dramatic swirl of dirt and sand not fifty feet away. Authorities must have been alerted by a Mayday call. The Raven and Kaya somewhere out there along the coast? My heart skips another beat, lurching in my chest.

"Uni diving, you say?" A medic with a stone-cold expression steps out of the chopper, immediately kneeling beside Jamie. She inspects a wound on his leg with practiced calm. "A dangerous sport at the best of times." As if I didn't already know that. "Good thing you kept your wits about you and your husband is physically fit. Otherwise, there's no way he'd have survived being tangled in kelp for much longer in these conditions."

I nod, trying to steady myself, though I can't help but feel the weight of her words. I'm sure Jamie would've grabbed his cutting device if he'd known he was about to be thrown in the water. I glance at her, trying to explain. "He's had years of experience with kelp forest preservation," I say, my voice trembling. She hands me two shiny mylar blankets, but it's no match for the cold that's settling deep in my bones. I wrap one around Jamie, but it does nothing to stop the shivering.

"That may be, but you two being present at the exact right time most certainly saved his life," she addresses River and me. It's sobering to consider she does this kind of thing on a regular basis—dealing with fools like us who have willingly put ourselves into the path of peril.

"Hypothermia is a concern. His body's been exposed to the cold for an extended time. We'll check his heart and respiratory system," she says.

I nod, though I don't bother mentioning my own medical training. Right now, I'm too consumed with Jamie's getting out of here to care about anything else.

"Conditions are prime for fatalities along the coast this weekend," she says, her tone flat but knowing. "People should stay out of the water when it's like this. With the highway blocked, air rescue is the only way we can respond."

Every nerve in my body feels electric, alive with tension. The team begins loading Jamie onto a stretcher when the medic pauses for a moment and turns back toward me, acknowledging the urgency in my eyes.

"A diver should never, ever dive alone," she says.

I don't know that it would have made any difference in these specific circumstances. Wouldn't it have put yet another life at risk if any one of us had been out there with Jamie from the outset? I hold my hand on my heart as I silently pledge to stay on his case for the rest of his diving life.

"Consider yourself lucky this time, Jamie my love," I whisper, my voice barely a breath. He's conscious, but barely—his eyelids fluttering, his body still cold. I brush my lips gently against his blue ones, then let go of his hand as they prepare to lift him onto the chopper. "Don't you dare slip away on me. I'll be there as soon as I can," I promise, my voice steady despite the tightness in my chest.

"Well. This little escapade quite literally blows our carbon footprint out of the water," Nate attempts to make light, breaking the tension above the din of the helicopter as it takes off.

"To think, the very thing Jamie was so hell-bent on maintaining, came close to taking him out," he adds.

We're all equally freaked out. Eva is staring blankly out into the ocean. Billy is the first to open up as we head up to the house, me and River trailing in our Mylar blankets, shivering and shaking wildly as the adrenaline wears off. Eva has our discarded clothes in her arms. My mind flashes to the journal pages that are undoubtedly soggy in the inside pocket of my jacket that was so hurriedly thrown onto the sand.

"So much for our survive-the-climate-apocalypse theme," Eva says. "I mean, how many boujee college roommate-reunions get to claim the triple whammy of a power outage, a series of mudslides and an air-sea rescue helicopter in their weekend itinerary?"

"Look, let's not forget, the forecast was for spring sunshine from Friday through Monday," Serena insists, her voice firm but laced with regret. She reaches for her partner's ice-cold hand, her thumb gently stroking their knuckles in a rare, tender gesture. Her body leans in to River's, a silent shield as if she's trying to offer warmth in a way that goes beyond the touch of her hand—offering herself, her presence, in the hope it might ease the chill between them.

River turns, gently pulling their hand away from Serena's and pressing a finger to their lips, signaling for us all to be quiet. "Jamie aimed to anchor in shallow water," they say, their voice low but steady. "We all know that. Who could blame him for assuming he was safe? It was an isolated freak storm is all." River pauses, their eyes scanning the turbulent waters, then adds with a quiet certainty, "The truth is that bull kelp restoration hotspot right here—it was way too tempting to pass up."

Before he left, Jamie had described his diving into a kelp forest for the first time as unlike anything he'd ever experienced.

"He only took up with this whole urchin effort of his after I moved out," I share as I do the math in my head. He had garnered almost a decade of kelp forest restoration in the years since we'd gone our own ways. This hits home as to how long we've been apart.

Nate turns his attention first to me, then to Serena. "I think we've all had more than enough of the ocean for today," he declares. He points to the house. "But do we really think it's safe for us to head back inside?"

A vast, displaced mass of mud and debris stretches down the slope on the highway in jagged, uneven layers. We stand in a line and look out at the scene. The highway we traveled to get here is now buried under thick sludge, loose rocks, uprooted plants and the remnants of trees half-sub-merged, their roots twisted grotesquely. The horizon is blurred by a cloud of mist stirred up from the slide.

There's a feeling of a return to awe as we witness the aftermath of some-thing so powerful and unpredictable. The sensation of the earth beneath our feet and the eerie sight of the damage done reminding us of nature's force and unpredictability. At the same time, there's the discomfort of the uncertain terrain beneath and the sheer unpredictability of the landscape. A palpable sense of danger hangs in the air.

"Yes. Are you sure we're okay to go back in, Serena?" Billy adds, his tone skeptical. "I mean, our lives are worth more than a pile of old hippy shit, surely?"

"Power's off," Serena replies. "River double-checked the gas line from the propane. We should be fine for now. Besides," she says, looking at River and me. "These two need to be warmed up immediately. Besides, what choice do we have for tonight? Unless you want to spend it out here on the beach?"

The scent of wet soil and decomposing organic matter fills my nostrils. An acrid tang of fresh mud mingles with a faint smell of plants and rotting wood. A mineral scent of the earth mixed with the sharp freshness of rain. I'm cold and faint.

"Let's get into gear, guys, put that woodburning stove into business," River urges. Their teeth are chattering like a pair of cymbals clashing in a fresh storm, frantic and uncontrollable. Mine too.

"Did anyone remember to pull out the plugs on the various appliances?" Eva asks.

"I turned off the main breaker," River replies. I look at my hands, which have taken on a pale, almost ghostly hue. My skin has turned a bluish white as if drained of color, veins standing out prominently, blue and purple tones contrasting against the flushed whiteness of my skin.

There's a numbness to the sensation of my feet, like there is ice beneath my skin. It feels like they are temporarily disconnected from my legs, unable to move with the same fluidity as I step clumsily forward into the house.

Sunday Early Evening

Hot water bottles are filled with water that's boiling on the surface of the wood stove, steam rising in the cold air. We're out of our wetsuits, River and me, each of us mercifully dry, wrapped in warm sweats and blankets as we snuggle together on the couch. Our bare feet, still cold and aching, poke out from beneath the covers, submerged in metal basins filled with the first of the warm water, my idea to help thaw us out faster.

Two pairs of thick, wooly socks sit ready, waiting for dry feet. With the power out and the electric water heater useless, there's no point in showering. So, we huddle close, clutching mugs of steaming hot toddies—whiskey, honey, lemon and hot water—to warm our insides and ward off the lingering chill from the ocean.

The shock of the risky open-water rescue lingers, settling into my bones. My hands tremble every so often and I grip the arm of the sofa to steady myself. It feels as though my heart was ripped out of my chest and carried over the hills to Santa Rosa in that helicopter with Jamie. I never dared imagine we'd reconnect like this—never thought I could resonate with another human being the way I have with him.

Kentucky bourbon, Nate informs—the base spirit of our hot toddies, a big and flavorful, pot-distilled bourbon from an open bottle he'd un-earthed from the pantry. I discover a slither of lemon peel in my mug and also, what is it? A clove, which slips through my lips as I raise the warming liquid to my mouth.

The presence of the others, along with the warmth of the alcohol, helps to ease my frayed nerves. But deep down, I'm still struggling to admit to myself that I actually saved Jamie's life—River and me, together. The fact that I had it in me, that I could step up in that moment, is a revelation, let alone the floating part. Minnie and Myrtle are curled up on River's and my laps, their tiny bodies warm against us as they doze peacefully, the soft rhythm of their shallow yelps escaping in their sleep. The warmth of our bodies and the heat from the woodstove surround them, and they seem completely unaware of the chaos that unfolded earlier. The dogs were inside during the rescue, blissfully oblivious to the drama of the afternoon.

My instincts tell me that it's too soon for any real sense of peace to prevail after such a close call. I know all too well how fragile Jamie was when they lifted him into that helicopter—his condition far from stable, his survival still uncertain.

The initial rush of relief is starting to fade and the weight of the situation is creeping back in. I know better than to fall for the false sense of security the warmth around me offers. This house isn't the safest place right now but as Serena pointed out, we really don't have any other option.

"You must be starving. What we all need is some comfort food, a little soul food, you know?" Eva says, reading my mind like she always does. "Serena, let's see if we can cook something up on the woodstove."

Nate and Billy urge us to close our eyes for a much-needed rest while the two of them assist Serena and Eva in the kitchen. I don't know about River but I must've dropped off, despite my anxiety, for the next thing I know there's a pot of lentil soup bubbling on the woodstove, hints of garlic, onion and cumin in the air. A cast iron skillet is brimming with biscuits that are browning nicely, filling the room with a buttery, toasty aroma. It's like waking up in a bygone time and what I imagine as the sheer, nostalgic pleasure of early beach-house-cooking.

I close my eyes and I'm transformed back as a small girl to my own grandmother's cottage by the sea. The sweetened British version of biscuits, Gran's tea-time raisin scones fluffing up in the Aga, my favorite treat, served with clotted cream and sweet strawberry jam. I'm grasping for a sense of stability, I suppose. Though the second I open my eyes, it slips through my fingers.

"None of us could've predicted this," Eva says, stretching out on the rug in a cat/cow yoga pose that opens up her spine and likely is helping to ease her own stress. "What happened here today is proof that we're going to called to be bolder, way more fearless and . . . creative going forward. What we used to consider rare, on the weather-front, is no longer so."

Billy joins her on the floor, straightening his back, stretching his arms out around him like tree branches.

"Imagine us a decade from now," he suggests, hands resting confidently on his hips. "A few more gray hairs. Maybe a little softer around the middle. But we'll be together in a place we've created—our forever home. This is the vision we need to hold onto, guys. We're fully capable of building a future that nurtures our creativity, our ability to innovate for the unpredictable future. The real question is, how do we best prepare for the crazy climate-driven danger zone that's coming our way?"

River chimes in, "And at the same time, we must be prepared to help others, don't you think? We'd better be ready for it. A whole new kind of life—one that is driven far less by greed and way more by our humanitarian efforts."

Nate drains a second hot toddy and sets his empty glass on a stack of books on the coffee table.

"What now?" he asks, eyes wide as he meets Billy's disapproving gaze. "I'm in shock. We all are. I'm not drinking any more than anyone else. Think of it as my last hurrah if that makes you feel any better."

He's rambling about being a grown-up, smart enough to know he'll need to scale back now that there's a baby on the way.

"Allow me one last wicked weekend," he pleads. "If you must know, I'm mentally prepping for my evolution into the zenith of model fathership."

Billy replies that he'd best start the training soon. "If you're setting your sights on American Dad, that is."

Nate laughs at this suggestion, rolling onto his side of the rug to catch Minnie as she leaps off my lap. I close my eyes, imagining myself sitting at a kitchen table, assisting Billy, Nate and Eva's child with their math and science homework. Maybe we'll be homeschooling, alongside any other kids born into our community. Maybe a child of my own. Though the plan, in so little that has been discussed so far is to send any offspring to mainstream schools, so they don't get labeled as "commune kids" and to give them a fair shot at being socialized.

The pandemic lockdown reminded us just how quickly everything can shift. And I can't imagine we won't experience at least another in our lifetime.

"It's as if this time is a kind of portal between the past and whatever comes next," I think aloud. I don't know where this came from. It's not like me, but then, honestly, I never, in a million years, would've imagined myself diving into the riptide like I did today.

It's shaken me to my core but at the same time, the rescue has filled me with an uncharacteristic sense of confidence for taking on whatever comes next.

Serena agrees that this weekend's experience feels like a major turning point in our lives. "I mean, we all know there are going to be huge challenges ahead," she says. "So many systems are broken. What an opportunity we have if we can come together now and forge ourselves a solid new path, create a better way of living."

Eva stretches. She raises her arms above her head, lowering them back down slowly to her lap. Then she sets about removing multiple chunky rings from her fingers, laying them on a dish on the coffee table.

"It's true," she says. "The idea of a stable, secure community, of being fully rooted, it's a shift back to the old times is all. Clean food, fresh air, surrounding ourselves with animals, nature. Who wouldn't want that?"

She holds her hands up to her face to inspect them. I notice how her fingers have swollen at this hour of day.

"But for now, let's eat," she says.

The first spoonful of lentil soup is like a warm hug. The broth is rich but not heavy, a deep, savory warmth that settles in and comforts me from the inside out. Then, there's the biscuit. The skillet has done its magic, crisping the edges just enough while leaving the inside tender and fluffy. I break it apart with ease, steam rising from the soft, buttery interior. The first bite is light but filling, with that comforting, slightly sweet and salty taste. I dip it into the soup and the two flavors meld together—earthy, savory lentils with the buttery, flaky biscuit. It's a perfect balance of textures and warmth, a bite that feels like home should feel. Each mouthful is both nourishing and indulgent, the kind of meal that makes me forget about the world outside. At least for the brief time it takes to consume.

I look down at my own hands. I think of my wedding ring. We'd picked out a cheap, gold-plated band with fake diamonds in a thrift store jewelry counter in time for the interview with immigration authorities. Jamie's was a plain, sterling silver band, heavier, more substantial. I bought it for him from a street vendor on State Street. We had a standing joke for years that we'd replace mine with a real diamond one day if we ever had any money. I still have the original, tucked away in the jewelry case I've had since childhood. It's in there alongside Gran's gold watch and the heart-shaped locket she was wearing when she passed.

The sound of waves crashing against the rocks is amplified in the gloomy last light of day. Shadows cast across the six of us as we sit, quietly, more subdued now, waiting for darkness to fall upon our cozy scene like the soft lid of the velvet-trimmed box.

"I'll grab the candles," Serena says. "I should've gotten them ready earlier. Not sure what I was thinking."

River insists she shouldn't go down to the basement alone in the dark.

However, "You stay here, stay warm. I'll take a flashlight," Serena replies.

Billy jumps up and joins her, regardless of her seeming independence.

"Well, if you're insistent, there's a box of assorted Mexican prayer candles down there," River instructs. "The Holy Family, Sacred Heart of Jesus, Our Lady of Guadalupe, Saint Michael Archangel . . ."

"I didn't know you'd taken up as a Catholic," Eva remarks.

River was raised on a lakeside dairy farm in southern Minnesota by Evangelical Lutheran grandparents. Since their grandfather died the year after we graduated, their grandmother, Betty Jo has apparently relied on her one living son, River's uncle, Jed, to keep the farm from going under. Last time we talked, River told me about the wide, flat land of neighboring farms being leased out to a West Coast solar developer. So far, Uncle Jed isn't having any of it, opposed to the idea of steel and aluminum panels taking over the green fields of the family's historic dairy farm.

"Lutheran agricultural roots run deep in these veins, even though I turned my back on it all when I left town," River says, twisting their hands in the dim light, faint blue veins along their inner wrists.

"Forget about religion, it's technology that's breaking the cycle of rural America," Nate says. "But the truth is, the country needs both solar and agriculture."

River leans back slightly, stretching their arms and rubbing the back of their neck as they talk, the weariness in their posture mirroring the strain in their voice. "It's hard to make any money out of small-scale dairy these days," they say, a sigh escaping as they glance down, hands fiddling with the hem of their shirt. "And Jed's getting older. Leasing to a solar company would undoubtedly bring peace of mind financially." They look up, meeting Eva's gaze, eyes soft but tired.

Eva tilts her head, intrigued, her fingers tapping rhythmically on the table as she shifts her focus. "What's keeping Betty Jo going?" she asks, her voice a little gentler now.

River chuckles softly, the corners of their lips twitching upwards, but the smile doesn't quite reach their eyes. They take a moment, looking out the window as if weighing their words, before responding. "God's love and grace are limitless according to Betty Jo," they say, nodding slightly, before their expression softens with a faint shrug. "And seeing as there is no limit to her and God's forgiveness, you'll be happy to hear she's seen fit to examine her past discriminations."

Eva's eyebrows shoot up, genuinely surprised. "Really?" Her voice cracks with shock, a spark of disbelief in her tone. She leans forward, hands resting on her knees, her posture unconsciously mirroring River's anticipation.

"Oh yes," River says with a sly grin, tapping their fingers together thoughtfully. "I'm pleased to report she has officially forgiven me my sins."

Eva's eyes widen further. She places a hand on her chest, pretending to be scandalized. "You mean you're no longer doomed to a state of everlasting shame and torment?" she teases.

River smirks, shrugging one shoulder. "Not devious enough after all, it appears!"

"I guess it was your determination to do your own thing in Lutheran preschool which was the first indication that you were not headed smoothly into the fold," Serena says, returning to the room with a cardboard box filled with candles in her arms. "Betty Jo had an idea of the wild ride she was in for with you and your unorthodox outfits."

I feel a sense of happiness and relief knowing that River has reconnected with what's left of their family. They explain how, over the years, they'd been testing the waters with occasional phone calls and short visits. Last year, it turned out that River's help was needed when Betty Jo had to undergo a double hip replacement. River and Serena took a month out of their lives to help Jed care for her. Betty Jo quickly warmed to Serena's charms—no surprise there—and never once after did she mention her previous issue with River's chosen identity.

"In fact, we even brought up the subject of the farm as a possibility for the pact," River says. "Serena explained the concept to Betty Jo, in-depth. Even Uncle Jed heard us out. It's just the two of them now and there's no shortage of space."

This is news to me. As I've said, I'd prefer we narrow in on a West Coast spot, regardless of cost.

"Seriously?" Nate asks, raising an eyebrow and crossing his arms, a hint of incredulity etched on his face. "I mean, come on, it could be interesting." He leans forward slightly, his voice lowering as he adds, "It's a pretty sizeable farmhouse, isn't it? If we were to buy in, we should think about building new units on the property for your family." He gestures animatedly with his hands as if sketching out the possibilities in the air. "Renovating the big house wouldn't be all that complicated, surely? And there'd be plenty of room to figure out additional units to suit our individual needs."

Billy leans back, nodding enthusiastically, his eyes lighting up with excitement. "If your uncle did come around to a partial solar lease," he adds, leaning in slightly, "it would be a no-brainer." He spreads his arms wide, envisioning the potential. "The rest of the land would be easily re-purposed for small-scale, self-sufficient farming. Plant a bunch of shade trees, beehives, an orchard."

Eva shifts in her seat, her brows furrowing as she looks from Nate to Billy. "Who will inherit the farm after your uncle passes?" she asks, her tone turning serious, a mix of curiosity and concern reflecting in her eyes. "What happened to your cousin?"

River leans back in their chair, arms crossed loosely as they stare off to the side, clearly lost in thought for a moment. Their lips twitch slightly as they reflect, eyes flickering with a hint of something difficult to name. With a sigh, they look back at Eva, shoulders relaxing as they continue speaking, their voice quieter now, more measured.

"It's ironic, since Jenny was squeaky clean as a teen," they say, shaking their head softly, almost as if the memory itself is a weight they can't quite shake off. River's gaze drops to the table for a moment as though they're trying to process the loss all over again. "She was the one they'd been counting on before it all went wrong. It was an accidental overdose. She passed way before her time."

Their hands gesture vaguely, like they're pushing the thought away, a slight shift in posture as they sit up straighter. River runs a hand through their hair, a quick motion that betrays frustration and uncertainty. "Don't know if I was ever written out of the will," they add with a sharp breath, their expression briefly hardening. "All I know is that Uncle Jed has since intimated it'll all be mine someday. For what it's worth."

The words hang in the air, River's eyes locking onto each of ours in turn, as though they're waiting for us to understand the gravity of what they've just revealed.

"What do you mean, for what it's worth?" Billy asks.

River leans forward slightly, their brow furrowing at Billy's question. They press their lips together, then let out a small sigh, their hands briefly rubbing the back of their neck. Their eyes dart around as if considering how much to explain before meeting Billy's gaze again.

"Not to get ahead of ourselves," River mutters, their voice more guarded now, a slight shrug of their shoulders. "I just . . . don't know how serious my uncle is about any of this. He's never exactly been the most straightforward dude." Their hands shift restlessly in their lap, fingers tapping briefly on their knee as they try to formulate their next words.

When Billy mentions the monetary proposal and the carbon-free goal, River's posture straightens, a flicker of interest crossing their face. They briefly glance at the ceiling, considering it. Then, a small, wry smile tugs at the corner of their mouth. They lean back again, more relaxed this time, but the slight tilt of their head shows they're intrigued by the suggestion.

"Yeah, Minnesota going for one hundred percent carbon free by 2040…" River trails off, letting the idea linger in the air. Their fingers drum lightly on the edge of the table, the thought clearly beginning to take shape in their mind. They look back at Billy, their eyes narrowing with a quiet intensity. "That *is* pretty damn enticing."

"People joke about our cold winters," River continues, one hand making a sweeping motion in the air, as if dismissing the concern. "But Minnesota is surprisingly well equipped to handle climate change. There's a low risk of floods for one." They cross their arms casually but their tone is confident. "The farm is nowhere near a forest, so wildfires are less of an issue as temperatures continue to rise."

Serena, who's been following the dialog quietly for once, raises an eyebrow and leans back in her chair with a slight smirk, a knowing look crossing her face. "That's because they logged all those pristine white pine forests back in your great-grandparents' day." She glances around the room before asking, her tone almost playful: "Did you know River's grandmother comes from saw-mill worker stock?" Serena's fingers tap the armrest of her chair as she watches the group, curiosity dancing in her eyes.

"Part Dakota, right?" Eva asks. "Down the line?"

River's posture is relaxed but upright as they lean into the chairback, their gaze momentarily distant.

"She sure is, a couple generations back on her grandmother's side." They reply. "They were the first farmers. No nonsense. And you should see her handle her old man's muzzleloader. It was enough to scare the pants off me as a kid, watching her march around with that single shot fire arm."

Their voice softens slightly with a touch of admiration as they speak about Betty Jo and they raise one hand, fingers slightly splayed as if holding a rifle in their memory.

"She took you deer hunting?" Nate asked.

"Not so much as hunting, more like stalking from an advantageous site."

"As in?" Billy asks.

"Any place where there are white acorns dropping from the oaks, less tannin. There was a secluded spot she favored down by the fruit orchard, by the pond." Their hands move in a slow, deliberate motion, tracing an invisible path in the air to show how she would position herself, their eyes narrowing slightly with focus.

"She waited until the wind was in her face to set up target practice and she rarely failed."

~

Serena moves gracefully around the room, her steps light as she carries a large box of matches. She pauses at each surface, lighting a dozen candles and places them carefully around the space. Her fingers flick deftly as she works, the faint glow of the flames reflecting in her eyes. We watch, mesmerized, when suddenly—

A small Black Widow spider, no bigger than half an inch, crawls up the edge of the box and onto the coffee table. The room falls silent as we all take notice. Eva, who's been sitting calmly, doesn't flinch. Without hesitation, she reaches over, her movements deliberate and unhurried. With an upturned water glass in her hand, she gently places it over the spider, her fingers steady and sure.

River's eyes widen in alarm and they lurch forward with a sudden, frantic motion, kicking off layers of blankets that had been draped over them. They're almost on their feet but their voice is filled with concern as they point towards the spider. "Jesus, Eva, don't be messing with a Black Widow for heaven's sake!" River gestures toward the spider's abdomen, their fingers trembling slightly as they motion to the small, red hourglass shape. "Look at that—she's dangerous."

Eva remains calm, her hand still holding the glass and she glances at River without a hint of worry in her expression. "Whoa, she's so beautiful," she says. "Like a work of art. Nature's masterpiece, she must've built a web for herself in the basement." Her eyes narrow slightly as she watches the spider beneath the glass.

Nate leans forward, his eyes locked on the spider, his fingers tapping nervously on his knee. "What do we do with her?" His voice rises with urgency as he gestures towards the glass. "Don't let her escape whatever you do. They're fast movers."

Serena, leaning casually against a nearby chair with arms crossed, looks over at the scene with a raised eyebrow. She smirks slightly rolling her shoulders in a relaxed motion. "Take it easy. Black Widows eat flies and mosquitoes." She tilts her head as she watches the spider through the glass, her fingers tapping gently on her arm in a rhythm of calm confidence. "Ants, beetles... she's busy down there in the basement."

Eva says that although the Black Widow is considered venomous, she is typically not deadly, especially to adults, since the amount of venom she can inject is relatively small. "She's like a little jewel."

Billy voices a genuine concern, "Hello? What about pregnant women?"

And Eva is quick to respond: "She'll want to escape more than bite. Although, cornering her like this is not a good idea."

"Note to self. Always wear gloves in a basement," Nate remarks. "I wonder if she has eaten her mate?"

River leans forward, their face serious as they warn us, eyes scanning the room as if assessing each of us in turn. "Nate's right. Don't think of going down to the basement barefoot," they say, their voice firm but calm. They fold their arms as they continue, pointing to an invisible spot in the air.

"The first sign of a bite is usually a small, local swelling, a couple of red spots in the center. I've been bitten a couple times in the past." River shrugs slightly, as if the bites were no big deal, but their eyes narrow as they remember. "It gets more painful after two or three hours. Am I right, doc?"

They all look to me for confirmation. River's posture is tense with the memory.

"I've never had a severe reaction, though, admittedly—just achy legs, headache, sweating, and a slight tummy ache," they say.

Billy, sitting up straighter now, scrunches his face in disgust. He shakes his head, his hands firmly planted on his knees as he leans forward. "No thanks," he mutters, voice tinged with urgency. "Get rid of her now."

I look around, recalling patients I've treated for Black Widow bites, my hands instinctively moving as I explain how I've treated several over the years, intravenously with a mineral supplement and medication called calcium gluconate to relieve and relax muscle spasms.

I pause, glancing around the room, my tone serious but practical. "But it would be impossible to get treatment tonight with the road blocked." I hold their gaze, in turn, making sure they understand the gravity of the situation. "The only thing we could do if any of us were to be bitten right now would be to clean the site with soap and water, apply a cool compress, take an ibuprofen or acetaminophen pill, elevate the affected limb to heart level."

I turn my attention to River, nodding toward the glassed-in spider. "Let's remove her somewhere she can't get back in," I add, keeping my voice steady but firm as I suggest the next step.

Serena hands River a set of gloves from the wood bucket next to the stove. "Here, put these on— and give them a shake-out first."

River follows Serena's instructions before swiping the back of a yellowing postcard with a French stamp from the bookshelf, slipping it carefully under the glass. The Black Widow gracefully navigates a faded image of the Eiffel Tower, her legs un-pinched. We hold our breath collectively as River flips the glass, carefully placing one gloved hand over the underside of the paper and the other on top of the jar.

"Maintain a little pressure each side," Serena instructs. "Don't jilt or jostle the jar—let her out into the long grasses away from the house."

Serena moves toward the front door, her steps purposeful as she pushes it open wide. River follows, moving with deliberate care as they shuffle outside, holding the glass over the spider as they disappear from our view to safely remove it from the house.

Inside, the tension begins to ease. Nate exhales loudly, his shoulders dropping in relief, and his eyes quickly shift back to the group, his curiosity piqued. "Phew," he mutters, his voice laced with relief. His gaze sharpens with interest. "So . . . what about her partner?"

Eva, standing now, her arms casually crossed, tilts her head slightly, tapping her fingers against her arm as she answers with a slight smile. "He'd be about half her size," she says, her fingers gesturing in the air to illustrate the comparison. "Usually, he'll have yellow and red bands with spots on his back. Legs way longer in proportion to his body."

Her posture straightens as she shifts into more of a storytelling mode, her hands moving gracefully to emphasize each point. "In some cultures, the Black Widow is said to represent danger, death, or fear." She pauses for a moment, then continues with a flicker of something more thoughtful in her eyes. "And in others, she represents feminine power, deception, betrayal."

She scratches her head lightly, her gaze drifting toward the floor as she extrapolates. "In Shamanism, on the other hand . . ." She looks back up, meeting our eyes with a hint of a smile. "Black Widows are considered to be protectors of the home and of the evolving spirit."

I watch as Serena moves toward the window, her gaze lingering on the darkness beyond, as if waiting for some sign. A silence thickens, the tension of the moment not quite dissipating.

"I don't know," she murmurs, almost to herself. "It feels like... like something's continuing to shift out there. Maybe it *is* time to talk more seriously about this idea of ours to find someplace to settle."

I catch her words, a chill creeping up my spine. *To settle.* As if this place, this moment, is just the beginning of something much larger. The air hums with uncertainty, the future hanging in the multi-dimensional balance, as though the choice of land could decide more than just our next step.

Serena's voice cuts through the silence. "It's not just about settling, though. It's about finding the right balance . . . between the land and whatever is within ourselves."

She looks back at the door, eyes narrowing as if sensing something I can't see. My heart beats a little faster. "And what happens if we can't come to a consensus?" I ask.

Late Sunday Night

R iver leans against the kitchen countertop, their arms crossed and their gaze fixed on the window, their mind clearly racing with possibilities. Their voice is steady but filled with excitement, as if the afternoon's dramatic events and having us as an audience has brought a new lease of life to their idea. They are increasingly adamant about taking on the challenge of transforming their family's ramshackle Victorian farmhouse into something entirely new—an energy-efficient, net-zero performer. The idea swirls around them like a blueprint waiting to be brought to life, from solar panels to reclaimed materials and the thought of using every inch of space to its fullest potential sparks a fire in their eyes.

"Shouldn't we sleep on it?" I ask. I'm not yet nearly convinced. "It's late. And it's been one hell of a day."

I've wandered in, blanket around my shoulders in contemplation of clearing some of the dishes, mugs and glasses amassed during the hours of our post-ocean-rescue.

"Yeah, I guess," River replies shrugging their shoulders and waving me away from the sink. "I guess the adrenaline is refusing to shut off."

The chill that dulled my blood pressure and rendered me dizzy and faint has, mercifully, subsided at this late hour.

I shuffle to the sink, ignoring River's instructions as I gather an assortment of vessels and empty wine bottles. I should've known better than to have started in on the wine after the hot toddy. It went down way too easily.

"We'd need a new roof for starters," River informs a newly attentive audience of Billy and Nate. "Solar would require a sturdy surface over the decrepit specimen that's served as a roof for as long as I can remember."

Billy asks about insulation. "I mean, Minnesota? In winter?" Billy knows a lot about this kind of stuff.

"You'd be surprised," River replies. "I've figured it out in my head. Rip out the interior plaster and replace it with fiberglass bats. Either that or punch holes in the walls and fill the cavities with cellulose. That'd do it."

Nate pipes in and says it all sounds terribly complicated. And expensive. "And the exterior and foundation walls?" he asks.

"Sure, we'd need to add exterior insulation as well as insulation to the foundation walls, disconnecting the natural gas line in order to go all-electric."

"Also, we would need to remove the old single pane windows and switch to triple glazed, plus replace all of the old brass lamps with LED lights."

Despite the mess of old plumbing and drafty walls, they're clearly not picturing a dilapidated house as I'm envisioning it, but rather a canvas, awaiting transformation. River's words spill out, filled with technical jargon and innovative ideas as they enthusiastically outline plans for rainwater harvesting, passive heating and natural insulation. For River, this isn't just about fixing up a house; it's about creating something sustainable, a home that could be as much a statement of the future as it is a refuge from their past.

"Worked out a rough budget?" Eva asks, circling in on the sink with an armload of stemmed glasses. "You guys sure made a dent in the wine supply tonight."

"May as well finish what we started. I'm planning on being out of here first thing tomorrow," I announce. "The minute they open that road."

Serena leans against the doorframe between the kitchen and living room, her voice steady but tinged with weariness. "By late morning, this nightmare will be over," she says. "Hopefully." But as the words leave her mouth, her expression falters, a shadow of doubt crossing her face. She sighs, her shoulders slumping slightly. "Let's face it, things can't possibly get any worse."

She pauses, scanning the room and meeting each of our gazes before her eyes settle on River. "I would've appreciated this level of support when it came to ideas for shoring up this place," she says, her tone laced with a hint of frustration.

"Sorry to say but it's a little too late for that," River replies, raising their eyes to the ceiling. "Time to let go, babe."

"And when I do decide to say goodbye, where do you think we will go in the meantime?" she asks, her voice tinged with skepticism. "It's no secret we're broke, we've nothing but this old shack to our name. Once this place slides off the cliff, you and me, baby, we won't see a dime."

River looks at her, unfazed. "I've never counted on anything from the beach house," they reply. "It's your legacy, Serena. The last thing you can accuse me of is being some sort of bounty hunter."

Billy steps in, sensing the escalating tension that has been building between River and Serena. It's not his place, or for any of us to take sides. Instead, he announces diplomatically that he thinks the Minnesota plan is certainly a sound idea worth further exploration. "Low-maintenance landscaping with drip irrigation, a grey water system centered around the communal house. Pathways leading to tiny, modular, or factory-built homes . . . I can picture it now."

We'd need to purchase at least four more modulars, he says, one each for Betty Jo and Uncle Jed and a couple more for work/study guests to tend the regenerative gardens, participate and learn from our model.

River's eyes brighten, their hands gesturing enthusiastically as they lean forward slightly, ever more animated by the idea. "Even an old ramshackle Victorian can make more energy than it uses if we plan it out correctly," they agree, their voice filled with of optimism and possibility. "Harnessing the exponential."

Nate, sensing the dreamy shift in the conversation, leans back in his chair, arms crossed tightly over his chest, a skeptical expression forming as he breaks the magical thinking. He glances around, his brows furrowed in confusion, clearly having a little more trouble picturing the idea than his partner and River. "Are we being real, or what?" His tone is grounded, almost challenging, as he looks from me to Serena.

Her eyes narrow in response, a flicker of irritation passing across her face. She flicks her hand dismissively, rolling her eyes, clearly unamused by the implication. "Yeah. Let's not get too carried away. Don't we all deserve an equal say in this?" Her voice is sharp, her shoulders tense with a mix of defensiveness and frustration.

River shifts slightly, uncrossing their arms with a calm yet firm energy, offering reassurance as they address Nate's concern before Serena's. "Nobody's forcing anyone into any of this," they say. Their tone is gentle but resolute, a small nod punctuating their words. "It's early days yet."

Eva, who's also been quietly watching the exchange, suddenly steps forward with a spark of support. Her face lights up as she speaks, her voice eager and bright. "The moment Betty Jo and Jed give the green light to regenerate the homestead, I say it's a no-brainer." Her shoulders relax with the confidence of someone fully committed to the idea, eyes twinkling with excitement.

"What about the baby?" I ask. "How soon would you be ready to relocate with a newborn?"

"It'll take some influx of capital to get this off the ground," River says, jumping in and speaking for her. "Eva's condo would sell in a hot minute. Billy and Nate fortunately have reserves so they don't have to sell their apartment in New York immediately and Jamie's already committed a chunk of his savings to whatever we do decide on. That leaves you, Tam?"

I'd need to sell my cabin, my safe-haven in the Santa Cruz mountains to buy-in. It's all I have. I bought it with a down payment a few years back which took all of the family money left me. And it was my sole refuge during the pandemic, which makes it all the more sacred to me. My chest feels heavy, my shoulders are rigid. The tension in my lack of movement speaks volumes with the struggle I'm having with the sacrifices I'm being asked to make. Giving up my hard-earned place in the medical practice and the trust I've built with my patients would be another huge ask. Who knows how long it would take me to re-establish the level of security I've created for myself. My reticence is evident.

"You made just as much of a commitment to the pact as I did, Tam," Serena says, her gaze locking with mine. "We all did, two decades ago. Though, to be honest, I'm not nearly as convinced by River's big green Minnesota program as they'd like me to be."

River's eyes widen. Their body stiffens and they lean back slightly, as if physically distancing themselves from the weight of her words. "You've waited until now to drop a bombshell like this? You knew I've been working on this idea." Their hands gesture outwards in a mix of exasperation and confusion, palms up as if asking for an explanation.

Serena holds River's gaze, her expression steady and serious, not backing down. She folds her arms across her chest, a subtle shift in her posture signaling the weight of what she's about to say. She speaks slowly, deliberately, her words heavy with meaning.

"After four generations of my family making their home out here along the Marin/Sonoma Coast, and aside from Santa Cruz, this is the only place I know," she begins, her voice steady and calm, her chin lifting just slightly as if bracing herself for the impact of her confession. "You must see that. You've said as much yourself. If you take me away from here, who knows how long it'll take me to let it all go, to adjust."

A lengthy debate erupts, each of us voicing our thoughts with growing intensity. Opinions clash, voices rise and fall and the tension thickens, hanging in the air like one more storm that is waiting to break. Some argue politics, others lean into economics or emotion, but all of us find ourselves caught between the pull of compromise and the weight of our convictions.

It feels as though our future teeters on the edge of every word spoken, each new point hanging like a thread we can't quite pull together. The debate spirals on and still none of us can let go, each of us pushing harder for what we believe is the right path forward.

Finally. "A word in private?" River's voice cuts through the noise, their eyes fixed on Serena. There's an unspoken weight behind it—a quiet invitation to step aside, to calm down and talk things through behind closed doors.

Serena, however, seems almost to relish the moment. With a small, knowing smile, she shakes things up further, clearly enjoying this latest dramatic twist. Her posture is playful but there's something behind her eyes—a challenge. She and River exchange a glance, then rise together, heading down to their bedroom without another word.

The room falls silent and we're left in an uneasy stillness. We look at one another, shrugging in a mix of confusion and uncertainty. There's a lot hanging in the balance and despite the debates, the weight of it all suddenly feels too much to ignore.

I'm secretly relieved I'm not the only one who can't quite believe we're really serious about doing this.

Last Thing Sunday Night

L ilacs in the moonlight. The sleeping porch is heavy with the soft, powdery scent of spring, drifting lazily from sprigs of purple lilacs I'd arranged earlier in a vintage crystal vase on the bedside table. The pale glow of the moon catches their petals, casting a delicate shimmer. Resting against the vase is a folded piece of paper—an unexpected presence. My pulse quickens as I focus the soft beam of my small flashlight, my fingers trembling as I scoop up the note. A flutter of anticipation rises within me. Jamie must have left me another of his poems before he headed out for the boat. I was too shaky to notice it earlier as I'd peeled off my wetsuit and underwear.

I fumble briefly for my reading glasses, the familiar, grounding motion offering me little comfort as my mind races. The narrow beam of the flashlight trembles slightly in my grip.

His handwriting is as distinctive as my recollection of his scent—warm, familiar, intimate. My hand steadies as I unfold the paper, the edges crisp against my fingertips. But as my eyes scan the page, something shifts. This isn't a poem ot another song. It's a letter.

I read it silently, the weight of the words sinking deeper with each line.

Hey Tamsin,

So, we kinda do fit back together, right? I really hope you feel that way too, 'cause it's not too late, I swear. I know, I know—it sounds like one of those cheesy things people say, but honestly, I can't help it. I'm sitting here this morning at the kitchen table, just totally stoked and trying to get my thoughts on paper, even if it is a little clumsy.

I'll just be straight with you: I'm offering myself to you, heart wide open, no holds barred. I messed up, I know that. I made mistakes I can't take back, and I'm sorry for the things I screwed up. But you know what? I'm feeling a new kind of hope, like maybe the stupid things that pulled us apart aren't totally impossible to fix.

To be real with you, I've never loved anyone the way I love you. I'm not some perfect hero—just a regular guy, honestly! But I'm here, all in, if you'll have me. So, what I'm asking is for you to say yes—say yes to us, to starting this next chapter of our lives together.

You're my person, Tam. My one and only.

Always yours,
Jamie xo

I read and re-read his note several times, tears welling, allowing the words to sink in. It's written on a lined sheet of a to-do list. I'd assumed it was enough that we'd already messed up our unconventional marriage once. I'm honestly stunned that this second chance is presenting itself for real. It's like he's proposing to me again—out of the blue but for all the right reasons this time. And yet, he almost got himself killed before I've had the chance to respond.

My stomach twists as I switch off the flashlight and lie down, closing my eyes in an attempt to steady my breathing. I remind myself not to overthink it—not to make things more complicated than they need to be. When we first got together, I was in a messy, fragile place—everything in my life felt off-balance. Would I stay or would I be forced to go? I wasn't ready for anything serious, especially love. I didn't even think I deserved it, even after we'd realized there was something real between us once the rush of our youthful chaos had faded.

This is the moment I've longed for, though I never fully admitted it to myself. Over the last ten years, I'd almost convinced myself that I was better off alone—living on my terms, traveling when and where I pleased, as long as work allowed, and answering to no one. No partner to negotiate with, no one to explain my spending habits to. No kids to embarrass. And yet here I am, clutching his note like some lovesick teenager, while he's lying in a hospital bed, a forty-five-minute drive away, with the roads impassable. I can't help but imagine his warm hand resting in the small of my back, his salty lips pressing softly against mine.

"Trust me, Jamie," I whisper as I hold the letter close. "We can do this."

If *he's* truly in on this wild pledge of communal living we made back when we were young and full of idealistic dreams, then I'm in too. As long as there's a clear boundary—some private space for the two of us. I have my limits, after all. It's a lot to ask of someone like me, an only child with a reserved nature, a loner at heart. Spending what's left of my life surrounded by six other people—these six people—soon to be seven, feels overwhelming. As much as we all may love each other, forgive each other for past mistakes, I know there will be huge challenges. And we're under no illusion that we have it all figured out.

I refold and clutch the note to my chest as I turn to my side and tuck it for safekeeping under my pillow, pulling the bedcovers to my chin.

The scent of the lilacs is comforting, a soft embrace. Purple lilacs, the first stirrings of love.

As tired as I am, sleep won't come. My mind refuses to let me rest, replaying the weight of the last twelve hours. I work my way through the events in chronological order until I get to the part where Serena let her cover drop—admitting that she wasn't nearly as on board with River's big "return-to-Minnesota" plan as she'd let on before.

I replay key parts of the heated debate in which Serena had stated that we'd essentially be: "Showing up in full force, overwhelming River's family and the community with our self-centered beliefs." And, she had a point.

It really does tread all over the people who live there. It's something we must consider.

There is something of a blatant and righteous element in all of this. I'm concerned that the idea of giving up our individual journeys for an eco-friendly, state-of-the-art, multi-family compound does, in all honesty, come across as an elitist ideal.

"Well, don't we all want to live our best lives? Plenty of open space around us. A carbon-neutral, shared community is arguably the best way to go," Billy had argued in River's defense, describing a multi-family compound as the way forward.

On the other hand, there's nothing pompous about reducing our carbon emissions, I get that. What we'd be doing is blazing a trail for the future by saving energy and money, as a group. Pooling our skills and resources makes sense in so many ways.

"I don't feel a need to go back to being too crunchy in our living quarters," Eva had said, adding that she's long past the student-digs stage.

River agreed.

"Whatever we do settle on with regards to the construction and design of our individual units," they'd said. "We'll need to hone in on making sure each house is as low-maintenance in upkeep as possible, with low operational costs for a healthier and more comfortable living space."

Serena had snorted at River's response, crossing her arms tightly over her chest and arching an eyebrow. "It's not much of a stretch when you look at this place," she'd remarked, her lips curling into a half smile. "But what I'd like to know is how you're planning on compensating me emotionally for giving up this view?" Her gaze swept the horizon, lingering just long enough to emphasize her point.

River had leaned back slightly, rocking on their heels, a soft chuckle escaping their mouth. "Well, you'll be safe from rising ocean levels for one," they'd replied, hands spread wide as if offering a grand vision. "There's thousands of lakes and waterways in Minnesota, all ripe for seasonal foraging, an infinite horizon on Lake Superior." They'd paused, then, their voice lowering, eyes locking with hers in a moment of earnestness. "And the main thing is, Serena, we'll be growing together, exploring. Sharing."

I speak from experience when I remind myself there's an all-too-common tendency in human nature to walk away when the pressure is on. I toss and turn beneath the sheets, running through the evening debate in my overly exhausted mind. I'd guess that Serena is the most likely to bounce now we're moving beyond the ideation phase.

As my mind begins to quiet in the darkness, a new, unsettling thought creeps in . . . what if it's Jamie who changes his mind?

Monday Morning First Thing

My bed is pressed up against a drafty, bare bank of weathered single-pane windows, offering a blurry glimpse of the dark blue Pacific. Soft light of a new day slips through the thin veil of my eyelids. As I pull my arm from beneath the pillow, Jamie's note sticks to my wrist.

It feels almost surreal to think that just 24 hours ago, he was lying next to me, bathed in the soft glow of our intimacy.

I reach out, my palm grazing cool cotton and this near-perfect memory slips away from me, like a corn snake sliding off the edge of a cliff.

My morning-brain moves itself into second gear.

A hangover isn't helping any, though it feels good to mute my brain somewhat before it shifts into an even higher gear. I rest the back of my hand on my reverberating temple, tracking a series of dull thumps that are pummeling against my brain like yesterday's raindrops on tarp.

A sharp, crochet-needle-like pain narrows in and hooks directly through the temporal muscle behind my eye, in-between my forehead and ear. Gradually, in part to distract myself from the ache in my head and in equal part my inner fear-mongering, I train my focus on the rising and falling of the surf. Its sound is one of measured ease, a respite of gloomy quietude after yesterday's rage-tempered waves. The physical storm appears to have passed. That's something.

Rubbing my eyes, I loosen my sleep-crusted lashes but everything is still a blur—just like the frantic events of yesterday afternoon. Part of me wants to block it all out, to stop replaying it endlessly. But I roll myself out of bed and face the day anyway, suppressing the strong urge to crawl back under the covers and curl up, waiting for someone to come in and tell me that the crisis is over and Jamie will be alright.

Has the power been restored? I fumble for the switch on the standing lamp. Nothing, although the shadowy, moss-green room comes into focus in the low, natural light. The window panes are pretty much fogged-up. Oxidation of air and moisture built-up over time, Jamie had informed me as he'd tested the levers. Decades of salt spray stuck to the exterior glass. I fixate on a permanent blur between the windowpanes where the sealing gel has failed.

The house has been without power since the storm. I'd known all along that it was a terrible idea for Jamie to take the boat out but I was foolishly reluctant to cramp his style.

Waiting for news is the absolute worst. How do I shake myself out of my stupor, to snap out of this sluggish, unproductive thought process? I'm not helping Jamie any by lounging around in a state of regret.

I stoop and reach my hand beneath the pillow where Jamie's head had rested in order to retrieve a crumpled white t-shirt. I raise it to my nose and inhale a heady mix of wind and earth, a Jamie-tang of lemon zest and sea-salt that helps soothes my still-thumping brain.

The house is quiet. I grab a handful of clothes, throw random items onto my disassociated body, and stuff Jamie's t-shirt into my duffle.

I wander, barefoot into the living room in search of my hiking boots which I had left to dry by the woodburning stove last night. All I can think of is that I'll not run the risk of losing Jamie a second time. It's not too late to shape the future as we wish. Jamie and me are my absolute priority this morning and going forward. The rest of them must willingly accept and embrace us a couple, Serena especially, otherwise this whole crazy pact would fall apart. There is no game plan between us without Jamie's steady presence. Everyone knows that.

~

It's brisk at this hour, the chill of the room cutting through my sluggishness. This does not prevent the dull thud of my hangover pulsing on in my brain as I move around a little more deliberately than at first. I grab a handful of small twigs from the basket next to the woodburning stove and toss them onto the smoldering remnants of last night's fire. A hiss and a sudden burst of flame flare up in seconds. I tiptoe back and forth, adding more wood to take the edge off the chill.

The fire is mesmerizing, vital to survival, a symbol of warmth, of hearth and home. I stare into the flames and I think of my grandmother's stone cottage, the steady flame of her cast-iron Aga burning day and night, year in, year out. There's a coal-burning fireplace in her living room, the one room my mother has kept exactly as it was—most likely out of financial necessity rather than any sense of cozy nostalgia. For the five or six warm weeks of summer, a stack of beach-foraged driftwood and dried flowers adorn the hearth, replacing the coal grate, a fleeting touch of the seasons in such a comforting space.

I step back, extending my arms toward the now blazing stove and warm my hands. As I stand there, I turn my head, taking in the space beneath the beamed ceiling. Serena's quirky California spot has always felt to me like a lifetime away from the familiar stretch of my native British North Sea. Whereas Gran's place, now Mum's, is a good twenty-minute flat walk past windmills and mudflats, leading to a wide expanse of sand and water—this cliff-top perch by contrast is other-worldly entirely, wild, compelling, untamed.

Let's say Serena's interior style is a tad Americana-grand-millennial, sometimes described as granny-chic. However, aside from the Summer of Love memorabilia and other valuables we tucked away for safety in the storm, she's purged a bunch of stuff since her mom passed. Serena and River have evidently spent a lot of time carefully curating, painting, and rearranging the furniture, creating a space that is best described as thoughtfully put together. My heart strings pull for the pair of them at the prospect of losing this gem of a place.

I'm grateful for the warmth as I'm eyeing a respectable pile of split logs stacked nearby—seasoned, untreated oak, rough edges holding the earthy scent of the forest. The wood carries a deep, rich aroma, free from pollutants, a crisp, woodsy edge that fills the room. I estimate it's enough of a pile to keep us warm for a couple more days, if need be. On top of the stove, a cast iron pot gently simmers with a fragrant mix of lemon peel and mint sprigs. Eva placed it here with its aromatic concoction, late last night. A sweet, citrusy tang mingles with the cool freshness of mint, adding a subtle, calming fragrance to the room.

I sink my bare feet into the dense, amber-toned rug over wide plank that's been painted, in contrast to the white walls, a dark and glossy, sea-kelp-green. There are a bunch of multi-colored handknitted blankets and throws lolling around to hand, abandoned where we left them late last night, casually strewn over an eclectic seating arrangement, the crackled-leather sofa and an assortment of wicker armchairs.

The scent of eucalyptus on ocean breeze greets me as I step through the sliding doorway into the outdoors. The old deck beneath my feet feels soft and damp, its surface slick with moisture. The morning air carrying a cool, dewy freshness. Though the wooden boards are soggy and yielding, they groan and shift beneath my weight as I carefully step forward, narrowly avoiding a large raven that swoops into view, its wings cutting through the air with precision as it darts overhead.

I hold on to the frail railing and gape at his four-foot wing span, the bluish-purple, iridescent sheen of a ruff of well-developed feathers at his throat, his violet, juvenile eyes, the light base of his long, strong beak. I continue to watch, transfixed as he glides through the veiled curtain of fog that hangs over the Pacific, the bird world's most intelligent trickster back again, playing with me as he makes his entrance center-stage.

He advertises his territory, calling "cr-r-ruck" "cr-r-ruck" as this ac-robatic flyer with his diamond-shaped tail soars upwards in a smooth and calculated flight path. It carries him above and beyond the shingle rooftop to a nest somewhere in the trees above the cliff edge.

Certainly, one of the most adaptable of the avian species. How many encounters have I had with the Raven this weekend? I'm pretty sure it must have been he and his mother who called in to emergency services prompting Jamie's rescue.

If he has come to teach me a lesson or two then his timing has been impeccable.

Behind me, the beach house rests quietly—the others sleeping off the aftermath of a late-night blur of lively, alcohol-fueled debate, a long-over-due release of tension and stress as we'd each made our individual cases for the future.

I reach over the railing, uncurling my hand. I release a single strand of Jamie's hair I'd plucked from the neck of his t-shirt. I watch as it floats away in the wake of the breeze. With luck, the Raven will weave it into a nest.

Jamie. Right now, I'd give everything for the promise of a life together. This plan, this pact, it isn't something any of us is entering into lightly. It's a monumental request—to let go of the security we've each spent years building and securing in our individual, adult lives for something so uncertain and bold. It's going to require a huge leap of faith from each and every one of us.

A faint, slate-blue line stretches across the horizon, barely discernible through the fog that wraps around the ocean like a jealous lover, holding tight to the water below. I zip up my rain jacket and tilt my head to the sky, fighting the pull of darker thoughts, determined not to let them disturb the fragile peace of this moment.

I'm interrupted just as I'm about to send a silent stream of bargains to the universe.

"Oh, you're up and about. Ever the early bird." Serena's voice is calm but there's a sharpness to her tone as she looks me dead in the eye, her posture relaxed but alert, as if she's already anticipating my response. "We should talk. I mean . . . if something should go wrong. With Jamie. Which it won't. But just in case." She tilts her head slightly, gauging my reaction.

I unfurrow my brow, trying to keep my expression neutral as I cross my arms. "What do you mean 'goes wrong'?" I ask, my voice laced with genuine concern. My fingers twitch, restless, as I attempt to make sense of what it is that she's implying. Is she insinuating he's in worse condition than we'd assumed, or rather that he might wake up and walk away from all of this? From me?

"He was pretty beat up." Serena thrives on the possibility of near-disaster. It's her thing and she always manages to spin it in a way that sounds like genuine concern. But the way she delivers it doesn't make it any easier to digest.

"I can't help but worry. He almost drowned."

I refuse to let myself go there. "Don't be so negative. And frankly, insensitive, Serena. He's strong. He's in good hands." I clench my jaw, biting back words I'll regret. Her bluntness is grating, her tactless version of her morning greeting.

I step back, putting some space between us. "You are *such* a kill joy."

Her voice may be thick and sugary, like she's swallowed a spoonful of raw honey, but it does nothing to soften the bite of her words. After all these years I should be used to it but I still feel a wave of distaste toward her demeanor—the way she leans casually against the sliding door frame like she owns the space. Which she does. Still, I can't help but look her up and down, my frustration written all over my face. She's barefoot, draped in a short, silken robe that clings to her sculpted thighs. The robe, a deep yellow, like the sun that hasn't yet made its appearance. It hangs open just enough to reveal her perfect frame, clad in a pale green vintage slip that draws further attention to the physical ideal she carries like a prize.

It feels wrong, shallow even, to focus on her appearance this morning when there are more important things at hand. I shift uncomfortably, guilt rising in my chest. Why do I care so much about the way she looks, how she presents herself? It's not her fault that she's . . . well, herself. I hate that I let it get under my skin, that I'm so quick to judge based on the surface. I scold myself for my own capacity for mean spiritedness, my superficial dark side. I should be better than this—better at seeing beyond the physical, at focusing on what really matters. But the image of her standing there, in stark contrast to the way I feel inside—imperfect, my thoughts so messy, her exterior so polished. I shift again, discomfort and regret gnawing at me.

She on the other hand, simply laughs my irritation off, aware of how annoying, how triggering she is. I turn my back to her but she's still very much there, loafing against the doorframe, staring at me.

I roll my eyes. It's not that I'm overly envious of her looks. Her sensuality, her brash self-confidence. There was never any competition in that department, we're so unalike. We've made an odd pair of bookends as friends. Serena the tall, willowy, flirty one. As for me, I'm average at best—pale-skinned, a freckle-faced English rose, unfiltered and unconcerned with artifice in contrast to her birthright of sun-kissed and tousled, California beach-babe.

People and animals flock to the cerebral, patchouli-scented Serena. She appears every inch as alluring as ever this morning, despite the insensitive drivel that bursts from her mouth.

What's more, Minnie and Myrtle trot out after her in unison, on-cue, like she's the Pied Piper of our collective pack, earthy, enchanting. Why be so callous, given all she has going for her? To me this morning? And to River, especially, last night?

They're identical, the dogs, even in their greeting as they move from her to me in unison and curl into my stance as a token of good manners. They've barely barked while I've been here even with a house full of relative strangers. I reach down and pet them as I peruse their contented faces in turn. I can't tell them apart. Serena's inseparable, side-kicks. Nuggets the size of a pair of stuffed animals.

"Go ahead. Vent. It's good to get it off your chest," she offers, her voice still dripping with sweetness. She leans back, casually, one arm crossed over her chest, the other loosely dangling by her side as she taps her fingers absently against the wood. Her gaze is steady, but there's a slight raise of her eyebrow, as if she's daring me to say more.

"Give it a break, Serena."

I can feel my frustration building, my fists clenching at my sides. She stands there, her posture relaxed but alert, a slight smirk tugging at the corners of her mouth as if she knows exactly how to push my buttons. Her eyes are locked on me, studying my every movement, savoring the tension.

"I'm not saying something bad *is* going to happen or that it already has. But he was out there in those conditions for a while before you found him. And then, when he went under again. You know how bad it was. We all do. It's . . . scary," she says.

"How do you do it?" My fingers are twitching at my side.

"What?" She tilts her head, eyes narrowing in curiosity.

"Insist that it's you who gets to say all this? To question his fate. That it's you who knows him best? His capabilities. Seriously, Serena . . .? Remember? Did anything we talked about yesterday sink in? You need to back off if any of this is going to work."

I doubt she'll ever stop consistently attempting to one-up me with Jamie. The past is the past. It's time to let go of the competitiveness that exists between us. I guess I have no choice but to accept who she is, her insecurities and leave it at that.

Yet she's a narcissist with a golden halo and I'm the one who routinely backs down first, sucks it up, retreats gracefully, as usual, leaving her to think she's stronger than me. Trouble is, I detest confrontation. She knows that. There's no one on this planet, other than my mother, who riles me like Serena.

Seething, I fix my sight on the grass bank atop the cliff along from the house. Swaths of fiddleneck—bright yellow spring flowers, as prolific as the abundant the California poppy, are swaying to the music of the breeze. Their coiled, trumpet-shaped flower heads resemble a fiddle's neck, hence the name. Beautiful to look at, bristly, irritating and toxic in large quantities. Like Serena. I tighten my lips and suppress a fresh urge to scoff at her audacity.

"Come on, Tamsin, don't be like that," she says, defending herself, regardless of all the other hurtful things she's said this weekend. "It's not as if I'm laying claim."

She repositions one hand on her hip and, rethinking her stance before it's too late, tipping her head to one side in the petulant woman-child-manner she favors. I fix on her nail polish, the exact same tone of shimmery, oceanic green as her slip, chipped at the tips.

"Anyway," Serena says, tucking a long, tangled strand of hair behind her pretty, silver-hooped ear, backtracking now. "Given Jamie's strength, his general level of fitness and all, he's the biggest fighter of our bunch. Right? I know that. You know that. No-one here is more of a survivor than him."

She's caught herself in her entitlement, her needling, softening a tad.

From my vantage point I focus next on the view of the cliff edge beyond a row of striking Monterey cypress. They're considered non-native to this stretch of the coast and invasive, but they've been left untouched by coastal naturists since they're on private property. Hot little tears well in the corner of my eyes though not before I register the fact the road looks even less promising than it did at dusk.

"He should have known better than to risk-take like that," I concede as I swipe a runaway tear with the back of my hand.

"None of us is perfect, I guess," Serena replies as she checks for any sign of service on the phone she produces from the pocket of her robe. "And the rest of us stranded here for another day at least. The only thing we can do for Jamie is to wait it out as a united front. Keep our shit together. We'll get some degree of cell reception eventually. And no matter how irritated by me you are, Tamsin, we're stuck here together, like it or not."

"His folks," I think aloud, before Serena takes it upon herself. "I wonder if they've been informed?"

Serena steps toward me, her narrow, bare feet padding softly on the wet wood. A long, green gecko, the tattoo around her left ankle. The motion of her foot makes it look like it's swishing its tale as she approaches. It's as if it's going to pounce off her skin and onto me any second now.

She reaches out assertively for my hand and she swivels me sideways, looking me directly in the eyes.

Nothing is going to stop her from her mission to dominate, clearly. "What makes you his point-person, Tam, given that you've been apart so long? I only ask as I've always gotten along so well with Jamie's family."

"Because I'm his wife. Legally. Remember?" Even though it's possible the last thing Jamie's folks are expecting is a call from me as they sip their morning coffee. But it *is* me who must make this call. They may not be aware of what happened during the isolated storm that hit here along the Northern Coast.

I squeeze her hand to emphasize my point and release it as I gaze out at the ocean for strength. It's not Serena's place to question the status of my relationship. We've been over it. How many times? I've lost count.

"Look, Tam. All I'm saying is it's not all on you. We're in this together, you and me. Isn't that the point?"

I'm tired of processing her ulterior motives. My patience with her has reached its daily limit and it's still early yet. But deep down in my heart of hearts, I know that if we are to move forward with our plan as a group, then somehow, I am going to have to find a way to make my peace with her.

"Don't push me so," is what I do say. "Don't forget why we're here. And if we're to continue on with what we've set out to do, then all of this finger pointing and one-upping must stop. Just give me some space for a few minutes, okay, Serena? You can start by making us a pot of your tea."

Monday Mid-Morning

W e're gathered around the breakfast table, four of us at first, two humans and two dogs. Minnie and Myrtle are curled by Serena's feet, snoring loudly when a call comes in on the limited reception of my cell. It's Jamie, much to my relief and elation. He is awake and sitting up in his hospital bed, responding encouragingly after a barrage of tests.

He reassures me he's okay as we talk, briefly.

I'm about to start processing the good news just as Serena's chamomile-lavender-honey tea hits the bottom of my empty stomach. It bounces, more of a liquid hand-bomb, a deep heat in the damp trenches of my guts than the calming tonic intended.

It's Serena who bursts my bubble. Naturally. She should be giving me the moment. Instead, she's acting nonchalant, like we all knew that Jamie would be fine. She's more intent on calling out any duplicity she can think of with regards to River's vision for a Minnesota homestead.

"Fear is a powerful tool," she remarks, backtracking and moving on at the same time. When the call came, she'd been in the middle of making her case to me that the Mid-West idea is a mere smokescreen for pushing her, personally, away from California.

It was Eva who had tipped the balance last night as she'd championed Minnesota's natural beauty, its uncrowded, friendly population. Though she'd claimed to have found it all most appealing, she'd admitted that she wasn't sure how long it would take for the state to be overrun with doomsday folk and climate change migrants such as ourselves.

"Rising temperatures are pushing us north as a population," Serena is raising her voice now, revisiting some of my own concerns, if I'm honest. "It's a fact. And mayors in Minnesota have made a slogan out of offering climate relief, but I wonder, are the people who were born and raised there ready for a mass invasion of their state?"

River walks into the kitchen, sleepy-eyed in shorts and a t-shirt with an *Always Fresh, Always Cool* slogan on the front. It's clear by the look on their face that they've heard Serena's latest assault on the Minnesota idea.

"On the other hand, I've not experienced too many places where the locals routinely stop in the street and talk to strangers," they say. "I love this about my home state. I feel like I'm being welcomed home."

Home being the operative word.

"That's because you're hardly a stranger, are you?" Serena is quick to point out. She's intent on playing devil's advocate and she's clearly enjoying it.

River counters that they may as well be since they've been living in California for more than half their life.

"Not too many folk recognize me as the awkward, pimply-faced teenager I was when I first took off to California."

Billy and Nate join us in the kitchen. River acknowledges the fact that as temperatures increase, cooler communities around the Great Lakes may well be amongst the few places in America where climate challenges might be more easily managed.

I mull this over.

"Basically," River adds, "by 2080, I think it's fair to say that any children and grandchildren we raise in Minnesota will be better set than any in America as far as comfortable summers. It's a given that the Great Lakes provide an abundance of fresh water, there's a lower risk of wildfires and winters are already becoming less intense".

"Right," I pipe in, attempting to make light. "Well, we're definitely going to need some serious on-boarding before and after we shift to the Mid-West."

Nate dives in, directing his attention to Serena. He wants to know what her biggest concerns are with regards to River's proposal. "Narrow it down."

"To be honest," she answers, "being coerced into caring for Betty Jo is a genuine issue. I'm having trouble with any idea of being handed an obligation to look after someone who basically booted River out as a vulnerable teen."

River is quick to respond to the double blow. "I've never suggested you'd be the one to take on my grandmother. Or my uncle for that matter. If either of them is in need of hands-on-care in the future, then that's up to me to figure it out."

Serena will not let it go. She has that look on her face when she's dug her heels in. She's insistent that the two of them are falling into an elder care trap. Hands on hips, she postures and pouts.

"I know we all got along great this last time. But why would you want to make it permanent when they turned their backs on you during such a difficult time in your life? That's what I don't get."

"Because," River explains, taking a series of deep breaths, their shoulders rising and falling with each inhale. They meet her gaze, their hands loosely clasped in front of them. After a brief pause, their fingers gently tap against the table, a sign of thoughtfulness. "I've moved past it. I believe they have too." They soften their expression, their posture relaxing as they continue. "It's different times. And I've forgiven them. We're family when all's said and done." They nod slightly, their tone steady but warm.

Eva steps in, raising a hand with a polite gesture, her expression expectant as she asks if she may offer a point. River nods in acknowledgment.

"My child—our child, Billy and Nate, me and all of us as an extended family, we would benefit in so many ways by integrating our elders in our daily lives. It's an important part of my culture and these relationships should be preserved at all costs. My mother, any of our parents for that matter, may need to join our community at some stage. We'll need to address this."

Serena punctuates Eva's statement with a loud, exaggerated yawn, stretching her arms overhead before letting them fall lazily to her sides. She rolls her shoulders back, her eyes half-lidded with mild disinterest. "Great," she says, her tone dripping with sarcasm. "Now we're talking about a senior living facility." She leans back in her chair, crossing her arms with a slight smirk.

She does have a point. It would be wise for each of us to explore this multi-generational scenario in more detail. We'd certainly need to meet River's family before we commit.

"Maybe show a little empathy for the elder orphans, the solo-agers out there in the world or you may end up that way yourself, Serena," River snaps back.

Ouch. Any one of us could end up alone. It's an epidemic these days. I'm not against the idea of welcoming our elders, though I'm not sure how I'd manage if my very British mother were part of the deal. The thought had never even crossed my mind. It would take a huge slice of humble pie for me and her to stomach what she'd dismiss as a "hippy-communal" way of life. Still, I get the general concept—after all, the pathways to singlehood seem to be multiplying by the day in the present culture.

"Growing old together would make life easier for everyone," River adds, trying to placate their partner. Meanwhile, Serena stomps around, tossing her hands up in exasperation as she declares that, for her part, she certainly doesn't consider herself anywhere near to growing old at this stage in her life.

"Don't you want to live a little? Be in the here and now? Where did you park your free spirit, River?" she asks, with a teasing smirk, her eyebrows raised in challenge.

River sighs, rubbing a hand over their face as if trying to summon some spark of rebellion. "I guess you must've worn me down, turned me into a planner," they reply, their voice tinged with a mixture of resignation and amusement. "Dependable."

Without waiting for a response, Serena flounces out of the kitchen, her bare feet making sharp, dramatic taps on the floor, before slamming the bathroom door with enough force to rattle the walls. The sound of it echoing through the house feels like a punctuation mark to their conversation.

As for me, I'm concentrating on my inhale, exhale. A series of long, deep breaths, composing myself as best I can. My head and heart are racing. Jamie is okay. My Jamie. T-J as Billy coined us, the odd-couple way back when. No matter what it may have looked like from the outside these past few years, in my heart of hearts, I never truly gave up on him and me, even though I'd tried so hard to convince myself otherwise. The relief is so intense, I vomit a mouthful of the warm, acidic liquid I've just imbibed back into my half empty mug.

"Grab some napkins." It's River who jumps to my rescue. Yes, dependable. Also, conscientious steady and giving. Serena should be so lucky. They're seated next to me at the table. Their bird-like hair swept to one side in what was likely a restless sleep. It looks like they've had an electric shock of the comic variety. I laugh, weakly, at the ridiculousness of it all.

Eva steps in behind River and seats herself across from me. She springs up and grabs a linen napkin from a folded pile positioned behind her amidst the jumble of the dresser. Zero-waste. Not a paper product in the house but an inordinate number of vintage cloth.

"Here, sweetie," Eva says, sliding a couple more napkins toward me. "These look like they've seen better days."

Eva is well practiced in stepping back and scrutinizing. Aside from figuring out which so-called sanctioned or home-brewed concoction might sicken or kill the future "us", her skillset for calling out any bullshit is guaranteed to be a big plus in our plans. Instead of spending her life bemoaning her relationship losses, she's evidently all the more positive and inspiring in her singledom. And here she is now in the early blooms of motherhood. I'm still processing that, too. I can only imagine what's going through Nate's mind.

Yet he and Billy, I'm relieved to see, are presenting together as an industrious, united duo this morning. They've set to work at the Wedgewood stove, their backs, one broad, one narrow, to the table. River must've reconnected the gas as Billy is successful in lighting the flame with a single match and the pair of them are intent on the making of what they announce grandiously as a forager's scramble.

I can't help but zone in as Nate stirs a jug of freshly whisked eggs into a fragrant sauté of emerald-green nettles, wild garlic, mushrooms, and dandelion greens. The rich, earthy scent of the greens and garlic fills the air and I instinctively raise my hand to my nose, filtering out the dense, woodsy aroma of the kitchen in order to settle my stomach.

"The *one* good thing about hanging on to an old gas stove is that it always comes through," River says. But the pervading smell of the gas and the mixture of mushrooms, eggs and greens isn't helping my nausea any despite the noisy vent running full throttle.

"Watch out, girl's gonna hurl!" Eva yells, her voice sharp as she shoves yet another stack of linens across the table, her movements quick and efficient. "I know how it feels," she says. I sense a wave roll through me, my stomach twisting painfully as I fight to keep it together. I'm clammy and dizzy, my vision blurring at the edges. The room seems to tilt, and for a moment, I'm afraid I might actually pass out right here, in front of everyone.

"Jamie's fine, everything's alright," I repeat over and over in my head, the words a mantra as I steady my breath. Gradually, my lungs begin to catch up, and my breathing slows, but my heart still pounds in my chest.

"I'm okay," I gasp, though it's clear that's an exaggeration. I must look like I've seen a ghost. Delayed shock and intense relief. My complexion, usually pale, is practically translucent this time of year, after a long, dull winter. Ivory, like piano keys, my Mum always says. If I'd truly forgiven her—and she'd forgiven me for the distance that had grown between us since Gran passed—she'd be sitting beside me, pinching my cheeks to bring back some color, just like she used to when I was a kid.

I promise myself this morning that I'll make things right with my mother, that I'll bridge the gap that's formed between us. It's time for me to let go of the lingering resentment and misunderstandings, to forgive and allow myself to be forgiven. As a thank-you to the universe for sparing Jamie, I vow to be more present, to rebuild the connections I once shared with my mother and Serena both, even if it means swallowing my pride and taking the first step. Deep down, I know that each relationship is too important to let it continue to fracture and I will endeavor to heal the rifts, no matter how long it takes.

Billy carefully serves the scramble into wide, brown earthenware bowls, his movements steady and deliberate. His eyes remain focused on the stove, keeping a watchful eye on the sizzling skillet as he ladles the creamy eggs with practiced precision. The scent of the food fills the air as he methodically arranges each bowl, ensuring the portions are just right. The countertop is cluttered with remnants of the meal—half-used ingredients, scattered utensils—but Billy doesn't seem to notice, his attention fixed on the task at hand.

I'm caught off guard by how my brain and body are reacting. I mean, I'm usually the stoic one in our little social circle—the Brit with the medical career, the good doctor with the stiff upper lip, the one who pulls up their socks and just gets on with it. I'm the no-nonsense archetype of our long-time Septenary Squad. In case that term sounds too obscure, let me clarify: it's a team of seven. Seven original eco-warriors. Only, right now, there are only six of us in the kitchen, because one of us took the sea foraging just a bit too far.

"Oh babe, it's okay," Billy says, his voice calm and reassuring. He turns toward me, flashing a mouthful of neat, white teeth. His eyes gleam with warmth, framed by lashes so thick they seem almost too perfect, set against the pale white and chestnut-brown of his eyes. I'm mesmerized by the soothing power of his gaze.

"Proves you're human, like the rest of us," he adds softly, his smile widening with gentle humor as he rests the spatula on the edge of the cast-iron pan and steps around the table.

Billy gently begins to work his fingers into the tight knots in my shoulders, kneading the tension away with practiced ease.

It's Nate's turn to analyze the shift in my demeanor. He eyes me curiously, a hint of surprise in his expression as he declares this is the first time that he's seen me so rattled.

"The doctor is clearly off-duty," he remarks, half-joking, half-serious, as he gestures toward me. Serena has rejoined the breakfast table and a loaded glance moves between the group. I can feel the tension in the air and trust my gut—it's now or never. This is my moment.

"Look, if we're all about being transparent this morning, then let me just lay it out here," I announce, my voice shaking slightly. I take a deep breath. "Jamie and I . . . well, we're no longer confused about what we mean to each other." I pause, the weight of the words hitting me all at once. "Basically, you all should know. We're back together. Officially." I feel my chest tighten, the relief mingling with a quiet concern of how they'll take it, but there's no going back now.

There. I've said it.

"I think it's safe to say we all understand what's at stake here," Nate responds, his tone measured. "The couples' game. The real question is, are we, as a group, ready to decide which version of the future we want—without Jamie's current input? Will you speak for him today, Tam?" He looks at me, a challenging edge to his gaze.

Billy releases his hands from my shoulders and, with a quick flick of a kitchen towel, playfully swats Nate across the exposed skin of his well-sculpted calves. Nate flinches, the unexpected sting lingering a bit longer than Billy probably intended—or maybe not. Either way, it's clear it caught his partner off guard.

"Nate and me, we're absolutely doing this," Billy, the businessman declares. He directs his gaze at Serena. "Jamie was all in, after all. And I for one will not allow this group to combust. He'd want us to move forward today as best we're able, take things to the next level."

I can't help but notice that Nate's eyes are slightly puffy, the kind of puffiness that betrays more than a late night or a lack of sleep—it's the mark of something deeper. He hides it well, but I can see through the tough exterior. Now there's a slight-pink welt on his calves from the towel flicking. He's been down to where we stashed the bulk of our stuff and dressed himself optimistically this morning in pale-pink tailored cotton shorts and a cream-colored, vintage cricket sweater draped over a baby-blue collared shirt. His feet are sockless in a pair of leather deck shoes, the put-together look they both seem to favor. It's still semi-fogged-in outside and the house is only partially heated by the woodburning stove, the cold creeping through the gaps.

"Is this an East Coast thing—the casual-preppy look?" I ask, trying to deflect the attention away from a more serious discussion, but my voice catches just slightly. Billy appears only slightly less immaculate this morning in jeans and a navy-blue cashmere crew-neck sweater. They're all about the polos, generally, these two. And they've clearly forgotten how cold it gets here along the coast with our natural air conditioning, even at the end of April. Despite his casual appearance, I can't shake the feeling that Nate's vulnerability is still simmering beneath the surface, hidden behind his effortless style.

"How will you manage to maintain this carefully curated-couple-style in a Midwestern winter, I wonder?"

Serena's eyeing their outfits also. She can't resist a tease: "You do know that once we're settled in Minnesota, River's going to mandate organic cotton work shirts for all. How'd you like overalls made with recycled fibers?"

"Sounds on-trend," Billy makes light in his reply. "Only no camo, please. I draw the line at camo."

They're an ambitious pair, Billy and Nate. The towel flicking episode a window into the playful edge that remains between them. A fire that propels them onwards, potentially. They've undoubtedly had to work through a bunch of cultural-ethic dilemmas over the years as they've figured out how best to live their life together. And, considering this weekend's developments, if they're still in on this crazy plan, then so am I.

I'm feeling a little better as I sip cold water from a bottle-green glass that Eva has placed into my clammy hand. Two slices of lemon and a sprig of mint float on the top. I spit a lemon pip discreetly into my lightly balled fist.

The violence of the storm has us all shaken. It's not over yet. The wind is picking up speed. Even if we'd heard a last-minute meteorological prediction of yesterday's thunder and forked lightning, who would've imagined such a powerful wind-speed intensity hitting at the exact spot where Jamie was out on the water?

The storm that hit was trapped by a downburst that had descended with cold air from the thunderstorm, according to the rescue team. All we could have done, we did, as we'd watched, transfixed and horrified by the powerful and brilliant half-circle that illuminated the horizon. And now it looks like we may be in for a second round.

It used to be jarringly unrealistic out here for such unexpected thunder and lightning, a storm such as this to hit so completely out of the blue at this time of year. Nowadays, it's the least of our worries. We're learning to be forever on our guard as to what Mother Nature may deem to throw at us next.

Monday Late Morning

We're huddled together outside, River and me, assessing the stability of the electric power line and transformer in front of the house. River is worried that the continued high wind has the potential to do serious damage given that there are so many trees nearby. We're looking at a row of fire-prone, towering Tasmanian blue gum eucalyptus, planted as windbreaks long before this house was built, their sickle-shaped leaves hanging from aging, high branches, deciduous bark peeling from thick, shaggy trunks.

"These giants are troublesome and super costly to remove," River explains as they gesture to the eucalyptus. A peregrine falcon swoops in a flash attack on an unsuspecting smaller songbird.

I lay my hands on my wind-blown hair as I switch my focus back to a pole-mounted transformer in its metal box.

"Serena's extra sensitive to electromagnetic fields," River explains. "They give her headaches and make her tired."

They're concerned that there may be sparks jumping gaps in the hardware. "Serena's been on at the utility company to check it for months," they say.

"The noise is worse during wet weather. Otherwise, there's definitely a detectable buzzy hum on a quiet afternoon when the ocean is calm. The crash of waves generally drowns it out by nightfall."

We talk about it as a common refrain amongst my patients, many of whom choose to live off-grid or as off-grid as possible. Electromagnetic fields being all around us.

"If you use a computer, cell phone, radio, an electric blanket, even a hair dryer or a toaster, then you're exposing yourself to various degrees of electromagnetic fields," I concur, my hands gesturing in the air as I make my point, fingers tracing invisible lines around the atmosphere.

River shrugs nonchalantly, their posture casual, one hand shoved into their pocket. "Yes, I get that it's difficult to avoid exposure but the further we live or work away from a power line the better, as electromagnetic fields decrease significantly with distance," they reason, lifting their chin slightly as if considering the idea. "If you're stuck with one nearby, it sucks."

"Crystals and harmonizing materials, though . . . that's another part of it. You should see our bedroom. Serena's all-in on their mitigating factors."

I tilt my head, narrowing my eyes as I bring up another point, my voice steady as I drive the conversation forward. "Your ancient refrigerator for instance," I explain, raising a finger in the air, then motioning toward the house. "Serena's electric sewing machine, those old light fixtures and lamps that date back to Marie's day. Electrical wiring problems no doubt. Best rid yourselves of all of that when making the move."

The wind howls, trees bending beneath its force as dark clouds gather overhead. The air feels heavy, thick with the promise of a storm. I pull my jacket tighter around my shoulders, feeling the gusts whip through the yard as I turn back to River.

"It's cool to hear your plans for clean energy," I remark, raising my voice to be heard over the wind. "A wind power element for this future homestead of ours? Sounds good to me."

River pauses for a moment, their gaze shifting toward the trees, their branches swaying violently in the gusts. They nod and exhale slowly, clearly grappling with the complexities of the situation. "There will be problems," they admit, their tone matching the tension in the air. "Wind and solar power generators get stuck in these tediously long bureaucratic lines just to connect with the power grid. And the fees . . . the fees are outrageous."

A distant crack of thunder rumbles in the background and we both glance up instinctively bracing for the storm to hit. River rubs the back of their neck, clearly not done with the weight of what's ahead. "This all speaks to the core of our communal culture and values." Their expression is thoughtful. "How we go about settling the issue of the ideal of living at least partially off the grid."

The wind picks up again, rattling windows. I find myself wondering if we're really ready for it—the shift to something so radically different. Could we really give up the electronic toys we've come to rely on? The gadgets, the endless distractions that make life appear so much easier. It'll be a huge challenge, a wild card, all of us figuring out how to compromise for the greater good. Could we really live without many of the comforts we've come to expect?

River breaks my train of thought, pointing toward the house with a hand braced against the gusts. "For instance, that wood stove in there," they say, their voice steady but tinged with a hint of irony. "A fixture of American life. There should be none of that in the next place in theory. Major contributor to air pollution. We're being total hypocrites keeping it fired up this weekend."

I glance back at the smoke trailing from the chimney, knowing they're right. I'm aware of the issues—wood smoke is damaging to the air we breathe. But it's hard to imagine a life where our basic instinct for survival doesn't rely on the primitive burning of wood. The wind howls louder and I shudder at the thought of a future without wood fires, especially since without it we'd have frozen our asses off this weekend, especially River and me.

"We can't solve the world's fundamental issues in one day, that's for sure," I reply, my voice barely carrying over the rising storm. "But right now, I'm interested to hear your take on the condition of that wobbly power line?"

I redirect the conversation back to the more immediate issue we're facing. The line is swaying dangerously in the gusts and I can't help but feel uneasy. It's just one more thing to consider in the storm of decisions ahead.

"It's flopping around way more than I'd like it to," River replies. They're leaning against a solid wood shed with a corrugated steel roof and a barn door attached to the side of the house.

"What's in there?" I ask.

"Surfboards," River says pushing the door open with the toe cap of their water-resistant boot. "A bunch of old boards, mostly."

I peer in. The structure holds a stack of dinged-up surfboards on slats that are open for airflow. There's a rack at one end holding several more wetsuits on hangers.

"Wanna know something else that's not cool?" River asks. "These old boards are about as nasty for the environment as the wood stove."

"In what way?" I ask. "What are they made of?"

"Polyurethane and polystyrene mostly. Coated in resin."

"And that's the standard board for ocean loving surfers?"

"Yup," they reply with a shrug, leaning back a bit as if the weight of the conversation is already getting heavy. "The design revolution has long moved on from local hardwoods. Redwood, pine, fiberglass… there are some companies trying to push eco-materials into the mix but honestly, it's still mostly these dubious, non-biodegradable boards that dominate the scene."

I gesture toward the wetsuits we wore earlier, back on their hangers. I am still experiencing the sting of the cold in my bones, especially with the absence of Jamie who nearly didn't make it out of the water.

"Neoprene," River explains, their face darkening slightly. They glance at the wetsuit as if it were a necessary evil. "Not very kind to the planet."

I throw my hands up in frustration. "Bloody hell," I mutter. "We're hardly hitting the mark this weekend, are we? So much for our green initiatives. It's like opening Pandora's Box."

River shakes their head, shoulders slumping as they push the door open against the fierce wind. "Afraid not," they say, their voice carrying the weight of reality. "We can't just summon new sustainable products out of thin air. It takes time."

I hold on to River by the elbow and steer them gently back toward the house. "You okay?" I ask, as we approach the door. "Serena's been giving you a tough time this weekend."

I understand the pressure they're under with the house and its pressing issues. But all the same, I don't think Serena's berating of River is helping her cause.

River turns, pulling me into a bear hug. They know I'm not much of a hugger, so the gesture carries weight. I feel the tension in their arms, a mix of frustration and something else, something deeper. We both linger there for a moment, the quiet of the embrace speaking volumes. After a long pause, River finally pulls away, their gaze a little distant, like they're releasing something from deep inside.

"You of all people know how Serena plays, Tam. It's a game to her. Getting her way. She needs to feel like this was all her idea. She'll come around."

River exhales sharply, the breath of someone who's been holding something in for far too long. "But it's more than that," they continue, voice softening, letting me in on something personal. "She's been there for me, in ways that… no one else has. People don't see it. They don't know the half of it." River looks off into the distance, their gaze far away, as if trying to capture a memory that's fading. "Serena's the kind of person who never asks for help, never shows weakness. But when things got dark at the start of lockdown, she didn't walk away. She stayed. Even when I pushed her to, even when I was at my worst. There's something in her that's… steady. She's not perfect and god knows we clash. But when it matters, she's there."

They look back at me, their eyes heavy with something unspoken. "So yeah, she can be a lot to deal with, but I've seen a side of her that no one else gets to see. And that's why I stick with her. No one else ever stuck around like she did."

~

Back indoors, the others are pacing the living room, their steps quick and anxious as they discuss the increasing velocity of the storm.

"What do you think?" Billy asks, his voice tense. "It's already windier than yesterday."

River shifts on their feet, hopping from one socked foot to the other, the slight movement betraying the restlessness building up inside. They scratch their head, raking fingers through their wind-tousled hair as if trying to brush away the uncertainty. Their eyes flicker toward the window, watching the trees bend in the wind, their jaw set tight. "It's only gonna get worse," they mutter, the words barely audible beneath the sound of the storm building outside.

"It's the wind that's freaking me out. I'm not feeling good about that power line," River admits, their voice laced with unease. "It's only a matter of time until the road is clear. I suggest we head down to the beach, play it safe, ride out the system until we can get out of here."

Serena stands near the window, her arms crossed tightly over her chest, watching the tree branches whip and crack against the fragile glass. She tilts her head slightly, brow furrowing as she weighs the idea. There's a slight hesitation in her stance, her foot shifting back and forth, unsure. Her lips press into a thin line, eyes narrowing as if she's trying to predict what could go wrong. The wind howls outside, rattling the windows, but she doesn't flinch.

"Erring on caution," she murmurs, her voice almost too casual as she glances toward River, her gaze soft but thoughtful. "But maybe it's not a bad idea." She uncrosses her arms for a moment, tapping a finger against her wrist as if mulling over the decision. Though something in her expression betrays that she's still not fully convinced.

I'm standing close to the woodburning stove. A thin trickle of fear runs down the center line of my back beneath my t-shirt and sweater. The fabric sticks to my skin as the tension in the room thickens.

"By the time this kiddo is running around us in circles, I'm gonna be all about the outdoors," Eva says, her hands resting instinctively on her stomach, but her voice betrays an undercurrent of unease. She's trying to sound upbeat but the tightness in her posture says otherwise. She's following her instinct and it's clear she wants out of here.

The walls feel like they're closing in. Every creak of the house, every gust of wind outside, makes it harder to breathe. I can almost feel the weight of our silence pressing down on us.

A deep, long, disturbing groan shudders through the house, halting us mid-motion as we gather snacks from the kitchen. It hangs in the air, unsettling, before it's followed by a loud, bone-rattling moan—a massive branch splits from the Monterey pine beside the house and, despite its weight, is violently whipped up and flung across the front deck. The sound is deafening, sending a second shiver down my spine.

Serena's gaze snaps toward the window, her eyes wide, her posture rigid. Without a word, she moves quickly, grabbing her jacket, her hands trembling just slightly as she pulls it on. There's no hesitation in her actions now. She's come to the same conclusion we all have. The tension in the room thickens, the air electric with urgency. The power line, still swaying dangerously in the wind, is no longer something to ignore. Serena doesn't wait for anyone—she's already halfway to the door, dogs at her feet, her voice sharp and quick, the words tumbling out in a rush. "Now's as good a time as any. Let's get down to the shore, away from the trees and the flying debris."

Her eyes lock with River's, the concern in them as palpable as the storm raging outside. It's clear: she's just as worried as River is about the danger of that power line.

Sand verbena carpets the ground in vivid magenta blooms, their delicate stems clinging to the sand beneath my feet, but the beauty of it feels sharp, almost suffocating. Everything around me is in such intense focus—the vibrant colors, the crisp outlines of California thistle, its light pink thistle flowers standing stark against the harsh, gray-green leaves. "Spring," the flora seems to whisper, a mocking tease as we descend the rocky path toward the beach. Summer feels impossibly far away, as the massive waves below crest and crash, their roar only amplifying the unease in my chest.

We reach Serena's makeshift shelter, a flimsy blue plastic sheet tied to stakes, valiantly shielding her family treasures. But even from here, I can see the tautness in the plastic, hear the snap of it against the wind—how much longer will it hold under this pressure? The wind picks up, biting at my skin as I scramble back up the path, my hair whipping across my face. I try to hold it back but it's futile. The world is spinning faster now, the air too thick with tension, as if the elements themselves are about to explode. Every gust of wind feels like a warning.

Nate slips, his foot catching on an uneven rock and his ankle twists at a grotesque angle. A sharp grunt escapes him, followed by a stream of complaints as he hobbles toward me, his face contorting with pain. The wind howls around us, adding a layer of chaos to the already tense air. I quickly sit him down, my hands moving on autopilot as I prop his leg onto the smooth surface of a large rock. His breath is ragged, the pain radiating from his swollen ankle.

I yank off his shoes and socks with a little more force than necessary, assessing the damage. His ankle's already swollen, darkening under my touch. In place of a proper bandage, I wrap his sock around it, the fabric tight against the swelling. It's a makeshift solution but it'll have to do for now.

"Rest here," I say, my voice sharper than I intend. I hand my water bottle to Billy whose anxious eyes are already darting between Nate and the horizon. "Billy, go get ocean water. It'll be cold enough to reduce the swelling so we can move him down to shore."

The wind picks up again, screeching through the trees almost as if the world is fighting us. We're each of us unraveling, struggling to keep it together. Nate groans, his frustration mounting as his gaze darts back up the path toward the house. "I wanna go back indoors. Wait it out," he pleads, his voice strained with desperation.

Billy looks at him with a raised eyebrow, his jaw set in a tight line. "Did anyone ever say no to you as a child?" He doesn't wait for an answer, his tone hardening. "You're staying put for now."

"I feel like Jack Torrance in *The Shining*," Nate mutters, his voice thick with both pain and dark humor.

Billy scoffs, rolling his eyes. "Tough old world, baby…" The words are flippant, but there's no mistaking the underlying tension in his voice, an acknowledgment that things aren't going as planned.

Eva and Serena push ahead, dogs running ahead off-leash, oblivious to the rising storm around us. River, ever the silent observer, follows them without a word but I can see the tightness in their posture, the weight of responsibility bearing down on them as the wind howls louder.

Myrtle stops in her tracks. I watch as she makes an abrupt about turn on the sandy spot where Eva, Serena and River have gathered and are spreading out the corners of a blanket. It's the first time I've seen either dog move at any speed and Myrtle's little legs kick into gear at an impressive, cartoonish pace for such a small animal. She races past Billy on his way to get water, darting between Nate and me on the narrow path, heading uphill, back in the direction of the house.

"Grab her!" Serena calls, her voice barely cutting through the shrieking wind. The urgency in her words is lost, drowned out by the relentless howl of the storm. Her plea falls flat, the small dog already making a beeline for the shelter of the house. I watch, helpless, as Myrtle's tiny body darts across the sand, moving faster than I thought possible, her instincts driving her straight toward the comfort of home.

Serena doesn't waste a moment. She scoops Minnie up, handing her off to River before turning and dashing uphill in pursuit of Myrtle. Her breath comes in ragged gasps as she reaches us, her face flushed, eyes wide with frustration and fear. "She never does that," she pants, wiping strands of hair from her face, barely keeping herself together. "Ditching me like this. Damn it, now I've gotta go back up there to get her."

Nate watches, his face set in grim concern. "Surely she'll turn around and head back as soon as she sees we're not following?" His words are cautious but there's no denying the edge of doubt creeping into his voice. "She's no dummy."

Serena shakes her head, her jaw tightening with both frustration and a deep, unspoken worry. "She knows her way in," she says, her tone flat, almost resigned. "There's a doggie door."

The words hit harder than they should, as we face the storm brewing around us. Every second counts. I glance toward the path, the wind pushing against us, feeling the tension in the air. It's more than just the dog, more than just the lost minutes. Something about this storm, this moment, feels like it's tightening its grip on us, pulling us toward an inevitable clash with forces we can't control.

I call out, my gaze flicking over to Serena, "You want me to go instead? Maybe she's just hiding under the deck?"

Serena doesn't even hesitate. "No," she says firmly, a determined glint in her eyes. "You stay put, Tam. Look after Long John Silver here." She turns, shoulders squared and strides toward the beach house, each step full of purpose.

Nate calls after her, his voice a little tight, "Not funny."

Billy reappears, trekking back with my water bottle—now filled with cold, briny seawater. He hands it to me and I remove the sock bandage and tip it carefully over Nate's swollen ankle, watching the water cascade down.

"How's that feel?" I ask, my voice low but concerned.

Nate opens his mouth to answer but before the words can escape, a crackle of sparks rips through the air, flashing brightly by the side of the house. We snap our attention to the sky, our eyes wide with surprise.

"What the hell?" Billy yells, his voice drowned out by the horrific shrieking of seagulls, a cloud of them swirling above us, their cries almost deafening.

"Serena…" Nate murmurs, his voice barely carrying in the wind as he teeters on one foot, struggling to stay steady.

"I'll go," I insist, my hand pressing gently but firmly across his chest. "Sit."

Billy grabs my arm and together we take our first step, heading back up the path. But before we can get far, a burst of flames erupts from a small brushfire setting the eucalyptus trees and the side fence alight, the flames painting the sky in a fiery glow.

My gaze darts down to River who's hopping frantically, clutching a trembling Minnie to their chest. They're screaming, their words a blur of frantic curses. Panic surges in me. Should I keep charging uphill or should I drag Nate down to the water's edge with Billy's help?

"Oh my God," I shout, the fear crashing over me. "Serena?"

A massive blast knocks me onto my back. I turn to one side, dazed but sufficiently aware to discover Nate and Billy laying flat-out beside me. The three of us are covered in a blackened cloak of smoking debris.

River appears in an instant, standing over us, horrified, peering into our stunned faces for an answer. Minnie whimpers and quakes in their arms.

The house is a mass of fire. Explosions blast out into the space around it in every direction. Uprooted trees shoot through the air like giant arrows. Blackened-wood crashes around us, smaller chunks clinging to our hair, our clothes, particles of objects I couldn't decipher if I tried. The air stinks of woodsmoke and chemical odor, burned plastic. We roll in the sand, covering our heads. It's hot, getting hotter as flammable objects ignite, plumes of black smoke darken the sky.

River is the first to face the smoke, hands shielding their eyes, but it's clear they're struggling to see. Their grip on the howling dog is like iron, the poor animal squirming, whimpering in fear. River's sobs tear through the air, a gut-wrenching sound that twists my stomach. Each breath I take is slow and labored, a toxic mix of smoke and chemicals from the burning beach house filling my lungs. The trees, the branches, the leaves—all of it is consumed by flames.

"Serena..."

I scramble to my feet, barely steady and reach to River, locking my arms around them. The dog is squeezed between us, trembling in their grip.

"Get back down to Eva!" I scream, the words cutting through the smoke. "The gases, the fumes... they're toxic! Don't go any closer, River. Listen to me!" The smell of burning rubber, like a race track caught in an inferno, stings my nostrils, thick and suffocating.

I can't shake the fear that gnaws at me—whatever Serena and Myrtle's fate, it can't be good. It's too much to even consider. Myrtle must've sensed something was wrong, felt the danger and rushed up to the house to investigate. I've heard of dogs trained for demolition running straight into danger, into simulated explosions. The thought twists my insides. It's all too horrific to process.

I pull Eva close when I reach her, offering her whatever fragile comfort I can summon as she rocks, her body trembling with shock, her arms wrapped around her knees as she slumps on the blanket Serena had laid out on the sand only minutes ago. The scene feels unreal, like time is slipping away, leaving us stranded in this raw, unbearable moment.

Without hesitation, I reach out, gathering Eva, a stumbling Nate, Billy, and River into a tight, desperate embrace—a circle of shared pain. We huddle together, clinging to each other as the world around us shatters. We try to look away, to escape the devastation before us, but it's impossible. The wind lashes at us, hot and harsh, flinging gritty, contaminated sand into our faces like some cruel reminder that it's not over. Not yet. As if we haven't already suffered enough, as if the universe isn't done punishing us.

Monday, Around Noon

We stand frozen amidst the chaos and devastation, unsure of what our next step should be. And then, impossibly, a figure emerges from behind the smoke and debris of the collapsed beach house. At first, we can't believe what we're seeing. It's Serena—alive, relatively untouched by the destruction that surrounds us. She stumbles toward us, dazed and disoriented, with Myrtle cradled in her arms, the dog's trembling form a fragile lifeline between them.

I blink hard, rub my eyes, but the sight doesn't fade. It's real. It's undeniable. She must've been down in the basement, deep beneath the house, where the bedrock shielded her from the full force of the explosion. How? Why? It defies all logic, all the rules we thought we understood. She shouldn't be here. And yet, here she is, standing before us, the impossible made flesh.

A stunned silence falls over us. Each of us is grappling with the miracle we're witnessing. My heart races as I look around at the faces of my friends—my family—still huddled together amidst the wreckage. How we'll pick up the pieces of this shattered moment, I have no idea. The future feels like a fog of uncertainty, but in this moment, one thing is crystal clear.

I am here. We're all here. And Jamie is not far away. It's enough to be a part of this beautiful disaster. I belong with these people, in all their chaos and noise. Commitment—this kind of reckless, all-in devotion—is the bravest thing I've ever understood and I realize now, as Serena approaches, that my place is with them all. Wherever they go, wherever it may lead, I am with them.

I swear that as soon as this is behind us, I'll call Mum. I'm her only child. And she's all I have outside of the mess of all this. It's beyond time to make peace in the midst of our mother/daughter battlefield. I'll find the words to finally explain to her how, all along, I've been searching for something bigger than myself, something beyond the world she's known. I am ready to stand up and show up as who I truly am, without hesitation.

And Serena . . . I realize now that she, too, has been searching. In her own way. It's like it took this destruction for a quiet truth to click into place. And I see it in her now, clearer than ever, how she has somehow saved me from myself one more time.

A fine drizzle falls, settling softly on our ashen heads. I glance up, past Serena, who's slowly making her way down to River and Minnie. They're already climbing the cliff path toward her, ready to embrace as the dogs reunite in a moment of utter relief.

And then I see him. The man who calls himself the Raven stands at a distance on the cliff top, his silhouette striking against the mist. I recognize him instantly—the long, black coat, the hat pulled low over his face.

Eva hands me her phone with trembling fingers. "Two bars," she instructs, urgently, her voice a whisper of panic, pulling a scarf away from her face with surprising calm. I take the phone from her, careful not to fumble and step away from the group, dialing 911 with a steady hand, asking for help.

~

Emergency services are already on their way—again. This time, it's an aerial firefighter and the Coast Guard racing toward us. Meanwhile, I'm told, ground teams are battling their way through the mudslide from the northern end.

The whole thing feels like a nightmare I can't wake up from. And all we can do is wait, stuck in the chaos on the beach. I fuss around, double-checking that Eva's scarf is tightly resecured over her mouth to protect her and the baby from the toxic fumes that are swirling in the air.

I'm silenced for several minutes. My mind is spinning. I've spent so long trying to make peace with Serena but it hits me again like a punch to the gut. If it weren't for her, I wouldn't even be here. I wouldn't be the one holding it together, keeping us all from falling apart. She's played me like a puzzle piece for two decades, shaping my path, positioning me again and again, dead center in the storm. And here I am—still here.

And right now, I'm witnessing her courage, her resolve, her steps shaky but determined as she makes her way down to the beach. I'm glad she's alive. I truly am. They say life is a collection of fleeting moments, none of which we can truly keep. But this moment—it belongs to Serena. She came so close to becoming the perfect victim in all of this yet here she stands, untouched.

A turkey vulture hovers overhead. First of the scavengers.

"Shoo," I warn waving my arms above my head, trying to push the chaos away. I lower my hands, pulling leaves and bits of debris from my hair. Nature has no sense of our human heartache, no understanding of how close we came to losing it all. It doesn't care. Nature is ruthless in its way.

The landscape is unrecognizable now. Dozens of trees lie shattered across the sand, their roots tangled with earth and rock, like massive, twisted obstacles. I can't even begin to understand how we managed to avoid being hit by any one of these deadly projectiles.

River pulls away from Serena, grabbing me by the shoulders with wide, frantic eyes. "It was me," they say, their voice frantic. "The stupid tea kettle. I reconnected the gas line this morning, I lit the stovetop. I may have left it on simmer."

"Shush," I cut them off gently, as a series of secondary explosions rip through the air, sending bursts of fire into the sky. A shower of sparks rains down and for a moment we're all silent, staring up at the spectacle. We huddle together, arms wrapped tightly around one another, our tears mingling into silver-gray streaks. "Don't be silly. That's not it," I insist, in my attempt to calm their racing mind.

"Look," says Eva, pointing to the surf and sand. "Wow."

A tide of ultramarine by-the-wind-sailors, blue, jellyfish-like creatures with translucent, triangular sails free-floats like a fleet of miniature, inter-galactic warships onto shore carried by the prevailing breeze. The wind is too strong for these peculiar little sailors to navigate their course and they're sailing onshore in startling numbers.

"Their coloration keeps them camouflaged on the ocean surface," Eva says, mesmerized.

We stoop to take a closer look at these weird and wonderful creatures that have washed up closest to where we're standing.

"They use their stinging tentacles to capture prey," Eva explains. "Once they're stranded, they're done for. Millions of cellophane-like sails and floats is all that will be left in a couple of days."

I feel a sense of peace begin to settle in my chest as we stand here together—battered, but unbroken—we are not alone, not anymore. We're bound by more than just history; we're bound by nature, the shared scars of the past, of this weekend, by the laughter, the fear, the quiet moments of understanding and by the pact that brought us back together. We've faced chaos and come out the other side and somehow, we've found strength in each other. Together, maybe we can take on whatever comes next—no matter how stormy the road ahead might be.

As the clouds part, the sun emerges for a fleeting moment, casting a golden glow across the wet earth before sinking into the horizon. I feel something shift within me. A flicker of hope, fragile but undeniable, burning brighter now than it ever has. The future is a hazy unknown but I do know one thing for sure: we will face it together. Our bond, imperfect but real, has been tested and in the aftermath, this—whatever it is, whatever it becomes—is worth fighting for.

In the end, there's a faint spark that holds on and determines our fate, even in the toughest moments. The path ahead is still unclear, but I'm certain we'll manage to face it together—fueled by grit, by hard-earned understanding, and, for better or worse, by the bond we continue to share.

Epilogue
Monday Evening, April 24

NBC Bay Area – Local News, Weather, Traffic

Sonoma Coast, Calif. — A devastating explosion from a downed powerline put the lives of a woman and her dog in jeopardy this afternoon when it obliterated a secluded beach house perched on a cliffside between Bodega Bay and Jenner.

Emergency responders, including fire engines, ambulances, and search-and-rescue teams, were unable to reach the site until after storm-induced mudslides had been cleared, blocking access to the area just 24 hours prior.

The cause of the explosion remains unclear, though officials with the Sonoma County Fire Department have suggested it may have been worsened by faulty appliances or a ruptured gas line from the property's propane tank.

A massive fireball consumed the 100-year-old home, reducing it to rubble along the cliff's edge.

Witnesses described the scene as nothing short of "catastrophic."

"It was a miracle we had evacuated earlier with the strong winds or we wouldn't be here to talk about it," said River Lee Hanson, the partner of homeowner Serena West, who narrowly escaped the blast after returning to the house to retrieve her dog. "The force of the explosion sent windows, doors, and belongings flying into the air and onto the beach below."

The fate of any salvageable items remains unclear. West is currently being treated for shock and smoke inhalation. For now, Hanson, West, their dogs, and four of their five weekend guests are counting themselves lucky to have been on the beach at the time of the explosion, not inside the house.

"This was Serena's grandmother's home," Hanson explained. "It's the end of an era." They believe the blast was triggered by a downed powerline that sparked a brushfire which then ignited a wooden fence and propane tank attached to the house.

Whatever the investigation reveals, for now, Hanson, West, and their friends are focused on returning to safety inland after what feels like a close brush with fate.

This marks the second near-disaster for the group of former college roommates in just one weekend. On Sunday, building contractor and fisherman James Foster from San Francisco was airlifted to Santa Rosa Memorial Hospital after his boat capsized in the Pacific during a sudden storm.

"James is doing well," said his wife and fellow house guest Dr. Tamsin Osborne from Santa Cruz. "Now that the road's been cleared, I'll be heading to the hospital as soon as emergency services give the all-clear."

While unsure of their future after losing the home they shared, Hanson added, "One thing I can say with certainty is that our friends—they're our family. If your world falls off a cliff, who do you trust when you hit the shore?"

In an era of coastal erosion and rare weather events becoming more commonplace, this resilient group of friends remains hopeful that there's still time to secure a future—one that's a little further from the edge.

Acknowledgments

Thank you to my support team—the people in my life who keep me focused, grounded and entertained through the many long months it takes to write a story. Beloved family, friends, my writing community, and loyal, enthusiastic readers continue to rally, book after book, encouraging my return to the desk—to zone out from the myriad attractions, distractions, and increasing chaos of the outside world in order to maintain the discipline it takes to bring an imagined world and characters to life.

This is my post-pandemic novel—channeling in to our collective need for community, purpose and connection. It is another story set close to home—along the Northern California Sonoma Coast, beside the crumbling cliffside easily recognizable to anyone who has visited or frequents the Pacific Coast Highway between Bodega Bay and Jenner.

I'm deeply grateful for the keen eye of early readers—especially my husband Timo Rivetti and longtime friends Carol McKegney and Cameron Carey for their careful attention to this story.

Special thanks to my concept and development editor, and oldest son, Rocco Rivetti, for encouraging me to tell this story in first person, present tense, and for offering your original, intuitive, and constructive insights into my early drafts. Thank you for gently pushing me to deepen my storytelling, to dig further into character and motivation, and to ease away from a natural tendency to extrapolate.

I have long admired the gorgeous work of West Marin-based science illustrator Laurie Mahan Sawyer, and I was beyond delighted when she agreed to collaborate on the cover illustration and design for this book. Laurie's intuition in translating my words into art is pure magic, continuing my legacy of working with regional women artists whose original work and cottage-industry ethics mirror my own. I have every confidence readers will adore this cover as much as I do—its beauty provides a significant boost as the book weaves its way out into the wider world. Many thanks to Laurie for being on board for such an integral part of sharing this important story.

As with my previous novels, the beach house in this story is entirely imagined—though inspired by a composite of several properties in the area.

I decided to write a British American protagonist in this story because, well, it's kind of like writing with a bit of home court advantage! While Tamsin is definitely not me, being able to tap into the blend of British and American cultures makes it easier for me to get into her head. The mix of humor, wordplay, and the little cultural quirks. Plus, writing a character who shares that dual identity lets me explore all those funny, awkward, and sometimes confusing moments that come with living between two worlds.

Why seven core characters? Six felt too symmetrical; five, too confined. Seven struck me as intriguing—more complex, slightly awkward, yet purposeful. The number seven has long held symbolic weight across cultures and disciplines: astrology, numerology, mythology, psychology, and spirituality. According to my research, its appearance in the seven colors of the rainbow, the seven chakras, the seven days of the week, the seven continents, and, of course, the seven wonders of the world make it an even more interesting number. In many ways, seven feels like the perfect size for this diverse, dynamic ensemble.

Furthermore, Shakespeare himself explored the seven ages of man; the number holds deep significance in Christianity and other religions. It's the foundation of Western musical scales, and even the Roman numeral system includes seven letters. In this story, seven symbolizes both exoneration and healing. When I created the seven main characters of *Floating in the Middle*, I aimed to form an unconventional, eclectic chosen family—imperfect and flawed, but undeniably real.

The Raven and his mother entered the narrative later in the writing process, but their presence became essential. Their arrival marked a turning point, adding depth and perspective to the original seven, aiding their journey of growth, support, and connection as they face an uncertain future together.

Mother and adult child relationships are a recurring theme in my stories. I appreciate my late British mother, Elaine, all the more as I write about complex family dynamics, especially for having supported my move to the United States so wholeheartedly and unselfishly when I was in my mid-twenties. Now that she is gone (sadly, while I was writing this book), I've been able to reflect with fondness and gratitude on the memorable visits we shared on either side of the Atlantic over the years. Although I draw deeply from the well of cultural knowledge in crafting Tamsin's imagined British mother, I'm fortunate my own adventurous and fun-loving Mum was far more loving and accepting than the chilly and complex mother in this story.

The house in this story clearly serves as a metaphor for global warming. None of us knows what lies at the bottom of the deep, dark well of the climate crisis. The world is warming at an alarming rate, and the ocean has absorbed most of the heat from the atmosphere. While I was writing early drafts of this story, my annual flight to the UK to visit family was canceled the night before departure due to runway reconstruction at San Francisco International Airport. Rising sea levels in the Bay had wreaked havoc on the runway.

We humans are 100% responsible for greenhouse gas emissions, and whether we like it or not, changing the way we live is not something to put off for the future. **Now** is the time to act.

We all know the drill—or we should. How do we think about the future? The future is **now**.

About the Cover Illustrator/Designer

Laurie Mahan Sawyer is a celebrated Northern California science illustrator based in Point Reyes, West Marin. She has lived and worked in places with an abundance of flora and fauna to explore in and around beaches and canyons, since birth. Her prolific artwork is deeply influenced by this rich, natural environment. Laurie hopes to share her concern for this beautiful place we inhabit, and through the creation of her pictures, to inspire understanding and respect for the world around us.

Find more of Laurie's work at www.newcompassdesigns.com
www.instagram.com/newcompassdesigns

About the Author

Frances Rivetti is a British-American author whose contemporary fiction has earned her multiple national indie awards, including a Gold Medal from the Independent Publisher Book Awards for her 2019 debut novel, *Big Green Country*. Her second novel, *The House on Liberty Street—Home of Second Chances*, was a 2023 finalist for the National Indie Excellence Award.

A former newspaper reporter from East of England, Frances has called Petaluma, California home since the early 1990s. Her deep connection to Sonoma County's landscapes and communities has shaped her work as both journalist and novelist. From 2010 to 2015, she wrote the popular South County Notebook column for the Petaluma Argus Courier, and her writing has appeared in publications across Northern California, the UK, and Australia.

This is Frances's fifth book and third novel set along Northern California's dramatic coastline. She lives with her British-Italian-American husband Timo and their rescue animals in a lively household that has welcomed three now-grown sons and countless overseas guests. Frances continues to explore the backroads of coastal Northern California, notebook in hand, drawn to stories that capture the area's wild beauty and the environmental changes reshaping familiar landscapes. Her latest work examines how climate upheaval affects the tight-knit communities she's come to know intimately through decades of coastal living.

Join Frances Rivetti's Reader's Club at www.francesrivetti.com.

Follow her at
www.instagram.com/francesrivetti/
www.instagram.com/floatinginthemiddle_novel/
www.facebook.com/fogvalleypress.

Fast-paced and suspenseful . . . A wild roller coaster of a story.

Rivetti explores family, relationships, adaptability, change, and acceptance in this immersive thriller. It's Christmas Eve. With festive tables set and a roaring fire warming her Northern California Victorian house parlor, Adamaria is looking forward to celebrating a cozy Christmas with her daughter Gracie and the latter's two little girls. When a stranger sneaks into the house in the early hours of Christmas morning, Adamaria finds her world turning upside down. Told in third-person omniscient perspective, the narrative is immersed in holiday spirit. With a keen sensitivity to familial relationships, Rivetti makes good use of her thrilling plot, keeping readers thoroughly invested. The pacing is swift, the prose crisp, and the characterization top-notch. A close-knit family, an adorable pup, deft use of foreshadowing, and a storyline that's just complicated enough make this an immersive read. A winner.

And for Big Green Country

Deeply moving, highly engrossing...

Two young women's trials of physical and mental abuse in Northern California's infamous emerald Triangle makes the heart of Rivetti's searing debut. When Mia and Jazmin left their homes to take seasonal jobs as trimmigrants in Northern California's Sonoma County to earn some extra cash, they had no idea the short escapade would change their lives forever. Though violence and the illegal marijuana industry of Sonoma County form the central theme of the novel, subplots of Maggie and Bridget's lives and their sisterly bonds along with issues of relationships, lasting friendship, and enduring family ties illuminate the story further. Rivetti's research is meticulous, the writing assured, and prose crisp. She portrays Jazmin and Mia with understanding and empathy, making the reader root for the flawed but courageous teens as they prevail their personal traumas through sheer will and resilience. A must read.

www.ingramcontent.com/pod-product-compliance
Lightning Source LLC
Chambersburg PA
CBHW020404120726
47904CB00002B/695